ILL STREET BLUES

Joe Martin

This is a work of fiction. Names, characters, and incidents are either the product of the author's imagination or are used fictitiously.

illstreetblues2009@yahoo.com

ISBN: 0-615-33877-1 ISBN-13: 978-0-615-33877-4

Artwork Designed By:
Pharaoh "Future" Paige
Future Grafx
716.884.1725

ILL STREET BLUES

Chapter 1

Bum woke up and wiped the sleep out of his eyes as he looked over at the clock. *"Seven in the fucking morning."* He thought to himself. He yawned as he stood up to stretch hearing several vertebrae pop as he reached for the ceiling. *"Got to get this money."* he exclaimed softly as he put his house shoes on to walk into the bathroom. While brushing his teeth, his phone started to ring. He ran back into the room and grabbed his phone.

"What up Homey. Where you at?" He mumbled into the receiver as he brushed his teeth.

"What up fam? I'm at the same house I was at yesterday. You coming through?" Lex shouted vivaciously as if he had drank a whole case of red bull. Bum spit into the sink then rinsed his mouth out.

"Yeah… give me 'bout an hour."

"Alright, fam."

"Alright."

As Bum hung the phone up another incoming call was coming in *"Fuck!"* he mumbled when he recognized his kid's mother number.

"What you want Keisha?" Bum sounded aggravated already.

"What I want? What I want? Nigga how 'bout some child support? How 'bout you spending time wit yo kids? How 'bout…"

Before she could finish, he laid the phone on the sink and continued getting ready to head out. He knew she could talk, or better yet *argue* forever, but it was too early in the morning for that.

Bum had two kids by Keisha, his son BJ was 6 years old, and a daughter Brittney who was 3 years old. He also had another son James, who was also 3 years old by another woman named Jasmine. Unlike Keisha, Jasmine was quiet and respectful. Jasmine was 22 years old, which was 3 years younger than Keisha, but she was more mature than her years.

Ever since Bum started getting his money right, Keisha couldn't leave him alone. She would constantly call for money or just to harass him. Bum would give her money for the kids and she would spend it on herself, she stayed with new designer shit. She was a trifling hood rat turned feather-weight gold digger. Bum was a good father, he took care of all his kids. He just couldn't stand Keisha with her scandalous ways.

After putting his clothes on, Bum picked the phone back up, "HELLO, HELLO!" Keisha yelled into the phone. He could hear her bamboo earrings clanging as she rolled her neck and her two inch nails clicked in the background.

"Yeah." Bum said as if he'd listened to her rant from beginning to end.

"What *I* want?" Keisha said followed by a deep inhale, "Nigga…you ain't SHIT!!" Keisha continued to talk.

"Bye!" Bum said as he aggressively pressed the *end* button on his cell phone.

At 24 Bum was getting his head right. He was getting paper. He grew up on the lower east side of Buffalo N.Y with his mother, aunt and her two kids, Gutt and Tamika. They didn't have much of anything growing up. It seemed like the great depression had yet to end in that household. He got his nickname of Bum as a kid. His wardrobe consisted of hand me downs and Goodwill clearance rack clothing. In school the other kids would often call him a bum because of his misfortune. As he got older, he took a liking to the name. It motivated him to get rich. He started selling crack and seeing money. Now, at 24, money is plentiful.

***

At 8:15am Bum pulled in front of Lex's house in his brown delta 88. Even though he had money, he stayed driving a hooptie; he also had a brand new Lincoln Navigator truck which he rarely drove. "Yo Lex I'm out front, open the door." Bum said on the phone while getting out of the car. By the time he got to the steps, Lex opened the door in the same clothes that he had on the night before. Bum respected Lex's hustle; he was about that money which was something they had in common.

"That's what I'm talking 'bout, right on time." Lex greeted Bum.

"Always. But yo...I got half a joint here. I know you only wanted 9 ounces, just see me with the rest when you get it." Bum said as they walked to the living room.

Lex responded, "I got it now, take it now." Lex pulled out an extra $6,500 and gave it to Bum.

"If I would have known you had it now I would have brought by an extra 9 o's on C." Bum said.

"Next time we can do that." Lex replied. Bum slapped him up.

"Next time."

Bum left and headed to Gigi's to get something to eat and spotted Loni. Loni owed him $1,000 for almost six months now. After fronting him the ounce, he hadn't seen or heard from him until now. He pulled over in front of the store where Loni was standing. "What up Loni?"

"Shit, what up?" Loni responded with an attitude.

"You... What you forgot about me?" Bum asked.

"Naw I ain't forget shit; if you want that nigga get it in blood." Loni said as if he was a gangster.

Bum hopped out the car, slammed the door and pulled out his Heckler and Koch four fifth, and with no hesitation he started smacking Loni in the temple with the barrel of the gun. "You bitch ass nigga, you better have ma money by midnight." He shouted while kicking Loni in the ribs and face. Loni just laid on the concrete in a fetal position as Bum got back in his car and pulled off.

***

By the time Bum pulled in front of Gigi's his anger had simmered down. He looked at his reflection in the visors mirror and said, "*Try to look out for a nigga now I'm gon have to kill him!*"

Bum placed his pistol underneath the driver's side seat and went into the restaurant. Gigi's was a soul food spot where the old timers and church goers patronized in the early mornings and Sundays after church. Late night, after most of the clubs closed, around 4am, was when the younger crowd came. It was like an after party there on Friday and Saturday nights. That's when Bum and pretty much everyone else carried their pistols inside the spot. Since it was a Wednesday morning, he could leave the pistol in the car.

As Bum walked in the door one of the waitresses recognized him. Most of the waitresses that worked there were older women with kids and grandkids from the neighborhood. "Hey baby you want your usual?" She asked with a fixed smile.

"Yeah, throw in some home fries and a half and half please." Bum responded.

"Turkey sausage, grits, cheese eggs, home fries and a half and half to go right?" The waitress asked.

"Right."

She went toward the back and gave the cook the order, "About ten minute's baby," She said after giving the order to the cook.

Bum responded, "Ok thanks." Just as he sat back in peace waiting for the food, his phone started vibrating and snapped him back to reality.

"Ayo, who dis?" He said as he answered the phone.

"What up fam? It's Will."

"Oh, what up Will, where you at?"

"Right now I'm at the gas station on Fillmore."

"Oh you driving?"

"Yeah."

"Come to Gigi's and holla at me." Bum stated.

"Be there in 'bout ten minutes."

"Yup," Bum responded as he hung up. During his conversation with Will he noticed two dime pieces toward the back eating. *Damn them bitches bad as hell.* He thought to himself. He contemplated which one to approach. One of the women had copper brown skin, long straight hair, pretty lips and a pretty face. She looked to be a little taller than her friend but they were sitting down so that was a guess. The other woman was caramel complexioned, had a short Halle Berry type hair style, pretty eyes and a pretty face. "Here you go baby," the waitress said handing him his food, snapping him out his trance. Bum got the money out of his pocket to pay for the food. He gave the waitress a twenty and told her to keep the change as he always did.

"You dropped this," a sexy voice said to him. He turned around and was surprised to see the two girls behind him at the cash register. The one with the long hair had a fifty dollar bill in her hand and was handing it to Bum.

"Oh...Thank you." Bum said while keeping eye contact. He then turned back toward the cash register; handed the waitress the fifty dollar bill and gestured that it was for the two women's meals and then left. He got back in his car and waited for Will. As he reached for his pistol the two girls came out. The one with the long hair smiled and waved bye to him. Bum threw the gun back under the seat and hopped out the car. "Excuse me, can I have a minute of your time?" He asked politely. She seemed classier than the hood rats he was used to dealing with. As she turned around Bum extended his hand. "My name is Brandon." He said giving her his government.

"I'm Misa," she responded in a soft sexy voice.

"Misa I was hoping that if you had some free time, I could take you out to a movie or dinner or something."

"Brandon why don't you give me your phone number and I'll call you when I have some free time."

"That will work." He said. Misa took down his number and promised to call. Bum watched as Misa got in her car.

Will finally pulled up, "Damn who dem bitches?" He asked excitedly.

"Some broads I just met, what up though?" Bum changed the subject.

"I need two O's." said Will.

"Where you gon be at?" Bum asked.

"I'm gon be on the block."

"I'ma see you in twenty minutes meet me at Peaches house."

"Alright." Will said as he pulled off.

***

Bum pulled into the parking lot of the apartment building that Jasmine stayed in. He had moved her to the apartments on the North side of Buffalo away from the crime ridden East and West sides of the city. Although there was crime on the North side, the East and West sides were notorious for most of the drug trade and 90% of the homicides in the city. Bum wasn't staying with Jasmine but she convinced him to keep some of his work over there instead of renting out another house to stash it in. That way she knew that her and her son would see him more often. It didn't take much for him to think about, he knew it would be better to keep the work spread out rather than in one location, plus he enjoyed seeing Jasmine. Even though they weren't intimate he still loved her, and he always wanted to see his son, he wanted to see all his kids.

Bum walked up to the apartment and rang the bell before he put his key in and opened the door, which he always did when he came over. He did this out of habit more than anything. He knew that Jasmine wouldn't dare have another nigga in the apartment around his son or his work. As he walked in his son ran towards him hollering, "Daddy, daddy!"

"What up little man?" Bum screamed as he playfully threw his son in the air.

"I got some new boots." Little James yelled out.

"Oh yeah, let me see them," Bum said as he put Little James down. As his son ran to get his boots Jasmine came in the living room. Jasmine was fly, she had a honey complexion and she stayed with her hair and nails done. She looked like a younger, thicker version of Jada Pinkett. She was 5-4 and 130 pounds. Bum couldn't help but notice how good she looked. She had on skin tight dark blue jeans with a tight shirt that hugged her perfect 32 c breast, paired with dark blue leather boots which looked like kids boots on her size four feet.

"Hi." Jasmine said in a shy voice. She missed Bum, even though he kept his work over there, he hadn't been there in over a week.

"What's going on?" Bum asked while staring at her.

"Nothing, I'm off of work till Monday."

"I know."

"See daddy?" James said coming back with his brand new timberland boots on the wrong feet.

"Yeah, them are hot. I'm gon' get me some just like yours," Bum said while bending down checking out the boots on his sons small feet. As Bum stood up he turned his attention back towards Jasmine. "So, where you headed to?" Bum asked.

"I'm going over my mother's house." Jasmine answered.

"James you going to see your grandmother?" Bum asked his son.

"Yeah I'm going to see my granny." James answered in excitement.

"I got to go handle some business. I might stop back through later." Bum said as he walked to the room where he kept his work. He closed the door behind him, went to the stash spot and pulled out half a kilo of crack. He then grabbed his digital scale and weighed 56 grams. Next he put it in a sandwich bag and placed it in his jacket pocket. He then put up the rest of the crack and the scale and walked out the room. Bum walked over towards his son, shook his small hand and said "See you later little man."

"Bye daddy." As Bum opened the door to leave Jasmine abruptly said,

"I missed you."

"Me too daddy." James added.

Bum paused in the door way then turned toward the both of them. "I'ma be back tonight...that's ma word." Jasmine looked at him as if she didn't believe him, but she knew he was a man of his word, most of the time.

***

As Bum got into his car he immediately threw in Young Jeezy's CD *The Inspiration* to get his mind off Jasmine, and back into the streets which is where he was headed. As he made his way from the North side to the East side he really paid attention to the difference between the two parts of town. The East side was a contrast to the calm streets of the North side. On almost every corner of the East side, there were abandoned buildings, hustlers, crack heads, dope fiends, whores being pimped by the high they were chasing, poverty and hopelessness.

Bum pulled into the driveway and Peaches met him at the door. She was a well known crack head in the neighborhood. The hustlers from the area would go to her house to bag up crack or just chill for a minute. "Hey Bum, I know you got something for me." Peaches said yearning for a hit.

"Peaches I'm fucked up right now, maybe next time." Bum said.

"Aw here y'all go with that bullshit, somebody gon give me something, one of you niggas," Peaches responded as they walked to the living room where Will was waiting. "Will you gon have to break me off something." Peaches yelled while walking towards the back room then added, "Shit all this traffic in ma shit…fuck that you got to hit house nigga."

Will just started shaking his head. "What up Bum?" he asked.

"You...Here you go." He handed Will the 56 grams.

"Two G's right?" Will asked as he handed it to Bum.

Bum didn't respond he just peeled two hundred dollars from the bundle of money and handed it to Will. "Nine a O now."

"Oh-alright." Will responded. Peaches came back into the living room with her crack pipe in hand,

"Give me mine now Will." She demanded. Will opened the bag, broke off about half a gram and threw it on the table. Peaches snatched it up and put damn near half of it in her pipe. She then put the pipe to her lips, and lit it taking her hit. She held the smoke in for about three seconds, and then blew the foul smelling smoke into the living room air. Her eyes were glassy as if she were in another world. She stuttered, "Tha-tha-that's some gooood sh-sh-shit, and it bu-burns cle-clean." Will looked up at Bum smiling and nodding his head yeah, as if to say thanks. Bum responded by winking at him.

***

By 9:40pm business was going as usual for Bum. He had time on his hands to check on one of his spots run by his boys Mojo and Bumpkin. As Bum pulled in front of the house, two crack heads were coming out. Bum walked toward the house while Mojo stood in the doorway.

"Hi Bum." The female crack head spoke as she was leaving the house. Bum noticed a box under her arm. "I got a brand new Sony DVD player for sale." She added.

"What you want for it?" Bum asked.

"Just two grams." She said as if she was giving him a deal of a lifetime.

"I already got three of them." Bum said letting her know he didn't need another DVD player, knowing she would drop the price.

"Give me one gram for it." She continued to play lets make a deal.

"Half a gram." Bum bidded to her.

"Come on Bum its brand new," She moaned. "Alright give me the half gram and ten dollars so I can get some cigarettes and a beer."

Bum walked to the door. "Mojo, what up?" He said walking pass Mojo.

Mojo was a little dude in stature at 5'5" and about 150 pounds, but he had the heart of a lion. He didn't take any shit from anybody. He always had his .50 caliber Desert Eagle on him and used it often. "Same shit. Man we downed seven ounces in less than 24 hours, its bleeding!" he excitedly whispered.

"Yo Bumpkin get half a gram fa me." Bum yelled to Bumpkin who was usually in the kitchen bagging up crack.

"How much work is left?" Bum asked Mojo.

"Shit, you brought over nine ounces last night." Mojo answered.

Bumpkin came to the front room. "Yo what up Bum?" he said handing him the half gram. "This shit movin' ma'n." He added in his country accent. He was a country boy from Alabama. He moved to Buffalo when he was 15 to stay with his aunt. He stood at about 6'3", 250 pounds. He had a strong country accent with a deep voice and he stuttered. He kept everyone around him laughing. Bumpkin was always the first one to gun and the last one to run. He was a loyal ass nigga, the type of dude you wanted around you if shit got thick.

"I heard y'all only got two ounces left." Bum said to Bumpkin as he handed the crack head the half gram and the ten dollars that he promised her. Mojo grabbed the DVD player and closed the door in her face.

"Yeah probably a little over." Bumpkin answered.

"I'ma bring back 6 more ounces that should hold till Friday morning right?" Bum asked.

"Eight ounces should hold us till Saturday night normally." Mojo responded.

"Alright I'ma be back in 30 minutes." Bum said as he walked out and headed towards his car.

As Bum got to the corner of the block he blew the horn and threw the peace sign up to the group of men standing there. They all knew Bum and spoke every other time, but tonight they all just had screw faces and ice grills. Bum figured the time would come when they would get mad because of how much money his crack house was making. They were losing out on money because of the quality and quantity of Bum's product. He knew that any day now, they would try and shut down his house by any means necessary but he wasn't worried about it. Bum, Mojo, Bumpkin and their young guns were down to ride, ready for war, although he hoped it wouldn't come to that. He wanted to keep the peace because war could mean losing out on time and time is money. So Bum just ignored their ice grills and just pulled off. Bum usually never went to Jasmine's apartment twice in one day while he was handling business but he decided to get rid of the work from there first since he only had another half a kilo at his other spot. He rang the bell as usual before he opened the door. The apartment was empty, Jasmine and little James were still out. He headed to the room with the work, got it from the stash spot; got the scale and weighed one hundred and sixty eight grams. He put the crack in a larger sandwich bag then put it in his jacket pocket. He then weighed the remainder of the work. *Two hundred and seventy six grams?* He thought to himself. *"What the fuck?"* He mumbled confused. He then remembered seeing Will with the two ounces earlier. Bum put everything up then left out the door, double checked that it was locked and headed on his way.

Bum got back to the trap house at about 10:45pm. As he walked in the house Uno was sitting near the window.

"What up big bra?" Uno asked.

"What's good wit you Uno?"

"Tryin' to make this paper." Uno answered. Uno was the brains of the three man clique they called their Young Guns. He was cool and smart as hell to be only 17. The other two were; Bull, who was the biggest and craziest of the three, and Pete, whom they sometimes called Pistol, was the wildest. They were in the front room playing video games and smoking weed. They all were only 17 years old, loose, and would do almost anything.

"What up Big Bra?" They simultaneously greeted Bum.

"What up y'all where Mojo and Bumpkin?" Bum asked.

"I don't know where Mojo at, but Bumpkin in the kitchen." Bull answered while puffing on the weed.

Bum walked to the kitchen, "Here is the six ounces." Bum said as he threw the crack on the kitchen table.

"Alright." Bumpkin said without raising his eyes from the crack he was packaging.

"Where Mojo?" Bum asked him.

"He went to the store to get some bags."

"What you boys getting into tonight?" Bum asked.

"Shit. We gon chill tonight. We went to Birchfields last night, might hit the strip tomorrow." Bumpkin responded.

"I'm gon take it in early tonight too after I go see the nigga Loni."

"Oh you finally seen that nigga." Bumpkin asked as he looked up at Bum.

"Yeah. I told him he gotta have mines by midnight."

"Want me to come wit you?"

"Naw I got this, I'ma see you tomorrow." Bum said as he headed out.

"One fam."

***

It was 11:45pm when Bum parked his car a few feet from the block where Loni hung out at. He sat in his car waiting on Loni and at 12:15am he was about to pull off. When he was about to pull off, he finally saw Loni walking up the block. When Loni got a few feet from the car and noticed Bum in the driver side, he immediately turned around and started to run. Before he could get too far, Bum got out of the car and started shooting at him. He caught Loni in the back thigh. Loni fell to the ground screaming, "HELP, SOMEBODY HELP!"

As Bum stood over him about to put one in his head someone screamed, "I called the police their on their way."

Bum looked into Lonis' eyes and told him, "Next time." He then hopped back into his car. As Bum got a block away, the police sped past him. He turned on the radio, the quiet storm was on, it was 12:37am.

He pulled into the parking lot of the apartment building at 1am. He turned the ignition off but kept the radio on listening to the quiet storm. He stayed in the car for another half an hour getting his head out of the streets, at least until the next morning. He finally headed to the apartment, he didn't bother to ring the bell, it was too late. He grabbed his son out of his bed and took him into Jasmine's room and laid in the bed wrapping his arms around them. He took a deep breath, closed his eyes and fell asleep.

Chapter 2

Lex pulled into the parking lot of the huge campus of the University at Buffalo. He started having second thoughts about his intentions for being there. Lex wanted to re-enroll into the University, but what he wanted more was to be back on the football team. Besides being a college student and the starting strong safety on the football team his freshmen year, he was also heavily involved in the streets. The son of Big Bank, one of the top heroin distributors in the town, Lex was born into the street game. His father, uncle and grandfather were all hustlers. Lex did his own thing, so while his father didn't want him in the street game, he himself *was* the game. Big Bank knew it was in his son's blood.

Instead of heroin Lex sold crack. Since he was doing his own thing, he never asked his father for anything involving drugs. Growing up Lex received all the things the son of a baller should receive. He always had the latest fashions first. When he graduated from high school his dad bought him a brand new Mercedes Benz. Now at 21 Lex was driving a 2008 Nissan Maxima with factory everything. He didn't like the spotlight from hustling. He only liked the spotlight on the football field.

***

After Lex finally got up the audacity to proceed with his plan, he headed towards the athletic department first to talk to his old coach. As Lex approached the athletic department, one of his old teammates happily greeted him. "So what's been going on, you gon get back on the team and help us out or what?" Trevor, the starting middle linebacker asked. He and Lex were the backbone of the defense which was the best in the Mid American Conference when they both manned it, now it was one of the worst.

"Yeah that's what I'm here for, I miss this shit." Lex responded while looking around the campus. As he turned back to face Trevor he added, "But damn son, I see you dun added about 20 pounds of muscle, I got to get ma shit up." Lex was in good shape in spite of the fact that he hadn't played football in over a year. Lex stood about 5'10" and 205 pounds of muscle.

"That's where I'm headed to now, the weight room." Trevor said.

"Alright I'ma let you go get that weight up." Lex said as he slapped Trevor up. "Oh yeah, is coach in?" Lex asked before Trevor walked off.

"Yeah he in. He gon be happy to see you." Trevor said smiling.

"Peace." Lex said before walking toward the building.

***

After meeting with the coach, Lex was feeling good about the future and the coach was excited to see him as well. He told Lex that he would have to pay his own tuition a semester and get back in good standing academically, then join the team as a walk-on until he maintained the grade point average required by the NCAA to be eligible to play. He wasn't worried about maintaining the GPA; he had always been an above average student. He just needed to concentrate on his attendance in the classroom rather than in the streets. Lex figured he could enroll in both summer semesters and get 24 credit hours with at least a 3.0 GPA and be eligible for the fall football season. So he went to the administration building to inquire about summer classes. Just his luck, the spring semester was close to ending and there were summer course books available. As Lex looked through the book he decided to pick some simple courses and take some of the courses which he had failed his last semester.

He had to go to student records to get a copy of his transcripts. After getting this, he saw that he got an F in Sociology. He decided to take that as well as Spanish 101, African American Studies and an art class. After completing his paperwork, he was officially pre-enrolled.

Feeling good about himself, Lex didn't want to leave the campus yet. He actually enjoyed being in such a positive environment. The University had some of the sexiest women in the city. Lex went to the student activity building to get something to eat. When he got there he saw many women in all different flavors. It seemed as if they were in packs throughout the large area. It wasn't that he didn't know about all the women at the University. It had been over a year since he stepped foot on the campus and he forgot how serious it was. All he could do was say to himself *Damn* with a smile on his face as he looked around the entire room.

"Girl who the fuck is that?!" A light skinned Mya look-a-like asked as the other girls sitting at the table turned to see who she was talking about. Lex was at the cash register getting something to eat when three girls looking like the black version of Charlie's Angels surrounded him. He looked from side to side then behind him. At first it looked as though they were ready to whip on him. The Mya look-a-like introduced herself as she stuck her hand out for him to shake. "How you doing?"

"I'm good. How y'all doing?" Lex asked all three of them, noticing they were a tag team. "My name is Lex."

"Oh shit, I knew I knew you from somewhere," one of the girls blurted out with her hand over her mouth. "You mess with that Caribbean girl from Canisius College, you Billy D's cousin." The girl added with a slight smile on her face.

Lex just looked at the girl trying to figure out how she knew so much about him.

"How you know Billy D?" Lex asked.

"How you know Michelle?" The girl asked as to say you figure it out.

"Michelle. Michelle who?" Lex asked, confused as to whom she was talking about.

"That Michelle." The girl pointed back to the table where Michelle was sitting with an evil look on her face. As Lex looked over and saw Michelle, he immediately recognized her. *Michelle.* He had met her his freshman year at UB. He used to fuck with her, well fuck her along with several other girls on campus. Michelle stopped fucking with him after she found out that he was fucking one of her friends. In a way, he was happy that she found out and stopped fucking with him because she was starting to become a bug a boo. Lex was a ladies man, good looking, brown skinned, wave cut with good skin and perfect white teeth. He didn't want any women hating him.

After Lex got his food, he walked over to the table with Charlie's Angels. He sat down next to Michelle who ignored him and turned her head away from him. "How y'all doing?" Lex asked the other three ladies at the table as they all said hello and introduced themselves one by one. Then he turned his attention toward Michelle.

"So. How you doing Michelle?" Lex asked.

Michelle continued to ignore him. After seeing her again for the first time in a year he wanted her again, if just for one night. Michelle looked better than he remembered. She was pretty with a nice body. She was short, light skinned, petite with nice suckable titties and a nice round ass and he remembered that the pussy was good. She had pouty lips and long hair with cat like eyes. As much as Lex wanted her at that moment he kept his cool and just made conversation with the other girls at the table. After about an hour of flirting with the ladies, the whole time he could see that he was getting under Michelle's skin, so he decided to leave.

Before he left, the Mya look-a-like told him that they were going to the Groove night club that night and hoped to see him there. When she said that, Michelle immediately sighed in annoyance. "Nice meeting y'all." Lex said to the ladies as they all said good bye in unison. "Bye Michelle." Lex said trying to make eye contact with her before he left. She still ignored him. Lex took that and breezed off.

***

While walking to his car, Lex decided to step his hustle game up until football season. Then he would slow down to concentrate on school and football. He called Bum. "Yo what up Bum?"

"What's good fam?"

"I need to holla at you," Lex said.

"Where you at?" Bum asked.

"I'm 'bout to be in traffic, where you need me to be?" Lex responded.

"Meet me at the car wash on Main and Bryant in a half?"

"Alright homey." Lex responded as he ended the call.

Lex pulled into the lot of the car wash beside Bum who was vacuuming out his car. Bum saw Lex pull along side of him and continued to vacuum. "What's good?" Lex asked walking towards Bum.

"What up fam?" Bum said as he stopped vacuuming to greet Lex.

"Yo I need a bird." Lex said, rubbing his hands together in front of his face.

Bum, with a business look on his face asked, "In a hour, where you gon be?"

"Over Shorty house." Lex said.

"Ya girl house?" Bum asked while putting the vacuum hose back on the wall.

"Yeah."

"See you in a hour." Bum said as he started his car up.

It took Lex less than 30 minutes to get to his house to get the money for the key and make it to Iyani's house where he was to meet Bum to make the transaction. Iyani was a good girl. She lived a couple of blocks from Canisius College where she studied elementary education. She was from Trinidad and Tobago, and had caramel skin, long curly hair, exotic eyes and nice lips. She was 5'5" and 135 pounds, and had a perfect body. In every aspect she was a dime. Lex had been with her for a year and a half even though he was a playboy. Iyani was the closest thing to wifey, he was definitely feeling her. She was the realest female he had ever dealt with. Iyani had her head right, had goals, and was mature beyond her 20 years.

Lex didn't stay with her, but he did have the keys to her house. He moved her there because he didn't want nosey roommates around when he came over. He knew Iyani was still at school at this time so he could handle his business while she wasn't there. Lex looked at his watch; he still had 20 minutes before Bum came through. He knew Bum was punctual so he decided to recount the money. Usually he bought a quarter for $6,500 or a half of a kilo for $13,000, but Bum only charged him $24,000 for a whole thing. Just as he got done counting the money, his phone started ringing. "Yo." He said, answering the phone.

"Yo son I'm getting off the 33 right now, see you in 2 minutes." Bum screamed into the receiver just enough to be heard over the music and traffic. By time Lex wrapped the money back up, Bum was at the door. Lex let him in. "L.E.X bonafide hustler. You tryin' to step it up huhn man?" Bum remarked as Lex let him in.

"Yeah, I'm gon turn it up a little." Lex responded as they exchanged the money and coke.

"No doubt, I'm feeling dat." Bum said as he handed Lex the key of coke.

"Good lookin' fam." Lex said.

"Holla back at me." Bum shouted before he got in his car and pulled off.

Lex watched as Bum pulled off, thinking out loud, *all that money dat nigga got yet he stay in a hooptie...Smart ass nigga.*

Lex didn't want to take any chances of losing on the coke so he called his man Smitty up. Smitty was an ex-hustler turned smoker, but Lex trusted him. They shared a mutual respect for one another. Smitty was an expert with coke, baking soda, water and fire.

Smitty first cooked three ounces of coke with a little baking soda. After seeing that the baking soda stuck he decided to cook 250 grams with more baking soda. This time he got back 300 grams. Smitty knew that the coke was pretty good because of how well the baking soda stuck and how quick it hardened up. He wanted to see if his intuition was correct so he tested it. Lex knew by his facial expression that it was pretty good. After coming down off of his high Smitty gave Lex his approval, and then he whipped up the rest.

After all was said and done, Smitty blew the 36 ounces up to a total of 43 ounces of good crack. Lex gave Smitty two hundred dollars and a half ounce for his work, and then sent him on his way.

"Good lookin' Smitty, I might need you again soon."

"Anytime Lex, anytime just call me up." Smitty said as he left. After Lex cleaned up, he was headed out to inform his usualls that he had that good. Now it was on. Get money.

Chapter 3

The club was pumping wall to wall women. It was a 4 to 1 ratio in favor of the woman. Four females to each male. There were four sections in the club, downstairs, upstairs, the reggae room and VIP. Lex and Billy D were moving throughout the club trying to find something to slide into later on.

"Ayo cuzo, shorty right there." Billy D screamed in Lex's ear barely audible over the loud music, while motioning toward his potential night cap. The young lady noticed Billy D and Lex watching her and started to dance more seductively. With her back to them, she started shaking her ass. Before she knew it Billy D was right up on her, in her ear. "Ayo ma you need to save me some of that," Billy D screamed over the music, his lips touching her ear. Shorty turned; as soon as she saw Billy D up close in front of her she started smiling.

Billy D was one of them niggas who didn't give a fuck about shit. He was known to bust his gun. Niggas knew he had bodies, but they didn't know how many. Billy D used to carry out contracts on niggas heads, murder for hire. By looking at him you could never imagine him to be like this. He was a pretty boy and he always had a lot of girls. He was quiet most of the time, except when he was in villain mode.

"Save you some of what?" Shorty screamed back in Billy D's ear. Shorty was stacked, 5'6" about 140 pounds, all ass with a pretty face.

Billy D grabbed her by her hand, pulled her in closer and lowered his head to her ear. "I'ma be frank, well actually I'm Billy D but I'ma be frank for a minute just to get ma point across… save me some of that ass." He said with all seriousness.

Shorty liked his directness. "Well frank I mean Billy D, I'ma be Trixie, and you could have at least started with a regular conversation, a phone number or something." Trixie said with a slight attitude. She was putting up a front, trying to play hard to get, knowing she wanted to give Billy D the ass and more, and Billy D had seen through the front also.

"Well Trixie I'm sorry if I offended you in anyway, but I get a little schizo sometimes. Frank just says the right shit at the wrong time." He said with an apologetic face.

This got another smile from Trixie. "You are funny, why don't you give me your number and I might call you… Billy D… not Frank." She said smiling.

Billy D wrote his cell phone number on a piece of paper, as he handed it to her, he asked, "What are you doing after the club?"

Trixie gave him a seductive look and responded, "I'm going home … alone, unless I get drunk."

Billy D immediately asked, "What you drinking?"

***

Lex was circulating throughout the club when he noticed Michelle. Michelle looked at him and then rolled her eyes. He laughed it off but he couldn't help but notice how good she was looking. She had on a skin tight skirt barely stopping below her ass, with a blouse that exposed her belly ring and some fuck me pumps on. He wanted to fuck her so bad that his dick damn near poked through his jeans, but he knew his chances with her were slim to none, but he had a game plan.

***

"Fam, what's good?" Mojo hollered with his hands in the air holding a bottle of Moet in one hand and a Corona in the other. He approached Billy D. Mojo and Billy D were tight, they did a couple of hits together a couple of years back. They both were known gun clappers. Mojo stopped doing hits and concentrated on the crack game, Billy D still did hits on occasion, basically for "therapy", so they rarely saw each other now a day.

"Ma nigga what up?" Billy D responded as he and Mojo embraced.

"Ain't shit. About to get pissy and fuck about four or five of these ho's namean?" Mojo shouted in a drunken slur.

"No doubt… who you here wit?" Billy D asked to make sure Mojo was alright and would get home safely.

"Just me and Bumpkin." Mojo replied.

"Let me get some of that Corona." Billy D said to Mojo.

"Ain't shit in this bottle, this bottle so I can smash it across one of these niggas heads if need be. Here, drink some of this." Mojo extended the bottle of Moet to Billy D.

"Naw I'm good." Billy D responded. Mojo shrugged his shoulders and took another guzzle.

***

Lex noticed Michelle watching him on the low, that's when he knew it would be easier then he thought. He decided he would get back to Michelle later, but now he needed to work on a back up plan just in case things didn't work with Michelle. Lex was in the ear of a dime piece. She was feeling Lex's conversation, when from out of nowhere Michelle slid in between the two. "Excuse me!" Michelle said to the girl with an attitude as she grabbed Lex's hand putting him against the wall and started grinding her ass on his dick. Michelle then turned around and shouted in Lex's ear over the music. "You's a ho!"

"Why you say that?" Lex responded.

"You all in that bitch face, while all of this is ten feet away from you." Michelle said while motioning her hands down her body.

"You was giving me the cold shoulder. I thought you was done wit me?" Lex responded.

"You still shouldn't be all in these ho's faces right in front of Me." she shot back.

"You buggin'." Lex said.

"Well I need you to give me a ride home tonight. Can you do that?" Michelle asked.

"Billy D driving." Lex told her.

"So what you saying, No?" Michelle asked while grabbing his dick.

As his dick started to get hard again he responded, "Meet me outside at 4:00".

By 3:30am damn near everybody in the club was good and drunk, especially Mojo. Mojo was walking through the club with a fresh bottle of Moet bumping and pushing niggas. He spilled some Moet on this one kid, "What the fuck nigga! I spent a buck on this shit and you made me spill ma shit!" Mojo screamed. The kid spit in Mojo's face. Before the kid could blink Mojo smashed both the Corona bottle that he still had in his hand and the Moet bottle over his head. The kid just started leaking. He was with about ten niggas though. Mojo didn't know this nor did he give a fuck. The kid and his mans just started pounding on Mojo. Everybody around the scuffle started to spread away from the melee. Bumpkin and Billy D were both in the ears of a set of double mint twins.

One of the girls said, "Oh shit." and pointed in the direction of the ruckus. Billy D and Bumpkin looked at each other then immediately ran toward the eye of the storm. They knew it was Mojo. Billy D just started hitting people trying to get them off his man.

Out of nowhere Lex joined in smashing niggas in the face. Then Bumpkin hit a nigga so hard you literally heard the man's cheek bone break over the music throughout the club as he dropped. That pretty much made his whole team pause for a minute.

By the time security got there three men were out cold. One was leaking like the Niagara Falls. Another guy's whole left side of his face was broke and swollen to about three times its normal size. Security gathered everyone that was involved and threw them out. The police were thick outside of the club, as they normally were close to closing time at 4:00 am.

Mojo was still talking shit black eye, bloody lip torn shirt and all. "You bitch ass niggas. Ya'll pussy, all you niggas!"

Billy D grabbed him and pulled him along. "Yo chill fa da police lock you up." Billy D demanded.

"Man fuck dem they pussy too." Mojo said.

"Where y'all park at?" Bumpkin asked Lex.

"Around the corner." Lex responded.

"We parked right up here, come wit us and we'll ride ya'll around the corner." Bumpkin said. While in the truck Mojo immediately reached for his pistol in the glove compartment. They pulled right behind Billy D's Yukon, parked, rolled a couple of Dutches and chilled. They were still chilling in the truck when Lex's cell phone started going off.

"Yo who dis?" Lex answered.

"It's Michelle, where you at? I still need that ride."

"Where you at?" Lex asked.

"In front of the club." Michelle responded.

"Stay there." Lex said before hanging up.

"Damn I almost forgot about shorty with the fat ass." Billy D said. "Come on Lex I got to see if I see her, after this shit I need some pussy." He added. Mojo was asleep in the front seat of the Truck.

"Ayo we out make sure ya'll holla at us tomorrow, one Bumpkin. Mojo call me alright?" Billy D said to Mojo.

"This nigga sleep, I'ma tell him to call you Bill, ya'll niggas be easy." Bumpkin said as Lex and Billy D got out of the truck.

As Billy D pulled in front of the club he didn't see Trixie anywhere in sight. *"Damn where dat bitch at?"* Billy D said thinking out loud while Lex was on the phone.

"I'm looking right at you, I told you I was riding with Billy D. I'm in the black Yukon in front of you." Lex told Michelle.

As Michelle got in the back seat of the truck Billy D's cell phone started to go off. "Hi Billy D." Michelle spoke from the rear of the truck.

"What's up? Hold on." Billy D respond as he answered the phone. "Who dis?"

"It's Trixie, where you at?" Trixie asked.

"Ayo I'm in front of the club in the black Yukon," Billy D told Trixie. *Pop pop pop pop pop pop pop pop pop pop* was the sound that came from a black Cadillac truck as it sped off. "What the fuck, who was dem niggas shooting at?" Billy D asked looking at Lex.

"I don't know they ain't hit shit… fucking clowns." Lex responded.

Tap tap

"Oh shit." Michelle screamed as she ducked down in the back of the truck.

"What the fuck you jumping for, wit your scary ass?" Lex said to Michelle laughing. Billy D rolled the window down to talk to Trixie, who had just tapped on the window.

"Trixie hop in the back…"

"Ayo take me to ma car." Lex told Billy D. Lex had left his car parked in front of Billy D's house.

"Trixie that's Michelle, Michelle Trixie." Billy D introduced the two.

"Holla at me tomorrow." Lex told Billy D after getting out of the truck and letting Trixie get in the front seat.

"Alright." Billy D responded as Trixie shut the door and he pulled off.

***

As Lex and Michelle got in his Maxima, Michelle had a change of heart. "Let's go to your house." Michelle suggested. Lex looked at her, turned the ignition and they were off. When they got to Lex's house Michelle started to doubt her decision. "I can't believe I'm getting involved in your web of deceit again." Michelle admitted. "Why am I here?" she added.

Lex exhaled in frustration. "Look here, I'm not forcing you to do nothing you don't want to do." Lex said while pulling some money out his pocket. "Here is twenty dollars there go the phone call you a cab and bounce if you want, I'm tired. I'm going to sleep." He added. While in the bathroom he listened to see if she was calling a cab. As he came out the bathroom with a towel over his face, he headed towards his bedroom.

When he got to the room, Michelle was at the edge of the bed with just her panties and bra on. Lex immediately started to remove his Tims and jeans. As he walked over to Michelle he lowered down on her and started to kiss her neck while undoing her bra. He slowly started sucking her titties. Michelle was singing in a low moan of pleasure. He proceeded to remove her panties, and then she took charge. She flipped Lex over on his back and started French kissing him passionately. She moved from his neck and to his chest as she removed his boxers, she then placed his dick in her hand and lowered her soft full lips and moist mouth in position to give Lex a blow job. She then put a condom on his dick. She mounted on top of him with his fully erect penis in her hand so that she could guide it to ecstasy. She began to ride his dick like a jockey in the Kentucky derby. Lex just grabbed her waist and held on for the ride. Lex then rose up and started to palm her ass as he sucked her breast again. He flipped her on her back and started pumping slow, and then he picked up the pace. At this point Michelle was moaning loud, and then they both came simultaneously.

***

Billy D was headed to Trixie's house. Trixie began to arouse Billy D as they were driving. She began playing with his dick as she sucked on his neck while he drove. At this point Billy D was thinking of all the positions he was going to put Trixie in and how that ass was going to shake as he pounded it from the back.

When they pulled up in front of the house, Billy D cut off the ignition and hopped out the truck faster than Trixie. Billy D and Trixie walked up to the door. As Trixie opened the door she put her hand on Billy D's chest to stop him from entering the apartment. "Thanks for the ride home, call me," she said with a teasing smile as she handed him a piece of paper with her phone number on it and kissed him on his neck then closed the door.

Billy D stood there for a second in disbelief. He just knew that he was going to get some pussy. *"Dirty ass bitch."* he mumbled to himself as he walked back to his truck tearing up the piece of paper with her phone number on it. *"Fuck that tramp."* he angrily added while his dick was on hard. As he got back in his truck he pulled out his cell phone and dialed. "Shoni. I'm on my way over." Billy D said to one of his young shorties. "*Well I guess I'ma have her give me some mouth to dick resuscitation.*" Billy D thought out loud. With that statement he was off to Shoni's house.

Chapter 4

"*Billy D come give me a hug.*" Billy D's father demanded as a young Billy D ran over and gave his father a hug. While on one knee his father embraced him. *"You want to take a ride with me?"* He asked as he let Billy D out of his embrace. As Billy D backed up, he back peddled with fear in his eyes as he saw his fathers torso riddled with bullet holes and blood all over his body. He then looked down and saw blood all over his clothes and hands.

This nightmare woke Billy D up out of his sleep. Billy D's father, Big Bill was a hustler in every "cents" of the word. He along with his older brother Bank had the east side of Buffalo on smash with heroin in the 80's. In the late 80's a couple of young crews wanted a piece of the heroin trade because it was so lucrative despite the crack boom. The young crews went to war against each other in 89; a lot of blood was shed. In 91 the two crews called for peace and cliqued up deciding to take Big Bill and Banks crew to war.

They went to war the whole year in 92. A lot of bodies dropped. By 93 the war settled down and both sides were seeing money.

One spring day in 93, Big Bill had just dropped little Billy D off at home after spending the day with him. As Big Bill was leaving out of the house Billy D watched his dad leave from the window. Just before he got in the car he threw the peace sign up to Billy D. As he turned to get in his car a black van pulled up and two masked gun men had the drop on him. He tried to reach for his gun but the two killers let off on him giving him no chance. Billy D watched the whole incident from the window.

***

Billy D woke up and it was still dark outside. He looked at the red lights on the clock which read 4:10am. Billy D went to the bathroom, splashed water on his face and looked in the mirror. In his eyes he saw hate and coldness. He never understood where the hate was coming from. The hate was like a beast and the beast fed off of blood shed. That's why killing came so easy to him. He had a job to do that day. He had been watching his Victim for over two weeks. He decided that the best time to get him would be at 5:15am, that's when the man's girl left for work. Billy D was going to catch her just as she came out of the door, put the knife to her neck and tell her to be quiet as he entered the house.

As Billy D was picking his tools for the job he looked at the clock. He picked his 9mm Beretta semi auto, and a 7 inch hunting knife.

He arrived outside the house at 5am. After parking his car down the street and walking to the house, it was 5:09am, and it was still pitch black dark out. Billy D stood on the side of the house waiting for the woman to come out so that he could enter the house. At exactly 5:15am she came out. She then ran back in the house as if she had forgotten something. The whole time she never saw Billy D. She left the door open which was good for Billy D and especially for her because now he didn't have to use her for entry. Billy D slid in the house through the open door and hid behind it.

"What the fuck? Stop all dat fuck'n noise!" Billy D heard the Vic scream to his girl as she hurriedly got ready to head out for work.

"Shut the fuck up...get a life." She mumbled to herself as she walked out of the door. Billy D watched as she hopped in a Lexus and sped off.

"And don't take ma car either!" the Vic yelled out about 3 minutes too late, not realizing she had already left. Billy D proceeded to the bedroom. The house was totally dark except for the light illuminating from the bathroom. This guided Billy D through the house, to the bedroom. Billy D stood outside of the bedroom as the Vic's snoring echoed throughout the house. When he entered the room he felt under the pillows for any weapons, careful not to wake the Vic. He pulled from under the pillow a glock 27. He had to keep it and add it to his collection. Billy D then pulled out his Beretta and cocked it purposely to wake the Vic up, which it did. The Vic immediately reached under his pillow feeling for his gun frantically. He couldn't find it, so he tried to charge at Billy D. When he charged, he lunged right into the blade of the hunting knife. This took all the fight out of him. Billy D then pulled the knife from the Vic's gut and spun him around, lifted his chin and slit his throat from ear to ear. Billy D then walked out of the house unnoticed to his car and pulled off. When he made it home, he seemed at peace. After taking a shower he decided to take a well deserved nap.

***

Billy D woke up filling like a new man later that day. It was 1:30pm and the sun was shining through the window. Billy D decided to head to the mall. After purchasing the usual; a pair of

Tims, a few pair of jeans, a couple of shirts, a CD or two, Billy D began to browse the mall. As he walked past the lingerie store, he bumped into, Trixie.

"Oh my God, hi Billy D." Trixie greeted him, she was happy to see him. He was still upset with her from the other night, so he greeted her with no emotion, just a head nod.

Trixie's friend was standing next to her checking Billy D out. "Oh, Porsche this is Billy D, Billy D Porsche. He's the one I was telling you about, from the club."

Both girls just started giggling. This made Billy D even madder. He figured Trixie told her friend how she played him that night. "Peace." Billy D said as he walked away.

"Call me." Trixie shouted at his back. Billy D kept walking and threw the 'peace' sign up without looking back.

Billy D was in the food court getting his grub on when his phone started vibrating. "Yo." he answered.

"Billy D this ya uncle, where you at?" Bank asked.

"What up Unc? I'm at the mall." Billy D responded while stuffing his face with tacos. Trixie just so happened to walk past. While walking she pulled out one of the outfits she purchased from the lingerie store pointing to it and then him.

"I got this just for you." she mouthed. She smiled seductively and motioned for him to call her. For a minute he was stuck-mouth wide open as he thought about Trixie in the outfit. Then he snapped out of it as he thought about the other night. He thought to himself, *fucking dick teaser.*

"I need to holla at you when you get a chance. I'm over your grandmother's house." Bank said.

"Alright. I'ma be over in about a hour." Billy D responded. After hanging up he thought about what his uncle needed to talk to him about. He thought to himself, *well I'll see when I get there.*

It took Billy D about an hour and a half to make it to his grandmother's house. She stayed in Orchard Park. A suburb of Buffalo, about a half hour outside of the city. She had been staying out there for about fifteen years. Her house was about fifteen minutes from the Buffalo Bills stadium. She was a neighbor to many Bills players over the years and she loved this as she was a Bills fanatic. Bank made it a priority to visit his mother at least three times a week. She was lonely out there in the huge house by herself. She lost her husband and son big Bill in the same decade. When Lex and Billy D were young they used to be over there all the time playing in the huge out door pool or riding their bikes up to the stadium to get autographs during the training camps. Now that they were grown, they might stop by once a month if that.

As Billy D walked up the drive way of his grandmother's house, he immediately smelled the aroma of lobster, steak and shrimp. This was his, Bank's and Lex's favorite. This was also her specialty, seafood and steak, unlike other grandmothers who cooked southern foods.

As Billy D walked in the house his grandmother was on the phone, but she immediately acknowledged him. "Hey baby come give me a kiss," she said while motioning with her free hand. Billy D smiled and walked over to give her a hug and kiss on the cheek as she sat on the sofa.

"Hi Grandma, where's Uncle Bank?" Billy D asked. She pointed to the kitchen as she resumed her phone conversation. When Billy D reached the kitchen, Bank was at the table finishing off a huge plate of steak, lobster and shrimp.

"Billy D... what took you so long?" Bank asked while devouring a piece of corn on the cob.

"I had to drop the ratchet off at the crib. I ain't riding with that out here." Billy D responded.

"Did you eat?" Bank asked.

"Yeah...at the mall." Billy D responded while looking around the kitchen impatiently, waiting for his uncle to get to the point. Billy D feared no one but he loved and revered his uncle so much that he respected him to the fullest.

Bank noticed his uneasiness as he looked at Billy D. "Billy D, the streets is talking…and you know I know of everything that goes on in this city…everything." Bank said to Billy D in his usual cool manner, pausing after almost every sentence for affect. "Niggas is snitching wit punk ass one to threes…niggas ain't built like they used to be, the city is fucked up." Bank continued to speak with out interruption. "You know me and ya father put in a lot of work...everything we did was for us, the family...so y'all wouldn't have to do none of this shit. When yo father got killed I lost my heart…but when I thought about you, Lex and yo grandmother, I realized I had to go at it stronger… for y'all…I love ya'll more than anything…I'ma tell you a secret…I never killed anybody until after ya father got killed. We was going to war with them niggas in the late eighties, I wasn't responsible for none of the casualties…ya dad put in work though... he was a gangster, he killed fa the cause…I guess that's why they went after him first." Bank said this last statement with some guilt in his voice. "He had the heart of a lion, and the mind of a genius…I was always good with the money, he was too, but I was always money first…so while he lead the team to war against them other niggas I was handling business…them niggas just caught him slippin'…they let the beef die down. The month after his death it probably was about…" Bank thought of the exact number. "33 homicides in that one month…we was responsible for at least 18... me myself accounted for 10…after that I haven't murdered since…I killed only because the niggas that was responsible for ma brothers murder was still living…and I couldn't live with that…now you on the other hand…what's your motive?" Bank asked not really wanting the answer. Billy D sensed this and kept quiet and listened while looking down at his hands. "I know you don't need money…let me ask you a question…do you know how much money we worth?"

Billy D looked up into his uncles eyes. He never really thought about how much money his Uncle was pulling in. He knew he was sitting on it though.

"Answer me…do you know how much money we, yes WE worth?"

Billy D shook his head no.

"Over 50 mill…easy." Bank paused for a reaction from Billy D. Billy D had an amazed look on his face. He never imagined the number to be that high. With that Bank proceeded "With the property and businesses we have up here and down south we all can chill and go legit…but I know that's not going to happen... this shit is in our blood... an addiction that only the street life can provide…" Bank completed this last statement with an expression of a defeated addict. "But what you doing…you have to stop. Sooner than later its gon be you they send the goons at."

Billy D tilted his head up as in a way to say, *I ain't worried about it, they come for me they better come proper.*

Reading his expression Bank added, "I know you can handle your self…but I'm not trying to see that happen…so what I need from you is to chill wit that shit…you can go down south live it up…you won't have to do shit, I'll give you an allowance of $10,000 a month, or get you started with your own business… it's up to you…if you just got to get dirty and you want to stay here…I'll set you out wit some raw dope." With that said Billy D again raised his head in interest. Bank already knew the answer before he asked the question. "So what its gon be?"

Billy D leaned in over the table and spoke, “Stay here.”

Bank just looked away. Billy D knew his uncle was upset with his answer, but it was his decision and he was ready to go at it hard.

Chapter 5

Bum sat back in the plush Italian made leather sofa relieving his back of the stress from sitting upright counting the $625,000. This was the amount needed to purchase his usual of 50 kilograms of cocaine. He was fortunate to have a connect down south. Little did he and his cousin Gutt know that when Gutt moved to Jacksonville Florida to stay with his grandmother on his father's side ten years ago that he would be Bum's cocaine supplier.

Bum grabbed his cell phone from the coffee table and called Gutt. "Guttaman, what's good?" Bum playfully greeted his cousin.

"Cuz'o, what's hap'nin?" Gutt responded with his acquired southern accent.

"I'm 'bout to head down there."

"Yeah I got to holla at you anyway cuz'o." Gutt countered.

"Ayo what up wit the bitch with the fat ass who you set me out wit last time I was down there?" Bum asked.

"Uh-oh yeah, the little stripper broad Kenya." Gutt answered.

"Oh shit the bitch strip?" Bum asked surprised.

"Man all these bitches down here strip, but yeah she been asking about you too." Gutt answered.

"Well make sure she around when I get down there. Bum demanded.

"Word. When you coming cuz'o?"

"I'ma leave about 9 tomorrow night, so I'm probably going to sleep damn near all day tomorrow morning that way I can just ride straight there. That's a long ass drive." Bum answered.

"Yeah, yeah, yeah nigga. I told you what to do. That way you can hop on the plane." Gutt said.

"Man fuck dat flying shit, I like to drive ma own vehicle that way I can pilot ma own shit." Bum replied. "But yo, I got to make some moves. I'ma see you when I get down there, one,"

"Alright cuz'o, one." Gutt replied ending the phone conversation.

Bum kicked his feet up on the coffee table and relaxed as he started to think about Kenya from Jacksonville. Bum didn't know she stripped, but she definitely had the body for it. She was brown skinned with a pretty face, but that body, it was proper. She was about 5'5" with a small waist. Her hips protruded to accommodate that fat ass of hers. She also had some sexy ass legs which Bum loved on a woman. Just as he started to feel fully relaxed, his phone started ringing. *"Fuck!"* He mumbled as he reached for the phone. "Yo." Bum said into the receiver.

"Hello may I speak to Brandon?" a sexy female's voice asked politely.

Bum was thrown off by the use of his government, but then he remembered. Misa, the girl he met at Gigi's.

"Hey, how are you doing?" Bum asked in a friendly voice.

"Do you know who this is?" Misa asked.

"Yeah, Misa right?" Bum responded pretty sure of the sexy voice on the other end of the phone. Very few people knew his real name; none used it, besides family.

"Wow that's interesting, this is my first time calling you and you knew my voice immediately like there are not a lot of females calling you on a regular basis." Misa sounded surprised.

"Actually I don't talk to a lot of females regularly. I usually focus my time and attention on one female at a time." Bum responded.

"Oh really, a monogamous, how rare." Misa said with a bit of doubt.

"Where would the time come from to spend with many companions? Someone's going to feel neglected." Bum added.

"That's true, well do you have time for little old me, or are you in a relationship?" Misa asked.

"I'm single and available." Bum joked.

"You're crazy, but smooth, I like that... You asked me on a date, I'm free tomorrow if you're free." Misa said.

"Well, I was planning on going down south tomorrow, I'll be gone for about 3 days, how about next week?" Bum asked.

"I'll give you my number and you can call me when you get back." Misa responded as she gave Bum her phone number.

"Definitely, if you're not doing anything right now you can come over and we can watch a DVD and order a pizza and chill." Bum suggested.

"Sounds like fun, but I'll have to pass. Maybe next time. Look I'm going to let you go so you can prepare for your trip. Have fun and make sure you call me when you get back." Misa said.

"Thank you and I'll call you when I touch back in town."

"Ok. Bye." Misa added as she hung up.

Before Bum could get any rest he had to stop by the house he just purchased to make sure the security company put the security system in that he requested. Bum was going to use this house as a stash house. He wasn't going to keep money or drugs in Jasmine's apartment anymore. He knew that was being reckless. He now had three stash houses to keep his money and drugs in. He was making too much money to keep anything in the same vicinity where he or his family rested. After checking on the house he decided to get some rest in preparation of the long trip.

***

The following day Bum got more than enough rest and he made it to Jacksonville in good time. He loved being in Florida. Not only did he enjoy seeing his cousin, he also loved seeing all the beautiful women there. Bum made this trip several times, from Buffalo to Jacksonville. When in Jacksonville he didn't feel the hate like he felt in Buffalo. People were to busy getting their own down there. Not only was Gutt getting it, but his whole family down there was getting paid, from his grandmother to his cousins. They had an organization in which the whole family took part in. Gutt's sister Tamika did a lot of the transporting. As Bum got closer to Gutt's house he called to make sure he was there. "Hello." A sexy female's voice answered Gutt's home phone.

"Hello is Gutt in?" Bum asked.

"Hold on." The sexy voice said as she called Gutt to the phone.

"Yo." Gutt said sounding half asleep.

"Yo, cuzin I'ma take ya player's card. You got bitches answering ya shit, what up wit dat?" Bum joked.

"Man I does dis shit. All mine know they place, ya feel me?" Gutt responded sounding fully awake now. "But where you at?" Gutt added.

"I'ma be there in like 10 minutes." Bum answered.

"Alright I'ma leave the gate open for you."

"Alright." Bum said as he hung up.

Gutt had a mini mansion just outside of Jacksonville. He had automatic iron gates, an outdoor pool with a waterfall and a maid who cleaned the house on the weekends. As Bum made it to the house, he drove up the driveway and parked behind Gutt's Jaguar and alongside his snow white Range Rover.

Gutt saw Bum pull in the driveway from his security camera. He came to the door to greet his cousin with only his boxers, house shoes and a silk Hugh Hefner style robe undone. "Cuz'n, I hope you ain't scratch ma Range." He jokingly greeted his cousin as he spread his arms to embrace Bum.

"Shit I be extra careful around shit I can't afford." Bum countered with a joke of his own as he hugged his cousin. As they walked in the house Bum found himself admiring its interior. "Damn son, this shit is proper." Bum said as he scanned his surroundings.

"This ain't shit; you should see ma grandmother's crib. She doing it big. Her shit should be on MTV cribs or some shit, I bullshit you not." Gutt said. Bum turned to admire the rest of the house. The sexy voice who answered when he had called caught his eye. He immediately looked at Gutt with an expression that needed no words. Gutt gave him a look saying *she's nobody* as though they were speaking telepathically.

"Yo cuzo I'm about to hop in the shower, Jessica make ma cousin some breakfast." Gutt demanded Sexy Voice. Even though it was 2 o'clock in the afternoon, Gutt had her make Bum breakfast. The only time Bum ate home cooked breakfast was when he stayed over at Jasmines'. Gutt went upstairs to handle his business.

"I'll make you breakfast only if you keep me company." Jessica told Bum as she walked toward the kitchen with him on her heels. Bum was starving. He only made a few stops on his trip and that was for gas. He had a couple snacks but his stomach screamed for a meal. He found a seat on one of the stools surrounding the island's counter. "So… *cousin* what's your name?" Jessica asked as she searched the refrigerator for the ingredients to prepare the meal.

"Bum." He answered.

"Where are you from Bum? I can look at you and tell you're not from here. And by your voice, I'd say maybe New York?" Jessica questioned.

Bum didn't know if she was asking questions because she really didn't know or because she was trying to figure him out by getting him to talk, so he decided to keep it short and sweet. If she didn't know now then she didn't need to know. "Buffalo." Bum answered.

"Buffalo? I never been there, how is it?" She asked still prying relentlessly.

"Alright." Bum answered, noticing his short answers were annoying her. She tried to play it cool though.

"I heard its cold." She said. Bum didn't respond to her statement. She looked at him as though she was waiting for a response. "I'm sorry I understand if you don't want to talk. After all you must be tired coming all the way from New York." She apologized.

"No it's..." Bum paused in mid sentence after noticing her reaction. As he was about to explain his lack of conversation, he had seen that she was still playing her game. She almost had him with the sweet innocent girl act. He was hip, but she was sharp and he liked that, he wasn't going to let her know so he stayed in character, short and sweet. "...It's all good," He continued. She was expecting more, but Bum played it cool. Jessica was as sexy as her voice was if not sexier. She looked to be mixed with Spanish and black. She had long silky hair in a pony tail with a mole above the right side of her upper lip. She had almond colored and shaped eyes with an hour glass slim figure. She was 5'8" with heels on. She had a slyness to her which was obvious to Bum, but in a way, this made her alluring.

"Make enough for me too." Gutt demanded as he palmed Jessica's ass as he walked pass to sit next to Bum. "Damn cuz'o, you look a little buff, what you been working out?" Gutt asked Bum.

"Naw, I don't have time to workout." He responded.

Gutt was handsome, but his personality is what made him even more attractive with the ladies. He was a gym rat. He owned a fitness center in downtown Jacksonville which he took full advantage of with his muscular 220 pound frame. He was 6'-2", could pass for a football player and was flamboyant. "Tamika just called me, she on her way back now." Gutt told Bum.

He nodded his head. When it was time for Bum to re up, whether he made the trip or not, Tamika would transport the work from Jacksonville to Buffalo. When Bum traveled to Jacksonville, he would bring the money with him. Tamika had a key to the drop off spot. She would place the work in the designated spot and return to Jacksonville.

"After we eat I'ma drop Jessica off, and we can talk after that." Gutt said. Jessica's 21 questions came to a halt now that Gutt was back in attendance. She prepared a breakfast of turkey sausage, scrambled eggs, grits and toasted English muffins. While Bum was eating he was thinking to himself. *Damn, this bitch can cook, she pretty, she sexy, she nosy as hell though, I wonder how the pussy is, she look like a freak.*

"Come on Bum." Gutt said snapping Bum out of his thoughts. "Stop savoring that shit and eat so we can bounce." Gutt was finishing off his orange juice to wash down the meal that he just devoured.

***

After dropping off Jessica, Gutt and Bum were riding the city in Gutt's white Range. "Ayo cuz'n what up wit that bitch?" Bum asked Gutt.

"What bitch, Jessica?" he asked.

"Yeah."

"Man she like…like ma professional head server. I fuck wit her when I'm in need of a proper blow job, and when I need a cook, but enough about that bitch, we gon fuck wit these otha bitches and kick it. You wit it or what?" Gutt asked with no answer needed.

Bum nodded his head and reclined in the soft leather of the Range as he observed the streets of Jacksonville. Gutt pulled in front of a cell phone store that he owned. The store was located in the hood, people loitered the busy street. Bum followed behind Gutt toward the store thinking the store was actually in a good location for such a store. It was obvious that most of the people in the neighborhood were "Street Pharmacists" Everyone had a need for cell phones.

When Bum walked in the store, he noticed there was only one male working there and he was security. The other employees were all female and all four of them were pretty. They were dressed in all black uniforms except for one, the manager. Gutt spoke to all the employees only introducing Bum to the security. Gutt was cautious, he trusted few. He felt it wasn't necessary for the other employees to be introduced. Besides the security was his man from high school, whom he trusted. Gutt then led Bum to his office in the back, before closing the door he asked the manager about some inventory which was suppose to arrive that day. She informed him that it had already arrived and she signed for it. The office was small; it wasn't much, after all Gutt didn't spend much time there. It had a small desk with two uncomfortable chairs on opposite ends, and a sofa which Gutt used to get real familiar with two of his employees. "Yeah son I had to stop by here to make sure these phones arrived. Later on we gon stop by this strip club, but I wanted to talk to you about moving down here, fa good... this coke moving so fuck'n fast it's ridiculous. Besides you need to get out of Buffalo, it's too many haters out there. You come down here, you can make more money and avoid all the bullshit. I know you getting ya head right in Buff, but you tell me all the time how fucked up it is. You need to come down here and you can fuck wit a couple niggas in Buff and hit them when they need to re up that way you can stay getting money from up there and here." Gutt proposed to Bum.

Bum just looked at his cousin before he spoke. He thought that it was a good idea also but he really had to think about it. As much as he hated Buffalo he loved it that much more. "I need to think about that cuz'n. I'ma sleep on it." Bum responded.

"Let's get outta here." Gutt said as he walked out of the office. "Oh yeah I told Kenya you was coming, she said call her." Gutt added as he handed Bum a piece of paper with Kenya's phone number on it.

"Damn son I almost forgot about her." Bum said as he walked out behind Gutt.

***

At 11:15pm Gutt and Bum pulled in front of the strip club. It was like a car show outside of the strip club. All types of luxury vehicles with 23 inch rims or better were on display. Inside of the club it was wall to wall ballers all there for the same thing, pussy. As Gutt walked through the club he greeted everyone he knew and everyone showed him love. Gutt and Bum then made their way to a table close to the dancer's stage. "These bitches proper cuz'n?" Bum asked over the loud music.

"This ma first time here. Niggas been telling me about this shit though," Gutt answered as they waited for the next stripper to come on stage. The first three strippers were average, but when you have a bunch of drunken men around a naked bitch they're going to overreact.

"Pull out them big faces, the next lady coming to the stage is Kandi!" The DJ screamed into the mic as he started playing Jeremiah's "Birthday Sex." Kandi walked out in a sexy outfit moving slow and seductively to the music. She was bad, about 5'-5" with a fat ass. As she made her way to Gutt and Bum's table they turned and looked at each other. They realized Kandi was none other than Kenya. About half way through the song Kenya recognized Bum. She approached him smiling ear to ear as she danced seductively in front of him. She then put one leg over his shoulder as she grinded.

She then straddled him and began to grind on him as she whispered in his ear "I'm happy to see you, and I can tell you're happy to see me also." She reached down and touched his dick. "Call my cell phone tonight at 2, ok?" she told Bum while still riding him. Bum shook his head in agreement. The song went off then Kenya danced on stage to T pains 'Can't Believe It'. She had the whole club going crazy as she made her ass clap. After Kenya got done performing the crowd simmered down. None that followed could compare to her. At 1:30am Gutt and Bum decided to leave.

"Damn son why didn't you tell me dat that ass was so fat?" Gutt asked Bum as they hopped in the Range.

"Yeah her body is ridiculous." Bum responded as he reclined in the comfortable seats of the SUV.

"Yo, you getting up wit that tonight?" Gutt asked.

"Yeah she told me to call her at 2." Bum answered.

Gutt looked at his watch. "Shit if you don't call her I will, you got 15 minutes." He said jokingly.

"Let's stop somewhere and get something to eat." Bum demanded.

"Man at 2 you gon have more than enough to eat." Gutt joked.

"Man quit playing I don't eat pussy." Bum responded.

"She put that leg on ya shoulder like she did in the club you is." he continued to joke.

"Man you wild'n." Bum said while laughing.

"Let's go to IHOP and get that shit to go." Gutt suggested.

After eating it was 2:20am. Bum decided to call Kenya. "Hey, what's up Bum?" Kenya happily answered the phone.

"What's up, how did you know it was me?" Bum asked.

"For one, nobody else better be calling me this late and you must have forgot about caller I.D. I saw the 716 area code." Kenya responded.

Bum thought he programmed his phone to permanently block his number. He made a mental reminder to check on that. "What up tho?" He asked.

"You. You coming to see me or what?" she questioned.

"Where you at?" Kenya gave him the location and he was on his way. First Gutt took him to get his own truck. He didn't want any interruptions from Bum to come pick him up from over Kenya's. Gutt knew he would be in some pussy himself, if he wasn't sleep.

When Bum arrived at Kenya's, he rang the door bell. Kenya answered with a silk robe on which hung just below the middle of her thighs. He was wondering what was up under it, he was hoping there was nothing.

"Give me a hug." Kenya demanded as she stretched out her open arms with a huge smile.

He embraced her, taking in the sweet aroma of her perfume. "You smell good. You just got out of the shower?" he asked.

"Bubble bath." she responded. She grabbed his hand and guided him into the living room where she had the lights dimmed, soft music playing and a bottle of bubbly with two wine glasses. Sitting extremely close to him on the sofa, she crossed her legs exposing even more of her thigh and some of her ass. They sat back drinking and talking for almost an hour. Bum was ready to fuck, but he decided to let Kenya initiate contact. *It won't be long now,* Bum thought as Kenya began softly caressing her neck and breast. The liquor was taking affect. He then started rubbing her thigh softly. She began to moan softly as the liquor heightened her senses. Not being able to control herslf, she immediately jumped on Bum and started kissing him. She then straddled him and took off her robe, leaving her with just her birthday suit on. She tore at Bum's jeans impatiently trying to get them off. After he helped her get them off, she started stroking his dick up and down as she lowered her mouth on top of it. Bum was enjoying this, as he reached for his jeans to grab a condom. Kenya was ready for penetration. She tried to immediately jump on top of his dick, but he stopped her so that he could put the condom on. She then lowered herself on his dick as she moaned in gratification.

The pussy was tight, moist and warm. In other words it was good. Kenya then turned around with dick still in her pussy and started to ride him reverse cowgirl style. This had him fucked up wondering how she did that without missing a stroke. He just grabbed her hips and continued to enjoy the ride. Kenya put her hands on the floor and arched her back so that she could feel every inch of him.

Bum then got off the couch and on the floor as he continued to hit it doggy style. This excited her even more as the moaning grew louder. She started screaming, "I'm about to cum. I'm about to cum. I'm about to cum…" After her tenth time saying it, she began to cum and so did Bum. When it was over he put on his boxers, and she went in her room returning with an over sized Jaguar's jersey on. They resumed talking and drinking. They made plans for Kenya to make a trip to Buffalo. To Bum's surprise Kenya had family in Buffalo and she visited often as a kid. After a while they noticed it was light outside. It was almost seven o'clock. Bum decided to leave, but not before hitting the pussy one more time. This time they did it the old fashioned way.

***

Bum made it to Gutt's house at almost 10 a.m. Exhausted, he crashed out as soon as he made it to the bed in the guest room, and didn't wake up until 6 pm. After showering he searched the house for Gutt. The house was empty. The phone rang. "Hello." Bum answered.

"Cuz'o you finally up?" Gutt screamed over the loud music in the back ground.

"Yeah, where you at?" Bum asked.

"Don't worry about it cuz'o I'ma be there in a minute to come get you." Gutt said.

"Alright." Bum said as he hung up.

Gutt came to pick up Bum from the crib. They hung out all night enjoying the city and having a good time. Bum really enjoyed his trips down there. He always had a ball with his cousin. He still didn't know if he wanted to relocate down there. He felt that he would be leaving too much behind, especially his kids. He couldn't leave them.

Gutt and Bum got home at six in the morning. Bum again slept all day. He was to leave that night so he decided to rest. He had a crazy dream. He was dreaming that Jessica was giving him some head. As he opened his eyes, his dream was a reality. Jessica was bobbing up and down on his dick. He bust right in her mouth and watched as she swallowed every drop. Jessica then walked out the room without saying a word. Bum was in shock.

As he was preparing to head back to Buffalo, he and Gutt embraced again.

"Cuz'n think about what I said, this is where you belong." Gutt said.

Bum looked at him, "I love you cousin, see you next time."

"Love you too cuz'o…oh yeah did you enjoy the wake up?" Gutt asked with a smile on his face referring to Jessica.

Bum just smiled ear to ear. "No doubt." he said as he headed to his Navi for the ride back to town.

Chapter 6

Lex had stepped his hustle game up dramatically. He went from moving a quarter of a key to moving two keys a week. He opened up a couple of trap houses which stayed busy with transactions. He had a few of the young hustlers from the neighborhood work the spots, and he paid each a weekly salary. Lex was due to start back classes at the University in two weeks. He knew he was going to have to focus on his education a little more. This was going to affect his paper a little, but he had to sacrifice one way or the other. He wanted back on the football field desperately which required good academic standing. He also needed to dedicate more time in the Universities weight room to prepare physically for the upcoming season. But until classes started his main focus was getting money.

***

Lex parked at the end of the block and observed one of his trap houses constant flow of activity. Lex sat in his car for a half an hour and watched as customer after customer entered and left the house. He often watched from a distance to make sure everything was going well with his investment.

Lex then decided to head to the gambling spot. He walked in the backyard were various hustlers from the town gathered to try their luck in a "friendly" game of dice. This was an everyday activity in the city. Somewhere in the hood hustlers from around town would gather and gamble. You had your dice games, dog fights and pick up basketball games where people would bet a $1000 a man. These social gatherings however were the cause of many beefs and homicides amongst the participant's. Hustlers hated to lose money. Often the loser would refuse to pay and that was a no no. Lex didn't like to gamble. He participated however as a way of keeping his ear to the streets. He greeted everyone as he walked in the backyard.

"Yo son you better get in now why this nigga got bank. His shit is suspect." Jay told Lex referring to Plump who was sweating profusely as he shook the dice.

"Naw son, I'm patient." He responded as he watched Plump roll two threes and a two.

"Fuck, that deuce gon hold. One of you niggas gon drip." said Plump as he pulled up one leg of his sweat pant's and got on a knee waiting for the next man's roll. Plump was fat, about 350 pounds. He was a paper chaser, moving about 4 or 5 keys, and a habitual gambler. He was known to lose over $10,000 dollars and come back with another bundle of money and break everybody. Jay ended up being the only one to lose to the deuce that Plump rolled. Lex joined in the game, and after about two hours he ended up winning a couple grand. He was satisfied. A two thousand dollar gain in two hours, good money.

While at the dice game Lex got a few calls from a couple of hustlers who wanted to purchase some work. He immediately took care of that. The last hustler whom he went to see wanted three ounces. He was 16 years old, young and hungry. He was on the grind calling Lex at least twice a day for two ounces or more. As Lex walked out the young hustlers house counting the money he just got from him, the young hustler spoke. “Yo Lex, I’m probably gon call you in a few hours for two more O’s.”

While concentrating on the money in his hand, Lex nodded his head in agreement. When he reached his car he put the money in his pocket and turned back towards the young hustler. “Try not to wait too late.” Lex said.

“If it get too late I’ma hit you in the morning.” The young hustler responded.

“Alright fam.” Lex said before he drove off. As he rode up the street he noticed his man, Gravy, sitting on a crate in front of the store. Lex parked his car so that he could holler at him. Gravy was Lex’s man from back in elementary school. There they grew real close, and as they got older they kept in contact. “What’s good fam?” Lex shouted as he walked toward Gravy.

“Ooh shit ma nigga, what up son, everything gravy?” Gravy joyfully accepted his company.

“What up wit you?” Lex asked as they embraced.

“Man I’m tryin’ to survive out here.” Gravy said as he tried drunkenly to sit back down knocking over the bottle of Hennessey that he was drinking.

“I’ve been hearing a lot about you in these streets.” Lex admitted.

“Word, you know ma name ring bells son,” Gravy responded as he sipped what was remaining of the Hennessey.

“Yo son spark dat.” Lex demanded.

“What son?” Gravy asked.

“That L,” Lex responded, pointing to the Dutch that Gravy had rolled up on the side of his ear.

“Oh shit son I forgot I had this.” Gravy said as he grabbed the Dutch from his ear and lit it. “Ayo…” Gravy’s voice sounded as in a whisper as he inhaled the marijuana. “Remember back when we was shortys, you always had the newest kicks…" Gravy asked not really expecting a response. "I was always jealous of you but you was ma man and I loved you even back then." Gravy emotionally continued. "Ya dad and uncle was the man's back then, they had the town on smash… I always wished they was ma dad." He passed Lex the Dutch. "I was hurt when Big Bill got murdered. I always wanted to be like them...They was real hustlers, but I ain't no hustler, I'm that dude that hustlers hate…I'm the predator...I did a lot of foul shit ma nigga…a whole lot of foul shit." Gravy paused as Lex handed him back the Dutch. As he took another pull he continued on. "A lot of niggas want to see ma demise." As Lex looked at Gravy it looked as though he was in deep thought, then Gravy lowered his voice and repeated in almost a whisper as though he was talking to himself. "I'm still here." Then suddenly Gravy jumped up and pulled out his gun and pointed it in the air and yelled. "I'm still here, because these niggas can't touch me!" Gravy was now in the middle of the street screaming with a gun in each hand and the Dutch held to his mouth by his lips alone.

Lex grabbed him from out of the middle of the street. "Come on son…Take it in before the police ride through." Lex suggested to Gravy.

"Yeah, you right son, it's getting late anyway." Gravy said as he calmed down. "I love you fam." He hugged Lex still with the pistols in his hands and Dutch still on his lips.

Lex walked him down the street to his house. As Gravy was about to walk through his front door Lex hollered out. "I love you son…like a brother, always."

Gravy still with the guns in his hands placed his right hand to his heart to show that he felted the same way about Lex as tears rolled down his face. He then turned and walked in the house.

Lex walked back to his car with tears in his eye's knowing this could be the last time he saw Gravy living. He had too many enemies in the town and word was out that he had a contract on his head. Lex was glad he had the chance to spend time with his long time friend, before the inevitable happened which was his murder.

***

Lex ran out of work sooner than he anticipated. He knew Bum would be gone for a few days, but he already sold out completely two days before. Lex was calling Bum nonstop, hoping he was back from down south, but Bum still didn't answer.

"Damn son we missing out on a lot of guap, you still ain't touched wit son yet?" The worker asked Lex as he walked in one of the trap houses.

He put a finger in the air motioning for him to hold on as he called Bum again. "Naw I'm still tryin'…what's been happen'n?" Lex asked as he put the phone back in his pocket.

"Shit, waiting to get back to work." he responded.

"I feel you. Sometimes I feel like I need that shit more than these crack heads." Lex said. "But yo..." Lex stopped in mid sentence as his phone started to vibrate. He answered. "Yo."

"Fam what up?" Bum shouted.

"You son, what's good?" Lex asked excited to hear Bum's voice.

"Meet me at McDonalds on Genesee and Bailey in 20 minutes." Bum demanded before he hung up.

"Yo son later on tonight we back in motion." Lex told his worker as he headed out the door to meet Bum.

As Lex pulled into the parking lot of the McDonalds, Bum pulled right along side of him in his Delta 88. They walked into the restaurant. After receiving their orders, they sat in a booth.

"What up Lex?" Bum asked as he pulled a handful of fries from the brown take out bag and stuffed them in his mouth.

"I need two of dem thangs, ASAP." Lex answered.

Bum stood up. "I got you. Where you gon be?"

"I'm gon be over ma girl's house."

"See you in a half," Bum said as he turned to head out to his car. "Oh yeah son ma bad fa not getting back at you sooner." he added as they both walked out the McDonalds.

"It's all good. See you in a half." Lex said as he hopped in the car not really trying for conversation. He wanted to get his hands on the coke immediately.

While waiting on Bum, Lex got the pot and the baking soda ready. He didn't need to count the money as he usually did while waiting on Bum because he counted it several times the past two days in anticipation of Bum's return. Lex also no longer needed Smitty to cook the coke for him anymore. After watching Smitty several times he got real good in the kitchen himself. Lex would cook a thousand grams to about 1200 grams. The coke was always good. It was good as or better than anybody else's circulating the hood. Lex was at the window when he saw Bum pull up in front of the house. Lex went to the door waiting for him as he walked up. Lex handed Bum a bag with the $48,000 dollars in it, the amount for the two bricks. Bum then handed Lex a bag which contained the coke. Lex couldn't wait to get back in motion; he had a lot of money on pause. Bum noticed his impatience "Alright fam good lookin, I'ma let you do you, get back." Bum said as he headed out of the door.

"Yeah, good lookin'." Lex said as he closed the door behind Bum. He then headed to the kitchen, got out the scale and got busy. He had one brick cooked and divided into eighths. He decided to handle some business before he cooked the other bird. He immediately took an eighth to each trap house to get them back in motion, then he went to hit a couple of hustlers whom he had on hold. After four hours back in motion he knocked off three fourths of the brick. He was now where he needed to be, back on full.

Chapter 7

Billy D was riding around thinking of his next move. He had sold heroin and coke briefly, but he got bored with it in the past. He preferred the action and rush of murder. He made a promise to his uncle however that he would stop taking out hits and get that dope money. The problem was that he had raw dope with nowhere to pump it. He was having second thoughts about changing his occupation, then he came up with an idea. His idea would allow him to knock off the dope and start some shit at the same time. He decided to go to one of the most notorious spots known for moving heroin in the city and post just outside of it and knock his shit off, knowing this would get the current hustlers hot and ready to kill him. The thought of making money on their block and taking them to war excited Billy D.

The next morning Billy D set up outside in the middle of their block. The current hustlers on the block didn't notice him until about after an hour. "What the fuck. Shit slow as hell! Where the fuck is all da dope fiends at?" one of the hustlers asked in frustration.

"Yo, yo what the fuck? It's jumping right here," another hustler yelled to a dope fiend as he quickly walked past them.

"I just copped from homeboy down the street," the fiend said as he continued to walk without missing a beat.

The group of young men looked at each other in disbelief. "Down the street?" one of the hustlers asked no one in particular. "Yo Chris, you and Preme take the ratchets and go see what the fuck the dope head talk'n 'bout." The young man ordered as if he was running shit.

The two hustlers grabbed their guns and walked down the street to check it out. Billy D sat on the steps of an abandoned house as he saw the two approaching. The whole time he just looked straight ahead as if he didn't see them coming. When they got closer, they saw on his lap laid a chrome Desert Eagle. He leaned back on the steps with his arms propped up on the steps behind him. Still without even looking at them he spoke. "What up?"

"What up? Nigga who da fuck is you coming on ma block, pistol exposed, hitting ma fiends like you Nino fuck'n Brown and shit?" Preme angrily responded as he was ready to pull the 9mm ruger from his waist band and kill somebody.

"My name is Billy D and you better watch how you talk to me." Billy D spoke calmly as he continued, still without looking at them.

Chris put his hand on Preme's arm to stop him from pulling out his gun. Preme immediately turned and looked at Chris as if he was crazy. Chris shook his head no to Preme and turned to speak to Billy D. "Yo son, I apologize fa ma man." Chris then motioned for Preme to walk back down the street with him.

As they walked back down the street Billy D didn't expect them to back down that easy, he was disappointed. *"Bitch ass niggas!"* He mumbled as he watched them walk away.

"Yo, what da fuck was dat about? I was about to clap dat nigga." Preme asked angrily.

"Naw son, that's Billy D." Chris said.

Preme Looked at Chris as if to say, *what the fuck dat mean*? "I don't give a fuck who dat nigga is. He should be Billy D'ceased right now." Preme angrily responded.

"Naw nigga dats OG Bank's nephew. If you would have clapped son, you, ya momma, ya baby momma, shit all y'all be dead before the week over." Chris replied.

"Man fuck dat! That nigga should respect that this our shit over here. Bank should tell dat nigga something." Preme added.

"That's why I stopped you. If it wasn't fa Bank I would have shot him as soon as I saw da Desi on his lap, but I know Bank gon tell the nigga to respect our shit and bounce." Chris said.

"Yo. Right here got that..." Billy D screamed to another customer as she hastily walked toward him while scratching profusely. "...Got that body bag, Yeah body bag." As he quickly came up with a name for his dope. Billy D thought to himself. *Yeah I'ma put dem bitch ass niggas in body bags if they come back down here.* As the dope fiend bought a couple of bags from him he told her, "Yeah ma I'ma be here all night."

"If it's good I'ma be back." She said as she sped off.

After about three hours Billy D had accomplished half of what he came on the block for. He was surprised at how much money he made in the short time he was out there on the block, but he was upset that they didn't give him a reason to pop off. *These soft ass niggas, all this cake out here and these dudes is pussy.* Billy D thought to himself as his phone started vibrating. "Yo." Billy D answered.

"Where you at?" Bank asked his nephew.

"Why, what up Unc?" Billy D asked in return.

"Yo, I know where you at and what you doing, you can't be over there doing that…" Bank told Billy D straight up. "So pack up and bounce." Bank added before he hung up.

This just made Billy D even angrier at the dudes whose block he was on. While walking to his car he thought out loud. *Pussy ass niggas didn't want no problem, so they tell on a nigga...bitches.* Billy D hopped in his truck and rode past the hustlers on the street real slow and ice grilled each of them. Preme mockingly waved good bye to him. Billy D just continued to ice grill as he stepped harder on the pedal and sped off.

***

Billy D took five days off. During that time he cut and packaged the rest of the dope while he searched for another spot to move his product. He chose a spot on the same block as one of Lex's crack houses. It was just two blocks and ten minutes in walking distance from the block in which he was on five days earlier. This street also had constant drug activity, mostly crack. Billy D was determined however to get it pumping hard with cliental for his dope. It was a slow go at first, but all it needed was for the word to get around that he had that shit! He promised a fiend a nice package if he would go on the other block and redirect Chris and Preme's customers to him. The fiend didn't think of the consequences of this small task. When the hustlers found out about this they immediately took action. Billy D was waiting at the end of the night to give the fiend the package but he never showed up. Billy D knew that something must have happened to him.

The next morning Billy D read a brief paragraph in the crime section of the Buffalo News. *"The body of 45 year old Nathan Brown was discovered burnt beyond recognition behind an abandoned house on Buffalo's eastside. Police believe Brown was doused with gasoline and set ablaze while still alive. Police were able to identify Brown by his identification that was untouched in his pants which was approximately three feet from the deceased. Police have no suspects."*

Billy D set the paper on the table next to his bowl of cereal and rubbed his hands over his head and face in frustration. He knew who killed Nate the dope fiend, the same cowards who were scared to approach him a week ago. "Fuck!" he yelled out as he banged his fist on the table knocking over a bowl of cereal. He wasn't mad about Nate's death, it was the fact that he sent him over there and those cowards killed him. Oh no, he couldn't let that slide, nor would he.

***

Business picked up for Billy D. He had everything organized. The workers were set in place and handling the hand to hand, all he did was count the money at the end of the day. The spot brought in so much money that day he decided to close up shop early. "Yo, shut it down, that's good for the day." Billy D ordered. After making sure that the dope was accounted for and every dollar was correct, he decided to play fire Marshall. Billy D was going to avenge Nate's death. He knew he had to be quick because they were heavily armed. He parked the car around the corner of the block and began to head in their direction. He changed out of his clothes from earlier and dressed in something less conspicuous. Wearing some old clothes to appear as a dope fiend, he walked hastily with a noticeable limp and scratching uncontrollably. The hustlers mistook him for a dope fiend when they saw him and continued with what they were doing.

"What you need?" A young hustler walked up to Billy D trying to make a sale.

Billy D continued to walk pass him with his head down. As he saw Preme he pulled out so fast that two shots were fired in rapid succession into Preme's forehead. Before Preme could hit the ground, Billy D was headed to his car. When he made it to his car he pulled off feeling alive again as he remembered the look of sudden death on Preme's face as he took the two shots to the head. Billy D smiled as he thought to himself, *Bitch ass niggas.*

Chapter 8

"Yo pull over I got to get a Dutch," Pete demanded as they rode down the street.

"Nigga you ain't got no weed, what the fuck you need a Dutch for?" Bull replied as he drove past the store.

"Them niggas got dro right there." Pete responded while pointing back at the group of young men in front of the store they just passed.

"It's all good, we go see son then we get the trees…matter of fact son might have smoke." Uno suggested to Bull and Pete. He was always the mediator between the two. Cool, calm and collective was his constant demeanor.

"Damn son look at dem ho's." Pete excitedly screamed from the back seat while leaning towards the front pointing at a group of young ladies getting out a truck, heading into a corner store.

"Now a good time to get that Dutch." Bull said while pulling behind the truck. All three got out of the hooptie simultaneously. Bull was always the driver because he was the only one with a license. Bum purchased so many different vehicles, he would often give them the hoopties after he drove them awhile. As the three of them followed the four young ladies into the store, Uno noticed one of them had a Buffalo State College hoody on, so he assumed they were all college students. He immediately separated himself from

Bull and Pete, knowing one of them would say something outrageous soon and it didn't take long.

"We got the bottles, we got the weed all we need now is y'all presence. Then we can get high, drunk, horny and fuck," Pete said to the group of young ladies. One of the girls turned in disgust and walked back towards the cooler. Uno was checking her out from the jump, so he took an opposite aisle and made it to the cooler just before she did. As Uno reached in the cooler to get a pop he turned and saw her up close. She was bad. She had an exotic look about her. Her skin was a brown Uno had never seen before, an orangish, milky brown. She was 5'2" with hazel brown eyes. She had on some tight low rise jeans, brown stilettos and a beige halter top exposing her belly button ring. Uno was stuck for a minute as he admired her beauty.

"Excuse me," She spoke waiting to get in the cooler.

"I'm sorry." Uno responded as he snapped out of his trance and backed away to let her get her item. He was checking her out as he took in the sweet fragrance she exuded. She found what she was looking for and she couldn't reach it, so Uno gladly volunteered.

"Let me get it for you." Uno stated as she backed up and let him get the bottle of pop for her.

"Thank you. I don't know why they put it all the way up there anyway," She responded with a slight blush of embarrassment.

She had the softest, sweetest, voice. "I don't know either, ain't none of them over 5 feet," Uno jokingly said referring to the Arabian workers. This got a smile from her. "My name is Uno." He said extending his hand.

"Aminah," She responded with a smile on her face as she shook his hand.

Uno held her hand firmly yet gently as he placed his other hand on top of hers and looked into her eyes. "Excuse me for staring but you have hypnotic eyes."

"Thank you," she responded, still blushing.

"I would like to see you again Aminah. Is there a way I can contact you." He asked still holding her hand.

"I would give you my phone number but you have to give me my hand back first," she jokingly responded.

"Oh…I'm sorry. It's the eyes…hypnotic." Uno stuttered as he talked.

"It's Ok," Aminah said as she wrote her number down and handed it to him.

"What's a good time to call?" Uno asked.

"Anytime tomorrow." She replied.

"Aminah, what you doing, you ready?" One of her friends yelled from the front of the store.

As they walked to the cash register Uno was surprised to see that Pete and Bull had the girls laughing. After paying for her pop, Aminah smiled and waved good bye to Uno. She walked out of the store with her friends who were still laughing at something Pete and Bull had said.

"A little while longer I would have had us all fucking them bitches tonight." Pete said while paying for his bag of chips and candy bar.

"Fuck all that. We got side tracked, we got business to handle," Uno said as he left the bottle of pop on the counter and headed towards the exit with Bull.

Pete then followed. "Oh shit I almost forgot the Dutch." Pete said as he ran back in the store. Uno and Bull waited in the car. Pete ran out of the store and hopped in the back seat.

"Y'all niggas ready to go see Son now or y'all got something else y'all need to do?" Uno asked sarcastically.

"Nigga I'm always ready. Pistol packing Pete." Pete said as he pulled out his chrome colt 45 and cocked it positioning one in the chamber.

Uno then pulled out his Kimber 1911 and did the same. He then looked at Bull and said. "Bull let's ride."

***

"Loni you gon see Bum wit dat money or what? The nigga got you hopping around the hood like a silly rabbit." One of the young hustlers who were standing on the block joked as the rest of the hoods laughed.

This made Loni angry. "Man fuck dat nigga, I ain't giving dat nigga shit." Loni screamed as he pulled a small 25 semi automatic pistol from his hoody pocket. "I'ma clap dat nigga. Beef on sight." he added.

The rest of the young men laughed at Loni knowing he had no wins with Bum. They knew and respected Bum and wanted no parts of Loni and Bum's beef. They knew Loni would be dead soon, it was just a matter of time. As Loni continued to rant on, one of the young hustlers received a call on his cell phone. After his phone conversation, he whispered something to his man standing next to him. He then told two of the other young men to take a ride with him. After they pulled off the first young hustler in which the one whom received the phone call whispered to, told the other two men to take a ride to Burger king with him.

As they headed to the car, Loni shouted, "Yo I'm coming, shit I'm hungry as hell."

"Naw, naw son what you want I got you," the driver told Loni.

"Get me a number two. Super size that shit." Loni requested as he handed the driver three dollars.

"Man this ain't enough." The driver said to Loni.

"Man I got you when I hit another lick." Loni responded. The driver rode off leaving Loni standing there. *"Fuck dem niggas now I got the block to myself, that's how it's supposed to be."* Loni spoke to himself as he hobbled on one good leg.

Loni was on the block by himself for a good 20 minutes. He managed to make over a hundred dollars selling soap. He had no crack. The crack heads knew Loni was known for this, but he was the only one on the block at the time. When they would come back to confront him he would deny it. Loni's heart skipped a beat as he saw a burgundy Chevy Celebrity pull just in front of him. For a minute he thought he recognized the car as Bum's, but he was relieved as he saw unfamiliar faces.

"What up homey you got trees." Pete asked Loni as he rolled down the window from the back seat.

"Na...Oh yeah." Loni was about to say no but forgot he had a nickel bag. He was going to sell it to them as a dime. "Yeah son I got one dime left," Loni responded.

"Let me get dat," Pete said as he got out of the car with his pistol concealed. As Loni handed him the weed he looked closely at Pete.

"Damn son, you look familiar. I know you from somewhere? Where you from The Belt?" He asked Pete.

"Naw," Pete answered not wanting conversation.

Uno then got out of the car. "Ayo son you can't get us no more of that?" he asked Loni.

"Naw, ma man left a bag but that's personal use." Loni answered.

"I'll give you fifteen for it." Uno told him knowing Loni's thirsty ass would go for it.

"Damn son, ma man gon be mad but fuck it." Loni said as he turned to get the bag. As he walked a few steps he realized he did know shorty and his man. They were Bum's people. He then turned back around and reached for his gun. Pete and Uno already were pulled out and aimed straight at his head. Before he could pull out, they let off on him and emptied both clips in his body as they stood above him.

As they rode off Pete was in the back seat rolling the Dutch, "Damn, we should have waited to body him till he came back with the other bag."

Chapter 9

Bum had been in town for three days now. The entire 72 hours he was kept busy and he hadn't had a second to relax. When his man, J. Brown asked him to come to the strip club to have a few drinks and chill with him, Bum jumped on it. He hadn't chilled with J. Brown in a while. J. Brown and Bum had been best friends growing up, their mothers use to be like sisters. They were both dime pieces in the day, until they got turned out and started shooting dope and prostituting. J. Brown's mom got killed by a local pimp when he was only 10. After his mother's murder he was placed in a group home on the west side. This was hard for him since he grew up on the East Side, and then having to relocate to the West. Not only did he lose his mother but they also took him away from his best friend, Bum. Through the years they found ways to keep in touch. Like Bum, J. Brown was involved in the drug game also. He moved heroin on the Westside. He was holding seven figures, easy, and had opened a few businesses on the Westside.

As the music played and the stripper was on stage doing her thing, the niggas in the club were wilding out just like the niggas in Jacksonville. Liquor and pussy, what a combination. Bum was mentally somewhere else. He just sat back in his chair with his arm relaxed on the table. He held his glass of Hennessey and thought about the proposition his cousin Gutt had made to him. He was thinking hard about moving to Florida. He knew he played long and hard in Buffalo. He was blessed to still be living and free after all the dirt he did in the city. The allure of the city kept him stagnated. As Bum came back to the club mentally; J. Brown leaned over the small table and screamed over the music, "Yo son, you alright?" His heavy platinum diamond encrusted medallion dangling from the platinum chain banged on the small table. As the medallion turned and shifted the little light that was in the club gleamed as it connected with the diamonds.

"Yeah son, I'm good." Bum screamed back as he nodded his head in agreement with his response. As the platinum chain caught Bum's eye he couldn't help but think of the good old days when he, J. Brown and Gutt used to hang in the neighborhood as kids. He always had to break up J. Brown and Gutt as they fought almost daily. The two would fight for Bum's attention. Even though they were all the same age, Bum had a superior aura, like a leader. He just thought about how close they were, like brothers. They were broke back then, now they're all grown and sitting on paper. This made him smile a bit as he sipped the last of his Hennessey.

"Yo son let's bounce, I got to get some sleep," Bum screamed to J. Brown as he stood up ready to head towards the exit. J. Brown was stuck for a minute as he watched the stripper on stage smoke a cigarette with her pussy.

"Yo son you see that shit, the bitch gon fuck around and get pussy cancer." J. Brown joked as he got up to leave the club with Bum.

As Bum and J. Brown were leaving, they said peace to niggas they knew and acknowledged niggas they knew of. Bum noticed one nigga, King, looking at him real grimy. They didn't really know each other but they knew of each other. Every other time King saw Bum he spoke out of respect and kept it moving, but Bum felt the hate as he looked in King's eyes. Bum just brushed it off and kept it moving.

"Yo son I'm going to Brazil next month, I was gon take ma little bitch but I seen some shit on TV about all dem bitches they got out there and I changed ma mind. I want you to come with me, you down?" He asked as they hopped in his 2009 yellow Corvette Zo6.

"Hell yeah, I been wanting to fuck some Brazilian bitches. We just got to be careful and take a lot of condoms. I heard a lot of them ho's got that monster." Bum replied.

"Yeah I heard that shit too." J. Brown said as he pulled off in the corvette.

"I don't have a passport though homey," Bum informed J. Brown.

"Don't even worry, I can get ya shit in 'bout two-three weeks," He smiled.

Bum shrugged his shoulders, "Then I'm down."

"So it's on, next month. Five days four nights." J. Brown said as he pulled in front of Bum's house.

"Yeah, I'ma call you fam, one." Bum said as he got out of the car and headed in the house.

Chapter 10

Bum finally got some rest in. He had J. Brown drop him off at around 2 am. When he got in he went right to bed. He got a good eight hours of sleep. This was the first time that he slept in his bed since he had been back, so when he woke up he felt rejuvenated. As he looked at the clock on the night stand it read 10:17 am. He then saw the piece of paper that he wrote Misa's phone number on laying on the night stand where he put it before he left for Florida. Bum decided that he was going to call her after he got out the shower. He had been so busy lately and forgot about Misa and everybody else, but he decided today would be a good day to make it up to her.

As Bum got out of the shower he instinctively looked at his phone to see if anyone had called him. He forgot that he had turned his phone off the prior night and left it off so that he could relax. He then turned it on and called Misa. "Hello." Misa answered in that familiar sexy voice that she was blessed with. Bum was intrigued by Misa. She was beautiful, she had natural long jet black hair, sexy cat eyes, flawless light copper brown skin, sexy legs slightly bowlegged to cap off her 5'6 frame and the voice of an angel. She favored the r&b singer Amerie.

"Hello may I speak to Misa?" Bum asked.

"Oh, Hi Brandon, what's up, how was your trip?" Misa enthusiastically asked Bum.

"It was ok, but the whole time I was thinking of you." Bum playfully flirted, not trying for game just playful conversation. "What are you doing today?" he added.

"Um…I don't have anything planned, I was going to just relax today. Why what's up?" She answered.

"Well, I was hoping that we could chill together if that's alright with you?" Bum said.

"What do you have planned?" Misa asked.

"Just be ready at one and I'ma come pick you up, okay?" Bum demanded.

"Well…" Misa paused as if she was contemplating a decision. "Okay I'll call you when I'm ready." she said before she hung up to get ready.

Bum was waiting patiently for Misa to call back. He couldn't wait to see her again and show her a good time. He looked at the time wondering what was taking her so long to get back, so he grabbed the phone and dialed her number. As the phone rang Bum still hadn't figured out where he was going to take her, he just wanted to see her.

"Hello." Misa answered the phone on the fifth ring.

"What's good, you ain't change your mind did you?" Bum asked hoping that they were still on.

"Oh, no I was just about to call you. I was just finishing up, take my address down. You have a pen?" she blurted out in one breath confirming that the date was still on.

"Hold on..." Bum said as he looked for a pen and paper to write Misa's address down on.

Before picking up Misa, Bum decided to stop by his man house to pick up some money he was owed. He was going to do this after the date was over but his man happened to stay two blocks from the address that Misa gave him. After handling that Bum wanted to drop the money off because it was no need to have all that money on him, but then he decided he would take Misa to the casino and gamble with it. When Bum pulled in front of the house he put the Navigator in park. With the engine still running, he called Misa.

"Hello." Misa answered, this time on the first ring.

"Hey, you ready?" Bum asked.

"Yeah, where are you at?" she asked.

"I'm in front of ya house..." he answered while reaching in his pocket with his free hand to review the address. "3261, right?" he asked.

"Yes." Misa answered as she walked to the front of the house to look out the window "That's you in the truck?" she asked.

"Yeah, come on out," Bum demanded as he hung up. Just as he hung up, the phone started to vibrate. Bum immediately answered it assuming it was Misa. "Yo." he answered.

"Hhiieee baby daddy, what you doing?" Bum's baby mother Keisha asked in an annoying hood leech way.

"Fuck!" Bum mumbled to himself not trying to hear her mouth right now. "Keisha, what up?" he asked ready to make this phone conversation as quick as possible.

"Damn, I just was calling to see how the father of ma babies is... I miss you boo." she annoyingly whined.

"Yo, quit the bullshit, what you want?" Bum asked.

"I need some more money so I can get the rest of yo son's school clothes." She responded with an attitude.

"I took him shopping two weeks ago he got shit to last him the whole year, plus the three thousand I gave you the other day," he responded knowing she just wanted some more money so she could trick it on herself.

"I used that for bills you cheap ass nigga. Just bring me some more money or else..." Keisha threatened.

"Yeah alright." Bum said ending the conversation. He sat back in the soft leather of the Navi and exhaled in frustration. *"Dumb bitch."* He mumbled with his head laid back on the head rest. Out the corner of his eye he saw the reason he loved woman. He was momentarily stuck as he admired Misa. She had on some open toe Manolo Blahnik shoes, with some jeans which hugged her hips and were fitting her as if they were custom made, with a matching blouse. Her hair looked as if she just stepped out of a beauty salon, skin was flawless and she had a walk that made him want to suck her slightly bowlegged thighs. She was edible. Bum finally snapped out of his trance when she reached the passenger side door. As she got in, she greeted Bum with a hand shake and a smile which exposed her beautiful teeth. Bum held her hand and checked her out from head to toe. She blushed while sitting in the passenger seat. *She even got pretty feet.* Bum thought which was a necessity for him. Pedicure, manicure she was styling. "You look… Damn!" Bum said excitedly as he searched for the right words to describe her beauty. He kept it simple "You look good." he said holding her hand and smiling.

"Thank you." She continued to blush.

He finally let go of her hand then put the truck in drive and rode off. "So, do you know how to shoot dice?" Bum asked Misa as he drove on the expressway headed to the casino.

"Uhh…yes." Misa responded unsure of what he was getting at.

"Good, because we are going to the casino." Bum said finally informing her of their destination.

"Oh, Ok that sounds like fun." Misa responded with a genuine look of excitement on her face. "But I don't have any money to lose, how about I just cheer you on."

"Don't worry about it, let's just have fun." Bum said as he turned to her and smiled.

Misa was equally intrigued by Bum as he was by her. When she first saw him at Gigi's, she watched him as he came in. She didn't turn from his direction until he noticed her and her friend. They both were plotting on him when he walked in. *"Girl these dudes in Buffalo is a trip. They walk around like they shit don't stink."* Misa's friend continued to complain. She was from Buffalo, and Misa was from Toronto. They were both students at Medaille College and were due to graduate the next year, and had become quick friend's freshman year. They remained close through the years. *"Then the ones with a little money run around fucking the same scandalous bitches."* She continued on. She knew this to be true because before she met Misa she was one of those scandalous bitches. Misa liked Nikki immediately. She was real unlike most of the other girls on campus.

"He's cute." Misa said referring to Bum as he walked in the restaurant. Nikki immediately turned to see who her friend was talking about.

"Yeah, he cute." Nikki agreed as she checked him out. *"I know him from somewhere."* Nikki added as she tried to remember where she knew him from.

"Girl he turning this way." Misa blurted out so her friend wouldn't get caught starring.

"Did he see us looking at him?" Nikki asked Misa, careful not to blow up the spot.

"I don't think so, but he's still looking." Misa spied from out of the corner of her eye as she observed Bum's attention on them now that he was off his cell phone. As Misa thought back to that day, she looked over at Bum. When he turned to look at her she immediately

turned away. Then she smiled at the thought of her and Nikki acting like high school girls about "Brandon."

While riding they talked and flirted with each other. Bum had the music low as they talked. Then his song came on "I don't know why, I...Get so high, on, get so high, on, get so high on –high off the life" the hook blared to Jay-Z's "Allure" as Bum turned up the volume and lip synched to the song. Misa looked at him with a half-smile half-smirk. Bum turned and saw her expression.

"What's wrong, you don't like Jay-Z?" Bum asked. He turned the music down.

"Yeah I like Jay-Z but I love Mary J… you got that?" She asked.

"Nah, I don't really buy slow music, I like it but I love hip hop." he answered as he got off at the East Ferry street exit.

"Oh. Ok. you sound like one of the actors from Brown Sugar." Misa joked as they both laughed. "I thought you said we were going to the casino." she questioned as she realized they were off course.

"We are I just need to make a quick stop." Bum responded as he parked in front of Doris Records and hopped out. Misa watched as he went in the store. She then looked over at the restaurant where she met "Brandon." Gigi's was directly across the street from where he had parked. As Misa started thinking about that day again, Bum came out of the store with a bag. "Let's listen to some Mary." he smiled at Misa handing her the bag.

She looked in the bag and to her surprise Bum had the whole Mary J. Blige collection from 'What's the 411?' to 'Growing Pains.' She immediately smiled as she turned to Brandon. "That's so sweet." She said as she grabbed his free hand as it laid on the divider. Bum turned to her as they made eye contact briefly, but it seemed like much longer.

***

They rode the rest of the way listening to Mary's 'My life' singing along to the lyrics, well Misa sang, Bum attempted to.

By the time they made it to the casino they were laughing and joking. Bum went straight to the counter to exchange his money in for casino chips. He then gave Misa $500 dollars worth. "You ready to win some money?" Bum smiled as he asked Misa.

"After you." She smiled as she responded.

Things weren't looking good for Bum as he was down to his last hundred dollar chip on the dice table. He lost $1,400 dollars in less than two hours. "This is it." Bum said as he bet the minimum allowed at the table of $100 dollars and rolled. Hoping for a five to match his first roll, it landed on seven. "Damn." Bum cursed as he swung his fist down to his side. "Well that's it for me, you not gon try yo luck?" He asked Misa as he stood there defeated.

"Here let me try," Misa said as she gave the man working the table a hundred dollar chip.

"The pretty lady is going to try her luck." The worker said as he positioned the dice in front of her.

"Better yet, Brandon you roll them." She said as she handed the dice to Bum.

"You Sure? Your luck might be better than mine." he said.

Misa then grabbed his hand with the dice in it and blew on them "For luck." She winked. Bum then proceeded to roll.

"Oh, Seven, we have a winner." The worker shouted. Bum then turned around facing Misa and saw her smiling as she shrugged her shoulders. He pulled out $500 dollars from the two thousand that he was holding for the remainder of the date. He put it with the two hundred they just won and bet it. He then turned back to Misa and put the dice towards her mouth so she could blow on them again, "Two in a row." The worker shouted as Bum won again. Bum then turned to Misa and whispered in her ear.

"Luck be a lady tonight." as they both smiled.

After it was all said and done, they won $22,000 dollars. Bum gave the chips to Misa to cash in. "Wow $22,000 dollars!" Misa said in disbelief as she handed the money to Bum. Bum took $200 dollars of it and handed the rest back to Misa. Misa looked confused as she took the money. "What, you want me to hold it for you?" She asked.

"No, that's yours." He said as he smiled.

"Uh Uhn Brandon, I can't take this." Misa said as she tried to hand it back to him.

"Why not? If it wasn't for you we wouldn't have won it." Bum responded.

"But, it's your money." she added.

"No... It's your money." Bum responded. "Now put all that money up before somebody tries to rob you." he joked as he took the money and placed it in her purse. He was turned on by her reluctance to take the money. Unlike many other women he came across through his years, Misa wasn't a gold digger. Misa and Keisha were like night and day. Bum literally shivered in disgust as he thought about Keisha. Bum looked over at Misa as they walked through the casino and noticed she seemed different than many of the girls from Buffalo. "You can't be from Buffalo. Where you from the suburbs? Amherst, Clarence, Hamburg, anywhere but Buffalo." He asked. Misa cracked a slight smile as she looked at Bum.

"Toronto." She relieved him of his confusion.

"Ooh, Toronto…Canada." Bum responded. He then thought to himself he has to cross the border more often. *Deborah Cox, Tamia, and Misa, Toronto give it up like that?* As they walked toward a jewelry store on the casino's lower level Misa window shopped, while Bum's attention was on the food court.

"You hungry?" he asked Misa with his eyes fixed on the plethora of fast food spots about 20 feet from him as he debated which restaurant to attack. Bum enjoyed many things, but eating had to be in his top three.

"Not really." Misa answered as she continued to admire the jewelry from outside the window.

"I'm 'bout to go get something to eat, my stomach is touching." Bum said as he picked his prey.

"Oh, Ok. I'm going to use the ladies room then I'll be right over." She told Bum.

Bum went to work on his food immediately after he received his order from Popeye's chicken. He almost forgot about Misa as he devoured the meal. *Damn, where Misa at?* He thought out loud as he looked towards the restrooms. Then he saw her as she walked out the jewelry store. *Should have known, she probably bought a diamond ring or something, bitches can't resist but to splurge.* He thought. While watching Misa walk the 20 feet from the jewelry store toward him, he again was mesmerized. *Damn...I got to have her.* He thought to himself as he slowly shook his head from side to side.

Misa noticed his expression. This only made her blush. Bum made her seem shy even though she was comfortable in his presence. It was something about him, she couldn't figure it out. *It must be his smile.* She thought as she sat down at the table. She smiled at him. "You have a pretty smile." Misa complemented.

"Thanks. Maybe I should smile more often." Bum responded as he got up from the table and grabbed Misa's hand. "Come on let's go." He said.

"Where to now?" Misa asked.

"Toronto." Bum answered.

Misa looked at Bum with skepticism. "Are you serious?" She excitedly asked.

"Yeah, it's only about an hour and a half away, you down?" Bum asked.

"Yeah let's go." Misa definitely agreed.

"Good you can show me around T.O." Bum said as they walked out of the casino toward the truck.

Misa usually went back to Toronto after every semester and on major holidays. Since she had enrolled in summer classes, she wasn't expecting to be back in T.O. until after the fall semester, so this was a pleasant surprise. She was going to talk Bum into meeting her family while there. Bum knew how to get there having been to the Caribana Festival a few times, but Misa's directions got them there in record time. Misa showed him around Toronto, they went to downtown Toronto, St. James Town, Regent Park, Moss Park and many other areas throughout the city. Bum never saw the whole city; he was surprised at how large it was. It was a nice city. Bum noticed the many different races and cultures that formed the city, it was more racially tolerant than the states. They then went to Misa's parents' house; it was a big house in Toronto's Rosedale neighborhood. When Misa introduced Brandon to her parent's he was surprised to find out that her mother was Korean and her father was Jamaican, which explained her exotic look.

After meeting her parent's, Misa drove the Navigator to a five star restaurant in Toronto's business district. It had valet parking and the whole nine. As they entered the building, Bum was surprised by the elegance of the building. At the top was the restaurant which overlooked the city. After they enjoyed their meal, they sipped on champagne as the sky began to turn from white and light blue to a dark pinkish orange and darker blue. They conversated while light jazz played in the background.

Misa was really enjoying herself, the whole evening. As she looked out at the beautiful sunset she was lost in the moment, then she remembered, "Oh... I almost forgot." She said as she dug through her purse and pulled out a jewelry box and handed it to Brandon who she learned was called "Bum." Bum took the box and looked at Misa wondering what was in the box. Misa had her elbows on the table with her chin resting on her clasped hands as she smiled. "Open it." She urged.

Bum then opened it and was surprised to see a designer watch with diamonds. Bum looked up at Misa in shock. "Where did you get th…? Oh the casino." Bum remembered Misa coming out the jewelry store as he smiled at her. "Thank you." Bum said.

"Do you like it?" Misa asked still smiling.

Bum just nodded his head and smiled as he put it on. "Thank you." he said again. Bum was really feeling that, first he had to force her to take the money they had won, and then she used it to buy him a watch. He was feeling Misa. He got to thinking maybe he was feeling her a little too much.

***

They finally made it back to Buffalo, Mary J. Blige still sang to them. When Bum pulled up in front of Misa's house she was reclined slightly in the passenger seat. She grabbed Bum's hand. "Turn the car off I don't want to go in the house yet." She said as she looked at him seductively. Bum complied and leaned back in his seat as Mary serenaded them. They sat in the truck for nearly 2 hours talking and flirting. "Well I don't want to keep you too much longer; you probably have other things to do." Misa said, ready to head in the house. "Well…bye," she said extending her arm's to give

Bum a hug. “Thank you for everything tonight.” She then opened the door to the truck and paused turning around to ask, “You want to come in?”

Bum thought about it long and *Hard* but he declined. “Naw I’ma go home and get some rest.”

“Well at least walk me to the door.” she said.

“Oh I’m sorry, where’s my manners?” Bum said as he got out to walk her to the door.

They got to the door; she unlocked it and turned to give him another hug. “Bye. Call me tomorrow,” she said. Bum then kissed her lightly on the lips and pulled back, she stood there eyes closed, stuck. Bum grabbed her waist and pulled her into him and started kissing her in a way that got her panties wet. This time he released her and grabbed her hand as he began to back peddle towards his truck. She didn’t want to let go of his hand. “You sure you don’t want to come in?” She tried again. Bum just smiled, released her hand and continued to back peddle

“I’ma call you tomorrow.” He smiled as he turned to walk to his truck. Misa then took a deep breath and exhaled the excitement from her loins.

As Bum drove off he thought to himself. *Damn that was one of the hardest decisions I had to make in a long time, I don’t know how I turned that down, oh well I got her right where I want her.*

Chapter 11

Mojo slept awkwardly, with his right leg laid across the arm of an old beat up, yet comfortable brown loveseat. His body pressed snuggly into the loveseats back. Bumpkin slept laid out on the old couch directly across from Mojo with his long leg's dangling off the end of the couch. They were both dead tired having just gotten in two hours ago from clubbin all night.

The humming of the old refrigerator was battling to be heard over Bumpkin's loud snoring. Neither Bumpkin nor Mojo were aware of any noise, not even the knocking at the door. *Boom Boom Boom*. The knocking continued from the porch of the trap house. It was Darlene a crack head from up the street, a regular. She knocked loud enough to be heard, but not loud enough to wake half the block like she usually did. She wasn't knocking lightly out of consideration for anyone, this was the knock she used when she didn't have any money and she wanted some credit. She knew that if she banged on the door they would get angry, eliminating any chance of getting credit. She was persistent, knocking for almost twenty minutes knowing that someone was there. Someone was usually always there, and Bumpkin's truck was parked next door.

Finally Bumpkin heard the knocking. He raised his head looking toward the window as the bright light from the sun beamed through a small crease in the window shades. He raised his arm trying to keep the sun light out his face as he squinted and grabbed his phone to see what time it was. 7:09 am. He then let his head fall back and hit the couch. The knocking continued. He sluggishly made his way to the window and peaked through the shade. He saw Darlene bobbing her head trying to see any movement at all through the shaded windows. Bumpkin immediately knew Darlene wanted credit by the way she was knocking because when she was spending money she would bang on the door.

Bumpkin made his way back towards the couch, purposely kicking the loveseat where Mojo was sleeping on to wake him. Bumpkin kicked the loveseat almost too hard because the loveseat moved slightly. Mojo popped up immediately trying to adjust his vision, because the heavy kick from Bumpkin frightened him.

Mojo looked at Bumpkin angrily, "Asshole." he said before he laid back onto the loveseat. Bumpkin turned on the TV and laid back down on the couch.

"Somebody at the door fa you." Bumpkin said.

"Fuck em." Mojo responded as he pulled his hand in which occupied a bottle of Hennessey and embraced it as if it were a woman. He then realized the bottle was all but empty so he twisted the top, turned the bottle up and let the remainder fall into his mouth. He gargled it before he swallowed "Ah." He then got up to see who was at the door.

"What up?" he asked with authority, opening the door for Darlene.

"Mojo I need a favor til the mailman come." she asked desperately noticing Mojo's expression of agitation. "Come on Mojo, I'ma give you double," she pleaded.

Mojo looked at her with disgust. She had what appeared to be dried up cum on the corner of her lip running down to her chin.

When she noticed him looking at her mouth, she tried to rub it off. This made Mojo sick. He stopped her and quickly gave her a twenty bag just to get her out of his sight.

***

Mojo threw a bag of weed on the coffee table as he looked for the Dutch that he was sure he had. He looked through the cushions of the loveseat, in the kitchen, on the floor, every where, he couldn't find it. "Fuck!" he irritably screamed. "Yo Bumpkin you seen a Dutch around here some where?" Mojo screamed from the bathroom as he began to take a leak.

"Naw." Bumpkin stated as he laid on the couch watching cartoons. Mojo walked out of the door in frustration. "Where you going?" Bumpkin screamed to Mojo as he closed the door behind him. "Yo get me some cereal and milk." He screamed knowing Mojo was headed to the store.

As Mojo got to the store on the corner of the block he noticed it was relatively empty compared to normally when there were at least ten niggas around the store. This early morning there were just two. Roney and...he forgot the other guys name, he was a younger guy. Mojo spoke "What up son?"

"Yo what up Mojo?" the young guy spoke back.

"What up Roney?" Mojo spoke. Roney just stared at Mojo and nodded his head up and down a few times as he rubbed his hands together. Mojo then walked in the store.

Outside of the store Roney spoke to the young guy, "Ayo I'm tired of these niggas, man something got to give, these dudes eatin' too good." he angrily vented to his man. The young guy just listened.

Inside the store Mojo began to joke with the Arabs, "Akhi, what's happening my friend?" Mojo greeted the Arab behind the counter in his mocked Arabian voice.

"Hey, how are you Mojo?" the Arab shouted back.

"Same shit." Mojo said as he headed to the back to get the cereal for Bumpkin. "Ayo let me get a Dutch, two AK 47's and a Mac 10." Mojo shouted as he continued to joke while walking to the counter.

"Ah, you crazy habibi, no AK's here." the Arab responded.

"Well just give me the Mac 10."

"No milk habibi?" the Arab asked as he rang up the items on the counter noticing Mojo had cereal but no milk.

"Oh yeah, good looking habibi." Mojo said as he ran to the back to get some milk.

"That's it?" the Arab asked

"Yeah that's it. Alright now habibi see you later." Mojo said as he was leaving.

"Peace habibi," the Arab responded. Mojo lit a cigarette as he left out the store.

"Ayo Mojo." Roney said leaning up against the pay phone on the side of the store. Mojo stopped and looked at him inhaling smoke from the Newport. "Yo look here son, you niggas gon have to shut down man. Y'all niggas doin' too much. I mean, ma niggas got to eat too." Roney was talking with his hands flailing in the air.

Mojo just listened and watched Roney's hands making sure he didn't pull out, or try to swing on him. After Roney got through talking, Mojo took a deep pull from the cigarette and exhaled right in Roney's face and walked off.

Roney stood there with a stupid look on his face. He was tight, but Mojo was tighter. He couldn't wait to make it back to the house to get the ratchet. As Mojo walked in the house he slammed the door and went right for the weed. While rolling the weed he began to tell Bumpkin what the nigga just said to him. As he lit the Dutch, Mojo grabbed his four fifth from underneath the cushion and cocked it.

"What you 'bout to do?" Bumpkin asked Mojo as he began to pour a bowl of cereal.

"Man you know what I'm about to do…push this nigga shit back that's what I'm about to do." Mojo angrily responded.

"Naw nigga chill, we take care of that shit later, right now all the nigga doing is getting shit off his chest, when he violate fa real that's when we pop off." Bumpkin explained.

Mojo puffed on the weed. Either the weed or Bumpkin calmed him down. He put the gun on the coffee table, sat down and smoked some more.

Chapter 12

"Yeah dog we gon cause some problems this year," Trevor excitedly told Lex while they were in the locker room getting out of their football equipment after practice.

"Fuck dat son, I'm tryin' to dominate… Some ESPN highlight shit every week…you feel me?" Lex responded amped up standing in front of his locker taking off his shoulder pads.

"Yeah dog you look'n like a animal out there in practice, don't look like you lost ya game, in fact you look better." Trevor said as he sat down in front of his locker which was right next to Lex's and took off his cleats. Lex just smiled at him confidently.

"Hey Lex." Lex turned toward the coach when he heard his name. The coach motioned for him to follow him into his office. When he entered, he saw the coach was seated in a chair behind his desk looking at him.

"What's up coach?" Lex asked still standing near the door.

"Close the door," the coach ordered as he stood up, walked around to the front of the desk and sat on the edge. "I just wanted to let you know that you're looking real good out there in practice, in fact you're looking great." The coach complimented.

"Thanks coach."

The coach continued on, "Now we're going to need your leadership on the field, I think with you at strong safety and Trevor at middle linebacker we can be a force on defense once again...possibly the best in the conference, with your speed and quickness. What is it you run in the 40, 4.37?" Lex smiled in agreement. The coach just shook his head in amazement. "We're going to put you in at punt returner also."

Lex nodded his head in agreement. He was feeling himself right now. Being at punt returner would give him a chance to make more highlights.

The coach then got up from the edge of the desk and walked to the door. "See you tomorrow at practice." The coach said as Lex walked out the door.

"Alright coach." He headed back towards his locker. The coach then called out.

"And Lex...we're expecting big things from you," he added. Lex smiled and nodded his head up and down.

Trevor was sitting down with a towel wrapped around his waist looked up at Lex. "What was that about?"

Lex continued to take off the rest of his equipment "They got me at punt returner."

"Oh shit, I'ma start calling you primetime nigga." Trevor joked. Lex winked at him.

***

After getting out of the shower, Lex got to thinking about the upcoming football season. He felt real good about it, however, he still had business to attend to in the streets. He still had work in the streets and his trap houses were still doing business. He was ready to abandon the drug game and focus solely on school and football. He decided that after he downed the remainder of the work he had left, he would be done with it. No more hustling for him. Even though he loved getting coke money, football provided a greater sense of enjoyment to him. Lex also wanted to start spending more time with Iyani. She was the most official girl he had ever fucked with. He decided to spend the rest of the day with her.

Lex wasn't the best cook, but he learned a few things in the kitchen from his grandmother. He and Billy D would help her cook occasionally when they were kids. He planned to cook Iyani dinner. *Lobster, pasta, sauce, olive oil, tomatoes.* Lex recalled to himself making sure he had everything for the meal. *Oh yeah wine, a nice bottle of Chardonnay.* With that he headed to the winery.

***

Iyani walked in the house and immediately smelled the aroma. "Lex," she called out as she threw her book bag on the couch and walked toward the kitchen. Lex greeted her at the entrance with his arms stretched out. He was holding both sides of the kitchen entrance stopping her from entering. "I can't come in the kitchen?" Iyani asked with a playful smile on her face.

"No, I want you to chill until I'm done. So go have a seat, turn on the radio, TV or whatever and relax until I'm done." She smiled as she grabbed the back of his neck with both hands; she lowered his lips to hers and gave him a kiss. Lex cooperated, "Now beat it." Lex joked. He smacked her on the ass as she walked away.

"Ouch…I'm going to take a shower." Iyani said as she looked back while provocatively moving her hips from side to side. He watched with a smile.

While Iyani was still in the shower, Lex finished preparing the meal. He began to set the table and the mood as he turned on the radio and inserted one of Iyani's favored slow jam CD's. "Wow!" Ianyi walked into the dining room with a blissful look on her face.

"Everything looks so nice, you did a good job." she said as she walked over and gave him a big hug. She had on some boy shorts, a wife beater and the care bear slippers that Lex had bought her. *She looks, so damn sexy.* Lex thought to himself as he squeezed her and took in the smell of nectarine and white ginger from her body wash. She had her long curly hair put up into a ponytail.

Lex took her hand as he sat her in a seat. "I hope you like it; I tried to make it exactly like my grandma makes it."

Iyani just smiled as she began to eat, "I love it, I love you." she said with all sincerity as she looked him in his eyes and grabbed his hand. With his free hand he poured her some champagne.

After finishing their meal Lex grabbed the bottle of champagne and walked over to the couch. "Grab the wine glasses." Lex told Iyani. They sat back sipping champagne and talking while they cuddled up on the couch and listened to the music that softly played in the background. They talked for almost an hour.

"I'm 'bout to get ready for bed." Iyani said as she stood up and looked at Lex. She walked toward the bathroom. Lex watched as she walked away thinking about how lucky he was to have the total package.

Looks, kindness, loyalty and brains, yes brains. He joked to himself referring to Iyani's exquisite blow jobs.

"Are you coming to bed?" Iyani asked Lex as she walked from the bathroom letting her hair down. She knew Lex loved to grab hold of her hair when they had sex, and she loved it as well. Lex picked up the bottle of chardonnay and took it in the bedroom with him. He placed the bottle on the night stand beside the bed and began taking his clothes off down to his boxers.

"Can you turn off the radio?" Iyani asked Lex. Lex walked in the living room and turned the radio off. When he arrived back in the room Iyani was at the bedroom door with her beautiful body exposed to greet Lex. She gently wrapped her arms around him and started to French kiss him, with a combination of love, lust and excitement. Lex returned the emotions and started sensually rubbing his hands down her side to her perfect round ass. Iyani guided him towards the bed while still kissing. She kneeled down and took off his boxer's, grabbing his dick; she teased him as she licked it from shaft to head. Lex just leaned back with excitement as the blood rushed to his dick and caused it to stiffen as hard as steel. She then placed the head of his dick in her warm mouth and proceeded to bob on it. He had to stop her, it was feeling too damn good. He helped her up and laid her down on her back. He got on top and started to kiss her. He started to kiss her neck, her titties, her stomach, her belly button, her thighs, and then he kissed her pussy.

She grabbed the sheets in her fist as she moaned. Lex then grabbed the chardonnay bottle and poured it on her pussy as he began to lick it off. He kissed it with the same passion that he did when he kissed her mouth. Iyani began to quiver as she came.

Iyani sat back for about two minutes to gather herself while Lex sat up to finish off the chardonnay. She started to suck his dick again as he laid back, she was determined to make him cum. Lex guided her hip's to position her pussy over his face. As she lowered her pussy on his face she began to attack the dick with conviction while her sensitive clit was being licked and sucked. She felt Lex's grip get stronger on her ass while his dick started twitching. Lex exploded in her mouth. She kept sucking his dick and licking it as she took in every last drop of cum. Lex got up, went in the kitchen, pulled out the Hennessey and took a long swig. *Ahh,* he said as he tightened his face from the strong taste of the cognac. *"Round two, ding ding."* He said as he went back into the room.

He immediately got on top of Iyani and started kissing her; she tasted the bitter taste of the cognac. Lex spread Iyani's legs, placed his dick head in Iyani and paused. She gasped, Lex continued to glide the rest of his dick in her warm, moist, velvety pussy. Lex and Iyani matched rhythms, she moaned, he moaned, both in pleasure. Lex turned her over and continued beating it doggy style. He grabbed her hair and pulled it with each stroke. This caused Iyani to moan even more out of excitement and pleasure. Lex started pumping in and out of her with even more force until he exploded inside of her. He felt her pussy begin to grasp his dick even more as she began to cum on his dick.

Chapter 13

"And the number 4 play is University at Buffalo's return man Lex Ferguson number 26 with a 67 yard punt return. This guy is amazing, this play helped Buffalo to a blow out win in their season opener." Lex had a huge smile on his face as he and his teammates watched Sports Center.

"Yeah son!" His teammates screamed out excited to see their team on Sports Center let alone the number 4 play in the top 10 plays of the week.

"You keep this shit up Lex and you gone be hot for the draft, first round money baby," Trevor yelled.

Lex just sat back thinking about the possibilities of getting drafted to the NFL. It was always a dream of his growing up, playing the game he loved. His first game back he had 10 tackles, a forced fumble, 2 interceptions and a 67 yard punt return for a touchdown. He knew in order to fulfill his dream's of the NFL he would have to keep this performance up. He had no doubt that he could, after all this was just his first game back. He knew the best was yet to come.

Chapter 14

"Damn, that dick feel gooood, sisss oooh shit," Trixie said with her face buried in the pillow. Billy D had Trixie on the edge of the bed doggy style as he stood up pounding the pussy from the back with a hand on each ass cheek watching his dick go in and out. "Smack my ass." Trixie ordered. *Clap* "Sisss ooh shit...again." *Clap. Clap.* Billy D smacked her ass hard leaving a red hand print on her plump ass. Trixie began coming on his dick. Each time he pulled out he noticed more cum on the rubber as he continued to pump. Billy D then placed his palm on the small of her back causing her ass to hike up. He started pumping harder and faster. Trixie joined in rhythm, her round ass jiggled with each stroke. Billy D pulled out, pulled off the condom and came on her fat ass. Trixie put her hand on her ass and started rubbing the warm cum.

A week ago Billy D told himself he wasn't fucking with Trixie because he felt she played him that night after the club. After seeing her at the mall, she began calling him and sending picture messages of herself in the outfit she bought at the lingerie store. After seeing the pictures, he had to hit it. He was glad that he did. "Want me to make you something to eat?" Trixie asked as she walked out of the bathroom drying her hand's off on the towel she was holding.

Billy D shook his head, *No* as he continued to put on his clothes.

"Want something to drink?" She asked.

"Water," he responded sitting back down on the bed. Trixie came back into the room and handed him the bottled water. He stood up and guzzled the whole bottle, put the top back on and set it on the nightstand. "Alright I'm gone." Billy D said as he headed to the front door.

"Wait." Trixie followed behind him. "Why are you leaving now? You should spend the night." She tried to convince him.

"Naw I got something to do…call me tomorrow." Billy D responded as he fumbled with the locks on the door.

Trixie stepped around him to unlock the door for him. "Can I have a hug before you leave?" She asked as she extended her arms. Billy D gave her a hug as he palmed her ass. "Can you please stay a little longer? Pleeease." She seductively pleaded.

"I told you I have something to do," he stated sternly as he broke her embrace and walked around her through the open door. "Call me tomorrow or whenever you get a chance."

"Bye." She said softly as she watched him walk to his truck.

As Billy D walked to his truck he noticed the car parked across the street a few houses down. The dude in the car was watching him. When Billy D got in his truck, the guy started his car up and rode slowly past Billy D with an evil look on his face. He looked upset, but for what? Billy D had no idea who this kid was, but he was going to find out and more than likely kill him. Billy D did this shit for a living. He got a real good look at the dude and the car he was driving. It wouldn't take him long to find out about him. As Billy D started driving, his phone started vibrating. He saw it was Bank. "What up Unc?" He answered.

"Hey what up with you…you good?" Bank asked his nephew.

"Yeah I'm good...been cooling out."

"That's good to hear…hey listen...you going to Lex game with me next week right?" Bank asked.

"Definitely, where is it gon' be at?"

"Texas." Bank replied.

We flying or driving?" Billy D asked.

"Flying, but I really called you to tell you to go see your grandmother. She misses you and really would like to see you." Big Bank sounded sincere.

"Of course, I'ma go take a shower and eat..."

Big Bank cut him off. "Eat…you know she gon make you something to eat…I don't even know why you said that. Just go take ya shower and go see ya grandma, and I'ma talk to you later. Love you."

"Love you to Unc, one." Billy D responded as they hung up. Billy D knew his grandmother got lonely out in Orchard Park in her big house by herself. He would visit often, but the visits went from often to seldom. Last time he had seen her was when Big Bank had the last talk with him.

***

Billy D got out of the shower and started to get dressed. The whole time in the shower he was thinking about dude who was watching him outside of Trixie's house. He never saw him before, but he knew he would see him again.

Billy D pulled into the huge driveway of his grandmother's house. He parked behind her Mercedes Benz. He, along with Bank and Lex, had the keys to the house, so he let himself in. He called out to his grandmother, "Grandma."

"In here baby." she answered from the living room. Billy D walked toward his grandmother as she stood up from the couch to give him a hug and a kiss. "Hey baby how have you been?"

"I've been Ok." He responded as he sat down on the couch next to his grandmother and looked at all the pictures spread across the coffee table. "How are you?" He asked.

"I'm Ok, just looking at all these old pictures of your grandfather, your dad, uncle, you and Lex's baby pictures."

"I see." He said as he picked up some pictures and started looking through them. After about 20 minutes of looking at the pictures, and laughing, Billy D noticed a baby picture. Not of him or Lex. It had a year on it, 1992. In 92 he was about 3 years old, and Lex was 4, but this was a baby in the picture. "Grandma…who is this?" Billy D asked as he looked at the picture. He then looked over at his grandmother who didn't respond. He noticed a saddened look on her face as her eyes welled.

"You hungry?...I'm about to go in this kitchen and cook something for you, you probably haven't had a decent meal in months." She ignored his question as she stood up and walked toward the kitchen.

Billy D didn't expect this reaction from his grandmother, but this made him even more curious as to who that was in the picture. The baby boy had the same features as himself as a baby, just lighter complexioned and finer hair. He wasn't going to ask his grandmother about the picture again because he had seen how upset she looked the first time he asked. He just put the picture down and walked in the kitchen. "Whatcha cook'n?" He asked as he sat down at the kitchen table.

"A little grilled shrimp and tilapia…Malawi style." She answered as she turned and winked at Billy D. She knew he loved that meal.

"Hmm. I can't wait." He said with a smile on his face. When the food was done Billy D devoured it. He loved his grandmothers cooking. They sat at the kitchen table talking for almost 2 hours about everything, girls, the Buffalo Bills, cracking jokes and just having a good time. Billy D forgot how much fun his grandmother was to be around. He was happy to see her in good spirits.

"I miss you boys. I'm happy to see both of you doing good." She told Billy D with all sincerity as she grabbed his hands. "I love you so much I just want you to always know that."

"I love you too Grandma." Billy D said as he got up and walked around the table to give her a hug.

"Now get out of here before you eat all of my food." She said jokingly.

"Ok. grandma, thanks for the food, it was good." He said as he rubbed his stomach.

"Anytime baby. I'll see you later, you let yourself out I'm about to clean up this kitchen." She said as she walked toward the sink to start the dishes.

"Alright Grandma, love you. See you later." Billy D said as he walked toward the door to leave.

Chapter 15

Bum hadn't seen Misa since their date to the casino, so when he saw her again he was mesmerized by her beauty. She had her hair in a ponytail and her lip gloss made her lips look as though they were glazed. She had on a sweat suit that accentuated her curves as well as air max tennis shoes. Even though her outfit was relaxed, she made it look good. She was one of those girls who could wear a nun's outfit and make it look sexy.

As she got in the car, she smiled at Bum. "Hi." She said shyly. Bum checked her out; he extended his arms to give her a hug.

"You look good." Bum said as he took in the pleasant aroma of Misa.

"You too." Misa responded while still smiling. "I'm not very good at bowling, so I hope you're going to help Me." she admitted in embarrassment.

"Then why did you want to go bowling then?" Bum asked while laughing at her.

"I like bowling…a lot I'm just not very good at it." She responded.

"Well don't worry I'll help you." He said as he turned and smiled at her.

"Ok... I see I have you listening to Mary J. now huhn?" Misa smiled.

"I put it on just before you got in." Bum said as his phone started vibrating. He continued to drive as he looked at the caller I.D. It was Keisha. Again. This was the third time she called. He already spoke with her earlier and told her that he would stop by later on that night. She called begging for money like she always did. He got aggravated every time he saw her number pop up on his caller I.D. He told her he would bring the money, which she didn't need. She would always say she needed money for the kids, knowing they were well taking care of by Bum financially. Bum was going to give her the money so that she would leave him the fuck alone for at least a week or two. *What the fuck this bitch need with $4000 dollars, I just gave her $3000 dollars.* He thought to himself. *Greedy bitch!* He ignored her call.

As they approached the door to the bowling alley, Bum opened the door for Misa. Manners? Yeah, ok. He just wanted to see her ass. He admired her physique.

"So, what size you wear?" Bum asked Misa as they approached the counter.

"A five." She answered.

"How you doing?" Bum spoke to the worker behind the counter. "Can I get a 10 and a size 5 for her, aannnd 4 games."

"You're on lane 26," the worker said as he sprayed the bowling shoes and handed them to Bum and Misa.

Once they arrived at the lane they sat down and put their shoes on. "Slow poke. I'm going to put our names in." Misa said with her shoes on already. She walked over to the computer to enter their names.

Bum was struggling trying to loosen the tight ass shoe strings. His phone started vibrating again. Keisha...again. He just ignored the call as he finally loosened the shoes enough to squeeze them on. "Ok... Let's go." Bum said as he stood up ready to bowl.

"You're first." Misa said as she sat at the computer. Bum rolled a gutter ball on his first roll. Misa put her hands over her face as she laughed at Bum. "Maybe I should help you." She joked.

Bum laughed, "Just making sure you're paying attention." He then rolled a strike. He stood at the lane with one leg back and his right hand still in the air displaying his strike pose. He turned and winked at Misa. She blushed. "Ok, your turn." Bum said as he took a seat. Misa stood up slowly and grabbed a ball.

"Ok, please don't laugh at me." Misa said while looking back at Bum.

"You laughed at me." He responded.

"No, I laughed with you." Misa said as she rolled. She knocked down one side of the pins leaving half standing.

"That's good. Now hit the rest of them." Bum encouraged her.

She turned and gave him a slight smirk. She then rolled. This time she didn't hit any pins. She turned her head immediately towards Bum to see if he was laughing. Bum tried to hide his smile. Misa ran over towards him with a smile on her face and playfully hit him. "I see you trying to hide your smile."

Bum finally let it out as he started laughing. "No, you did good." Bum said as he stood up to bowl again. Strike. He did his strike pose again. He walked back past Misa with a smile on his face, as she grabbed a ball and bumped him purposely. "Come on Misa get a strike." Bum cheered her on. She rolled and knocked down the same pins from her first roll. Bum then got up and walked over to Misa. "I see what you're doing wrong." He said as he turned her back around facing the pins. He put the ball in her hand and stood behind her to help her with her form. The whole time he was enjoying the close proximity of her ass near his dick. His phone started vibrating again.

"You getting excited back there." Misa joked as she felt his phone vibrating. Bum pressed the ignore button seeing that it was Keisha again. As Bum guided Misa's hand, the ball hit the remaining pins and they fell. She looked shocked as she turned facing Bum with a smile on her face. "I did it! Oh I forgot to do the pose." She said as she turned back facing the lane and mimicked Bum's strike pose. Bum started laughing.

After they finished bowling, they turned their shoes in and decided to get something to eat from the little diner inside the bowling alley. "I'm going to wash my hand's, I'll be right back." Misa said as she walked to the bathroom.

Bum's phone started vibrating once again. It was Keisha, again. Bum decided to answer it so she would stop calling. "Yes Keisha." Bum answered.

"Hey I was calling to find out what time you was coming."

Bum closed his eyes as he raised his head in frustration. "In a few hours Keisha."

"Well, what time?"

"Three hours Keisha." Bum responded.

"Its 7:30 know so at 10:30." Keisha asked.

"Yes, at 10:30." Bum responded.

"Ok. see you then." Keisha replied as though they were two close friends setting up a meeting for brunch. Bum just hung up.

Bum sat at the small table in the diner looking at the menu. They didn't have much of anything he would eat, so he decided to get Buffalo wings and fries. Misa came walking towards Bum at the small table with her sexy walk. He got to thinking why he didn't fuck her the night after the casino. He knew if the opportunity presented itself again it was going down. Misa started blushing and smiling as she saw the look on Bum's face. He handed Misa the menu as she sat down. "You see anything on there you want?" Bum asked.

Misa looked up from the menu at Bum. "What are you getting?" She asked.

"Buffalo wings and fries."

"Me too." She smiled at Bum.

Misa only ate three of the seven wings and maybe a handful of fries. Bum didn't mind, more for him. He was already starting on her food after he finished his. Misa took a sip of her apple juice then began to wipe her hands on the wet wipe. "So... what do you like to be called?" Misa asked Bum as he looked down at the food as he sucked it in.

"It don't matter, you can call me whatever you like...as long as you call me." Bum looked up at Misa and winked.

She smiled. "Well...Brandon, I know we haven't known each other that long, but I enjoy the time we've spent and the conversations we have, and I would like to spend more time with you." Misa decided to let Bum know how she felt about him.

Bum looked up at her as he finished the last wing and took a sip of his water. "That sounds good. I would like that." Bum said as he smiled. He then wiped his hands as he stood up extending his arms for Misa to get up and give him a hug. She got up and hugged him. Bum pulled out a twenty dollar bill and threw it on the table as he grabbed Misa's hand and walked out of the bowling alley.

***

After dropping Misa off, Bum headed to his spot to get the money to drop off with Keisha. After counting the money Bum wanted to say fuck Keisha and give her nothing, but he decided he would give it to her to shut her the fuck up.

Bum hopped in his car and headed to Keisha's house early. It was 9:40pm; she wasn't expecting him until 10:30. He wanted to hurry and give her the money so that she would leave him the hell alone. As Bum rode up Keisha's street he saw the nigga King riding down. King broke his neck as he looked at Bum ride past. *What the fuck that nigga looking at?* Bum thought out loud. He reached at his waist to feel the handle of his gun just for reassurance. He pulled in front of Keisha's house and saw Keisha in the upstairs window looking out at him. When she saw him she immediately ran from the window. Bum noticed she had a worried look on her face. He got out and walked to the front door. Keisha met him there.

"Hey what's up, you early." Keisha sounded nervous. "Come upstairs real fast." She added.

Bum just wanted to give her the money and bounce, but for some reason he followed her upstairs. He thought he heard the door to the downstairs apartment open. Bum owned this house before he gave it to Keisha. It was always in her name anyway. The door to the apartment downstairs made a funny noise whenever someone would open it. Bum knew the house in and out.

"Was that the door down stairs?" He stopped on the steps heading upstairs and listened.

"Naw that's probably next door or something." Keisha responded as she continued to walk up the steps.

Bum looked back and listened for a second and started walking upstairs behind Keisha. As they got upstairs, Keisha picked up a manila envelope from off the entertainment system and handed it to Bum. "What's this?" He asked as he turned it over looking at it.

"Its pictures of the kids." She responded while avoiding eye contact. Bum thought maybe the bitch was high or something. The kids weren't there so he didn't give a fuck what she was doing. He then gave her the money and walked toward the steps. "Thanks Bum." Keisha said as she walked behind him down the stairs.

When he opened the door he noticed that somebody was in the hallway. Keisha pushed him off the last step and locked the door. She pushed him right into the person who was in the hallway. As Bum slammed into the masked person, he felt the hardness of steel. Then he heard a shot go off. Bum was pressed up against the barrel causing it to point downward as the shot hit the floor. Bum felt the heat coming from the barrel. He then heard another shot but this time it was from another gun and another direction. Bum immediately pulled his gun from his waist as another shot went off. He heard the masked person gasp as blood dripped onto his face from the person's head. The shots were coming from behind him. He immediately turned as another masked person was aimed right at his head. He began to shoot until he had no bullets left. Bum was now in the small dark hallway with two dead mask gunmen. He felt his heart beating as though it was trying to burst out of his chest. He looked from one to the other to make sure they were both dead. He grabbed their guns, and then knocked on the door to get Keisha. "Keisha. Keisha…" He wanted to yell but he remained in a low tone.

Keisha came to the door with her hands over her face with tears in her eyes as she opened the door. "I'm sorry. Bum I'm sorry." Keisha cried as she stood at the door.

"It's alright, just…I'ma need you to help me put these niggas in the basement until I figure out what to do." Bum said sounding in control.

"I'm sorry Bum." Keisha continued to cry.

"It's Ok...Just be quiet and help me...go get me some sheets and a couple garbage bags." Keisha continued to cry as she went back upstairs to get what Bum asked her for. Bum stood there with his mind racing thinking, *who the fuck was these niggas*? What were they doing there and how did they know that he was going to be there? Then a light bulb went on in his head. *Keisha.*

Keisha came back down with the sheets and garbage bags. "I'm sorry Bum." She continued to cry. Bum just looked at her not saying a word as she continued to cry. "I'm sorry they made me do it." She started sobbing. "They just wanted to rob you, that's it. Nobody was supposed to die. I'm sorry."

Bum knew what he had to do, but for now he had to deal with the situation at hand. "Keisha…Keisha its ok, its ok." He assured her. "Just help me get these niggas in the basement."

Keisha began wiping the tears from her face as she stepped in the hallway. They continued to put both dead bodies on the sheets and plastic. Bum carried one down at a time. When they both were down there he pulled off their masks. Bum recognized both of them. They were King's men. Then he thought back to the night at the strip club with J. Brown when King was looking real grimy. Then the he just so happened to ride past Bum on Keisha's block less then 30 minutes before? But why was this man trying to come at him like this? He had no idea, but it didn't matter now. *My turn,* Bum thought to himself. Bum couldn't wait to get a hold of King, but he knew he had to do it right. As Bum came back upstairs he told Keisha not to do anything that night, but chill, go to sleep and relax.

"I'm so sorry Bum." She said for about the hundredth time.

"I said it's ok...I'm not mad at you. Just do what I told you to do. Don't tell nobody what happened. I'ma have somebody come over and clean this shit up…it's alright." Bum said as he gave Keisha a hug. He wanted to fucking strangle her, but he needed her for now. Bum smiled at her before he left out the door and looked to make sure the police wasn't around. "Remember…don't worry." Bum then walked casually to his car and drove off.

Chapter 16

"Number 26…Lex Ferguson on the tackle." The man spoke over the loud speaker in the huge stadium.

"Yeah Lex!" Bank and Billy D both screamed out as they watched Lex make another tackle. It was only the start of the third quarter and Lex already had 6 tackles, a forced fumble, an interception and a 77 yard punt return for a touchdown. His team was up 17 to 10. "That boy balling." Bank commented to Billy D with a proud smile on his face.

"Uh oh, they 'bout to punt it." Billy D said in anticipation of Lex returning another for a touchdown. "Come on Lex run this shit back." He screamed waiting for the other team to punt the ball to his cousin.

The punter tried to kick the ball as far away from Lex as possible, but Lex ran all the way to the sideline, caught the ball in bounds and headed up field. The crowd got silent except for the few hundred fans that traveled from Buffalo to watch their team. The Buffalo fans along with Bank and Billy D yelled in excitement as Lex made his way through the would-be tacklers, maneuvering through the pack of players like a fleet footed cheetah. Lex tried to accelerate through the last bunch of players, but one dove at his ankle and tripped him up just 15 yards short of the end zone.

"Damn." Bank yelled as he smacked his hands together.

"Shit, it's all good Unc. He returned it, what fifty two yards?" Billy D said.

"I know. I just wanted him to get that TD." Bank explained.

"He gon get another one before this game over, I can feel it." Billy D said being the optimist. Lex's punt return led to a UB touchdown just two plays later.

Nearing the end of the third quarter, the score was 31 to 20. "Unc I'm 'bout to get something to drink, you want something?" Billy D asked as he stepped around Bank.

"Naw, hold up... I'm coming with you." Bank responded as he reached to answer his phone. "Hello." He answered and remained silent as he listened to the caller. Billy D turned to look at his uncle. He saw his uncle's expression and immediately knew something was wrong. "I'ma be back in town tomorrow." Bank said as he hung up. He shook his head as he cursed.

"Everything alright Unc?" Billy D asked concerned.

Bank took a deep breath "We'll see." He responded.

"What's the deal Unc?" Billy D continued to try and see what his uncle was upset about. Bank stopped on the steps as he looked at Billy D.

"Big John got knocked coming up." Bank continued to walk after he said this. His worried expression still remained.

Billy D started back up the steps behind his uncle. This happened to his uncle before when his load of heroin being transported from down south up to Buffalo was seized, but he didn't react like this, so Billy D was confused. As they made it to the concession stand, Bank remained silent. "Unc, it's nothing, shit you gonna bounce back." Billy D tried to lighten him up knowing this loss wouldn't hurt his uncle's pockets.

Bank shook his head "It's not about that work…it's the feds, so this ain't just no random traffic stop and search, soon as we get back

I have to contact the lawyer, because I know…I just know I'ma need him."

Billy D understood why his uncle was reacting like he was. "Sorry Unc… if it's anything you need me to do, anything..." He emphasized, "Just let me know." He meant that with all sincerity and Bank knew this.

He just smiled at Billy D. "You just don't worry about this." Bank responded as he looked Billy D directly in his eyes. Billy D looked at him. He was worried for his uncle.

As they made it back to their seats, their moods were dampened because of the phone call Bank had received and the possible consequences behind what happened with Big John. They were there for Lex, so they tried to put it off until after the game.

At the start of the fourth quarter, UB punted the ball. The opposing player ran the ball back. The crowd began to get excited as he crossed the end zone. "Damn I know they ain't gon let these fools come back and win." Bank said as he had his focus back to the game.

"Fuck…Lex got one more touchdown in him, they ain't gon blow this shit." Billy D said as he started clapping his hands. "Come on UB, let's go." He yelled.

As the game went on, it was now only one minute and twenty three seconds left in the game. The other team had the ball on UB's 8 yard line. When they lined up, Lex came up to the line as though he was going to cover the tight end. When they hiked the ball he immediately blew past the tight end while the running back tried to block him. He knocked the running back down as he eyed the quarterback. The quarterback saw Lex coming from out of the corner of his eye, and he tried to avoid him by running to his right, but Lex immediately hit him.

"Hell yeah Lex!" Billy D and Bank shouted.

The sack forced the clock to continue to run. The opposing team immediately came back to the line and hiked the ball. This time Lex did cover the tight end, but the quarterback found the receiver in the back of the end zone. "Touchdown!" the man screamed over the loud speaker as the crowd went wild.

"Fuck!" Billy D and Bank both yelled. It was now only fifty three seconds left in the game.

"Damn I hate to see them lose like this." Bank said as he watched the people all around the stadium go crazy.

Billy D stared onto the field looking at the UB players who had their heads down. As UB lined up to receive the kick off, Billy D noticed Lex was out there to return it. He usually only returned punts, but they needed a big play by their best player. "Oh shit, they got Lex back there for the kick off. I told you he got one more in him...this is it." Billy D smiled at Bank. When the team kicked it off, they kicked it right to Lex. Lex immediately cut towards the middle of the field. When he got past the first wave of players the crowd began to get silent. The players on Buffalos sideline began to rush toward the sideline to get a better look. They felt it. Lex then cut toward the right side of the field as the pursuit was following in the opposite direction. He then picked up speed. The sideline started jumping up and down going crazy as well as the UB fans.

"Oh shit." Billy D said as he grabbed Banks arm in excitement. Lex had one player to beat, the kicker. He blew right past him with no problem. Touchdown. Billy D started yanking his uncle's arm as he screamed. "I told you Unc, he had one more in him."

Bank smiled as he nodded his head. "How that boy do that?" He said in amazement of Lex's abilities.

There was a faint roar of excitement in the huge stadium coming from the few UB fans. The home team fans began to file out of the stadium, sensing the game was lost for their team. It was now thirty eight to thirty four with only forty one seconds left. The kicker for UB kicked the ball short causing it to bounce, giving his players time to get down field to make the tackle. The returner retrieved the bouncing football at his 25 yard line. He was able to return it to his 35 yard line, with only twenty eight seconds to go. Lex and the rest of the defensive players came back on the field ready to stop the other teams attempt at a victory. The quarterback got behind the center, looked over the defense and called the play. The center then hiked the ball. Lex watched the quarterback's eyes as he looked to one receiver then he looked over at another, his eyes got big. Lex immediately ran in that direction. The quarterback threw the ball, he knew he probably shouldn't have thrown it because Lex was running in stride as he located the ball in the air and jumped to snatch it out the air. The UB sideline began celebrating as Lex kneeled down. He then tossed the ball to the referee and began to run towards the sideline as his teammates congratulated him.

"Man, he is good, damn good." Bank smiled and shook his head admiring his son's game. The rest of the home fans that remained began filing out. Billy D and Bank made their way down the stadium to get closer to the UB players on the sideline. As they got close enough they called out Lex's name. He was hugging and celebrating with his teammates when he heard his name. He immediately spotted Billy D and his father and ran over toward them.

"Yeah cousin good game." Billy D leaned over the railing to give his cousin a hug.

"Good lookin' man, I'm glad y'all came." Lex said with a huge smile on his face.

"Man you looking like a super star out there." Bank said as he leaned over to give Lex a hug.

"I appreciate that." Lex responded.

"Our plane leaves first thing tomorrow so we'll see you when we get back." Bank told Lex.

"Alright see y'all tomorrow, love y'all." Lex said as he jogged back toward his teammates. He ended the game with 11 tackles, a sack, a forced fumble, 2 interceptions a 77 yard punt return and an 88 yard kickoff return for a touchdown.

***

It was 9:27am when Billy D and Bank pulled in front of Banks house coming from the airport. "Remember what I told you...this is not your problem, so don't stress it." Bank told Billy D while they sat in the car.

Billy D just looked at him. "I'ma handle it. I love you." He added. Billy D nodded his head in agreement as he got out the car and walked to his truck which was parked in the driveway. He got in his truck and rode off. As he made his way into the city, the whole time he was thinking about his uncle and the situation he was in. He just wished there was something he could do. This made him upset knowing he couldn't really help. He then thought back to the day at Trixie's when dude was watching him. Now was the time to deal with him to take his mind off his uncle's situation.

Chapter 17

As Bum and J. Brown made it to the hotel, they both were tired from the plane ride. J. Brown slept on the plane, but Bum couldn't sleep. He never flew on a plane before, and this had him restless the entire plane ride. He figured it was worth it. He wasn't going to let his reluctance of flying stop him from going on the trip.

"Yeah this is what's up!" J. Brown commented as he toured their hotel room which looked more like an apartment, the room was huge. They had their own separate rooms for privacy and a deck overlooking the beach. "I'm tired as hell son. I'm 'bout to lay it down." J. Brown told Bum as he walked into his room.

"Alright, I'm too amped to sleep. I'm gon hit the beach." Bum responded as he put his luggage in his room.

"Alright son wake me up when you get back, we got to figure out what we gon do tonight." J. Brown said as he flopped on the soft bed.

"Alright." Bum responded while unpacking his personal items from one of his suitcases. As Bum was heading out the room he heard J. Brown snoring. *I hope this nigga don't snore like that all night.* He thought to himself as he left out the door. Bum made his way through the hotel. He had never been in a hotel like that. It was huge. It had huge chandeliers hanging in the foyer, the floors looked so clean that you could eat off of them and the restaurant and bar area looked classy.

Bum headed to the bar to have a couple of drinks to get his mind off of the past few days he had in Buffalo. He wanted to enjoy this vacation because when he got back he had a full plate of business to handle.

Bum made his way to the bar, the pretty bartender smiled at him. She was gorgeous. She looked to be Brazilian. She had long curly hair, a honey complexion, exotic eyes, and a slim body with a nice ass.

"Ola, O que posso fazor por voce?" She spoke. Bum had no idea what she said. She just smiled. "Hello, what can I get for you?" She then asked with an accent.

Bum smiled back. "Let me get a Mango margarita." He ordered.

"Ok." She smiled again as she walked off to prepare his drink. He watched her ass as she walked away. Bum liked what he was seeing. "Here you go." She placed his drink in front of him. "Would you like anything else?" She asked.

"Yes." Bum said as he took a sip of his margarita. "I would like to get to know you." He said looking at her, waiting for a reaction.

Her honey cheeks began to blush as she smiled exposing her perfect white teeth. "Well, I'm working now." She said as she raised her shoulders and looked around the bar.

"I know...and you're supposed to keep the customers happy, besides there's nothing wrong with a little small talk." He said as he took another sip of his drink.

"What's your name?" She asked.

"I'm Brandon, Jazmeen." he said as he read her name tag. "Is that how you pronounce it?"

"Yes, Jazmeen." She smiled. "Where are you from Brandon?"

"Buffalo." He responded. He noticed the confusion on her face. "New York. Buffalo, New York." He added.

She then smiled in agreement, recognizing New York. "Are you from Brazil?" Bum asked.

"Yes…Rio de Janeiro, but originally from Sao Paulo." She answered. "One second." She said as she went to take another customers order. Bum liked to see her walk. She had a sexy ass walk, along with her nice ass. "So, how long are you going to be staying here?" She asked as she came back over.

"Five days." He responded while finishing his drink. He didn't want another drink, but he ordered one anyway just to see her walk again. She came back and placed his drink on the bar in front of him. "Do you work here everyday?" Bum asked.

"Well I usually work nights, the day worker called off." She answered.

"Maybe one night when you get off we can hang out." Bum suggested.

She began smiling. "Maybe. We'll see." She responded.

Bum took a sip of his drink as he got up. He put a hundred dollar bill on the bar as he said goodbye and began to walk away.

"What about your change?" She asked while holding the hundred dollar bill up.

"Keep it. I'll see you later...Jazmeen." He said as he smiled and walked off.

She smiled back as she waved goodbye.

***

It was now almost 9 pm. Bum and J. Brown showered, got dressed and headed out.

"How I look?" J. Brown asked Bum as he adjusted his platinum designer frames.

"Like a million bucks." Bum replied. He literally meant that as he looked at J. Browns outfit. He had on Gucci shoes, a Gucci hat to match, two platinum chains with chunky diamond encrusted medallions hanging from them, a watch on each wrist, one gold one platinum and a ring on each pinky finger. With his clothes and jewelry, he had to be wearing about $160 thousand dollars. Bum's attire held it's own, but he couldn't compare to J. Browns. He also had on Gucci, but he had only one platinum chain and the watch that Misa bought him. That was their personality differences. Bum was more humble and reserved, as oppose to J. Brown who was flamboyant and flashy.

"Man this shit look like its popping." J. Brown said as he looked around at all the people and busy atmosphere.

Bum nodded his head in agreement. They walked the busy strip packed with tourist and locals. "Right there son...let's check that spot out." Bum said as he watched the three sexy Brazilian women walk in the night club. When they walked in the night club all eyes were on them. They made their way to the bar while checking out the women who were checking them out. After ordering their drinks and sitting at the bar it didn't take long before a group of women approached them. All three looked to be Brazilian. They all had nice bodies, except for one of them. "Ola," one yelled trying to get as close as possible to be heard over the music.

Bum and J .Brown both spoke. "Hi,"

"Are you guy's rappers?" She asked now in broken English.

Bum and J. Brown laughed. "No, no we're not rappers."

She was sexy. Her skin was a golden bronze color, she was slim with a nice shape, and she had on a short skirt which showed her sexy golden bronze legs.

"Are you here on vacation?" She asked.

"Yes we are." J. Brown answered while looking her up and down.

"Are you having fun?" She asked with a smile on her face.

"So far, yes," he responded.

"So who are your friends?" Bum asked while staring at one. She was short with long jet black hair, a sexy body and pretty face.

"These are my two cousins, Gabrielle…" She said pointing to the big one. "And Tabitha."

He greeted both of them, but focused on Tabitha. "Do you speak English?" Bum asked her.

"A little." she answered.

The big girl walked away noticing she was the odd one out. J. Brown continued to talk to Tabitha's cousin, while Bum talked with Tabitha.

"You want a drink?" Bum asked.

"Sure, Tequila." She smiled. J. Brown started dancing with the other girl. Bum and Tabitha talked and had a couple more drinks. After about her third Tequila, she began talking about marriage and how she could please her lover. Bum thought she was crazy, but he still was going to fuck her. As the night went on, she wouldn't let Bum out of her sight. She followed him to the bathroom and all around the club. He couldn't get at any other females. He was cool with it though because he wanted to fuck her. "Yo lets bounce back to the hotel and fuck these bitches so we can get rid of them." J. Brown spoke loud enough to be heard over the music but not by the girl as she stood behind him holding his hand.

"Let's go." Bum agreed as he stood up. Tabitha immediately stood up after him. They then left out of the club.

***

"Oh, se sente tao bem!" Tabitha started moaning in Portuguese as she rode Bum.

Bum had his hands on her hips as her wet pussy stroked up and down on his dick. She rode his dick from every angle. Front, sideways and backwards. *She wasn't lying...* Bum thought to himself. *She knows how to please.* Bum loved her body. She had nice titties and a nice ass. As Bum was fucking her she was completely nude. He saw her tan lines. Her titties, ass and pubic area were all lighter than the rest of her body. This turned Bum on. He then began to fuck her mouth as he stood over her. He pulled the condom off and came on her titties.

***

The next morning they finally got rid of the two Brazilian cousins. "Man them hoes was fucking crazy." J. Brown said as he and Bum ate breakfast by the pool.

"Man who you telling, the bitch was talking about marriage and all type of crazy shit." Bum added.

"The bitch wanted me to take her back to the States wit me." J. Brown said as he finished his breakfast. "But yo, you ain't finish telling me 'bout that shit wit Keisha." J. Brown changed the subject.

"Oh yeah." Bum said as he guzzled his orange juice and wiped his hands off. "Yeah, I told you the bitch was calling me all day that day about money for the kids. So I told the bitch I'ma be through later, you know I was on a date wit the bad little chick from T.O. I was telling you 'bout...but anyways, I get over the bitch house and she acting kinda nervous, I just ain't pay her no mind. As we going up the steps I hear something downstairs, she try to tell me it's probably nothing, probably next door or some shit, so I let it go. I give her the money and I'm ready to bounce, and I head downstairs.

Soon as I open the door I see a niggas boots, the bitch push me out the door and lock it."

"The bitch did what?" J. Brown asked with a surprised look on his face.

"Hold on... so when the bitch push me, I'm right up on the nigga, the nigga shot his pistol off but by me being on him so close the pistol is pressed in between us and it's pointed down, so the bullet hit the floor...I guess his man panicked or something cus he just start shooting. He tried to hit me but he hit his man right in the head."

"Wow!" J. Brown said in shock.

"So dude blood get on ma face that's when I realize somebody behind me, so I pull out, stayed low as I turned around and started dumping on the nigga...the whole clip. So now it's two dead niggas in the hallway, stanking ass gun smoke, shells and blood all over. I'm knocking on the door calling the bitch name trying to get her to open the door. She come crying and shit talking 'bout she sorry. At first I didn't know what the fuck was going on. You know ma mind racing and shit. These niggas tried to kill me, the bitch just kept talking 'bout she sorry. Then I calm down and realize the bitch set me up. So I tell the bitch to get me some sheets and garbage bags so I can put these niggas in the basement."

"Hold on son, who was these niggas?" J. Brown asked.

"The niggas had mask on, so when I put them in the basement I lift them up and they was the nigga Kings people." Bum said with revenge in his voice.

"Word?" J. Brown asked in surprise. "Dirty ass niggas." J. Brown added.

"He's a dead man." Bum said.

"So what about Keisha?" J. Brown asked.

Bum just looked at him.

Chapter 18

Keisha was in her room rummaging through her drawers and closet hastily, trying to pack whatever she could in a single suitcase. She was scared. She was avoiding King's phone calls and she didn't know if Bum truly did forgive her. She just knew she had to get the fuck out of town. Her cousin in Atlanta told her that she could come down there and stay with her. She even had a job lined up for her at the strip club she worked at. Her kids were staying with her mother for the moment. She figured she would work at the strip club down there for awhile to save up some money and get her own place, then come back for her kids. She was tired of Buffalo anyhow. After she filled the suitcase up, she stood in the middle of the room and looked around making sure she had everything she needed. She put her hand in her jacket pocket to feel for the $4000 dollars Bum gave her the day the drama happened. She had the money and a suitcase full of clothes to hold her down until she started working at the strip club. She grabbed her suitcase and headed down stairs.

***

"Yo, right here." Uno pointed at the house. "Back into the driveway." He ordered Bull. "Pete get the gasoline from out the trunk," he told Pete as he took the keys from Bull and handed them to Pete in the back seat. Uno and Bull then walked to the front door of the house.

"Oh shit!" Keisha screamed as she dropped her suitcase and placed her hands over her chest. "Uno, Bull y'all scared the hell out of me." She said as she recognized the two.

"You alright?" Uno asked as he walked into the hallway.

"Yes. I'm ok. I was just about to leave." Keisha said as she reached down to pick up her suitcase. She then thought of a lie real quick. "I'm going to stay at my mom's house until things calm down, you know?" She asked hoping Uno was falling for her lie.

"I understand." Uno said. "But come upstairs wit me, I need you to help us real fast then you can be on your way." He added as he took the suitcase from her. Uno noticed fear in her eyes as she turned back around to head back upstairs. She just wanted to get the fuck up out of there. She then saw Pete walk in behind Uno and Bull with a gas can. She didn't know what was about to happen, but the sooner she was gone the better.

"So..." Uno said as he looked around the house while standing in the front room, "Take us to the basement."

"Want me to leave this up here?" Pete asked referring to the gasoline.

"Yeah." Uno replied as they followed Keisha.

As soon as she opened the basement door the foul smell hit them immediately. "Shit." Bull said as he covered his nose to avoid the smell.

"How long these niggas been down here?" He asked Keisha. She was in shock from seeing the two dead bodies again. Uno, Bull and Pete walked past her and wrapped the bodies tightly and carried them up the stairs. When they got back upstairs, Bull and Uno placed the pistols back in the two dead men hands as they positioned them across from each other. The guns and shells from Bum's gun were wrapped in the sheets as well. The two gunmen had revolvers. Uno scattered the shells from Bum's gun and placed it in the ones hand that Keisha pushed him into, and the other one had his own gun. "Keisha pour the gas on them." Uno sad as he pointed on the floor at the two bodies.

She looked at him sick to her stomach. Pete handed her the gas can. She reluctantly took it as she slowly walked towards the bodies. The sight and smell of the bodies overwhelmed her as she began throwing up. "I can't." She sobbed as she stood slouched over while gagging.

"You have no choice." Pete said with a stern look on his face. She began to pour it on the bodies.

"Pour it all over this bitch, we gon burn the whole house down." Bull demanded.

Uno then took the gas can from Keisha purposely getting some on her and poured the gas out leading towards the exit. Keisha stood there crying not knowing what was going to happen next. "Come on lets go." Uno told Keisha as he grabbed her arm to lead her to her exit. As they made it to the bottom of the steps, Uno looked at Pete. "Go ahead Pete." Pete pulled out a match, lit it and threw it on Keisha. She immediately ignited due to the gasoline on her. She began screaming. Bull then pushed her and closed the door as she burned and ignited the gasoline trail leading back up to the dead bodies and the rest of the house. They stood in the hallway looking through the window as Keisha's body perished in the fire. They walked to the car and rode off. The house was became engulfed with flames and smoke.

Chapter 19

Bum and J. Brown decided to party outside of the tourist district one night. The club was different than the previous ones. It was more hood. The women were still sexy, but they looked a little bit more street. Bum and J.Brown walked to the bar, ordered their drinks, took a seat and faced the dance floor. Bum wasn't feeling the clubs atmosphere as much. It kind of reminded him of the bars in Buffalo.

"What up son, you wanna bounce?" J. Brown asked noticing Bum wasn't enjoying himself.

"Naw, whenever you ready." he responded not wanting to be a party pooper.

J. Brown looked to be enjoying himself. All eyes were on them. Two girls then walked up on J. Brown. One was short and slim with big titties; the other one was tall with a big ass. The lighting was poor in the club and one couldn't get a good look at anyone unless they were right up on them. The tall one began to grind her ass on J. Brown as he continued to sit at the bar stool. The other one began to whisper in his ear. J. Brown ordered the two ladies and himself a drink. "What you drinking?" He asked Bum.

"I'm good." Bum responded. The two girls were all over J. Brown as he continued to order the drinks.

"Hi." The Brazilian girl spoke to Bum as she sat next to him. Bum turned around to face her.

"Hi." He spoke back.

"Where are you from?" She then asked.

"New York, Buffalo New York." She smiled. They continued to talk. She was pretty, but she wasn't sexy like the women from the other night. She schooled Bum on Brazil. She told him about the "real" Brazil. The slums in Rio de Janeiro. She told him don't go anywhere near them.

"Yo son these bitches both trying to fuck me." J. Brown slurred in Bum's ear. He was pissy drunk. "I'm gon take them to the telly and fuck these bitches, you can stay here." He added.

Bum didn't want to leave his man while he was that drunk. "Naw son I'ma come wit you."

"Naw son chill, chill." J. Brown insisted.

Bum reluctantly agreed. He watched as J. Brown walked out with both ladies, one on each arm. He staggered a few times. Bum sat back down and continued to talk to the Brazilian girl.

"Was that your friend?" She asked Bum. He nodded his head yes.

"He knows one of them isn't a girl, doesn't he?" She asked.

Bum looked at her confused. "What?" He asked.

"The tall one is a transvestite." She added.

Bum immediately ran out the bar to get J. Brown. He made it outside, but J. Brown was nowhere in site. He immediately hopped in a cab and went back to the hotel.

He was furious as he made it back to the room. He was outside the door thinking about whipping the trannys ass. When he opened the door, it was silent in the room. He walked to J. Brown's room, empty. His room was empty. The bathroom, empty. *Where the fuck is he at?* He thought out loud. He knew he shouldn't have let J.

Brown leave by himself. He looked all around the hotel for J. Brown. He walked to the beach, no J. Brown. Bum was hot. He knew his man was pissy drunk, he probably didn't know what the fuck he was doing. Bum didn't get a good look at the tranny, but from what he saw, he thought the tranny was a female. J. Brown was so drunk; he wouldn't have been able to tell. This had Bum tight. He just went to the bar in the hotel and hoped for the best.

Bum wanted to talk to Jazmeen, the sexy bartender he met the other day, but she wasn't working. Bum had a few drinks before he made it to his room. Still no J. Brown. Bum didn't realize how much he had to drink, he was wasted. He fell on the bed and went right to sleep.

***

"Yo Bum." J. Brown screamed as he came in the hotel room. Bum immediately woke up when he heard J. Brown scream his name. He noticed that it was morning time. He stretched as he walked out of his room and saw J. Brown standing there with just his wife beater, pants and socks on. "Them fuckin' bitches took all ma shit!" J. Brown screamed as he threw his hands in the air.

"What the fuck happened?" Bum asked.

"Man, I don't even know. All I remember was waking up in a fuckin' shack wit two Brazil niggas standing over me wit guns." J. Brown paused to light his cigarette. "The nigga wit the A.K started speaking that Portuguese shit pointing the K at me and pointing at the door." He continued in between puffs. "So the niggas walked me outside, the shit looked like the ghetto fa real, the shit was fucked up. Then the niggas walked me up the road and stopped. The one holding the pistol spoke English. He told me go up the street, I should find a cab to get me up outta there. Then the nigga was like don't come back." He took another puff. "Man they got ma jewels they even took ma fuckin shoes." J. Brown said in frustration as he sat on the couch dumping the ashes in the ash tray.

Bum sat on the loveseat across from him and put his hands over his face, "Damn son I should have never let you leave." Bum said with his head down.

"Man it ain't yo fault. I remember at the bar, I told you to chill and stay there with the little bitch you was getting at." J. Brown responded. "But...man I'm so pissed off and tired I'm 'bout to take a shower and go to sleep." J. Brown put the cigarette out and stood up.

"Yo son…did you fuck those bitches?" Bum asked hoping he said no.

"Naw." J. Brown lied. He didn't want to admit that he fucked them both. Bum sighed in relief. He figured he wasn't going to tell J. Brown about the tranny since he didn't fuck them.

Bum took a shower and went right back to sleep. This was their last night in Brazil, but he didn't feel like partying after what happened last night.

***

Bum woke up at 8pm. He threw on some clothes and decided to go to the bar downstairs and see if he saw Jazmeen. He walked out his room and heard J. Brown snoring from behind his room door. He wasn't going to wake him after what he went through.

Soon as Bum walked in the bar he saw Jazmeen. She looked up, saw Bum and started smiling. "Como este?" Bum smiled as he sat at the bar.

"Hello Brandon," she smiled.

"You were off last night?" he asked.

"Yes, I worked today from 1pm... and I'm off in twenty minutes thank God." she sighed in relief.

"Twenty minutes? Maybe we can hang out." Bum suggested.

"Okay, but what are we going to do?" she asked.

"We can go up to my room, order something to eat and relax." Bum responded.

"Is it okay if I take a shower in your room?" she asked.

"Sure." Bum responded with no hesitation.

"Okay what's your room number?" she asked as she grabbed a pen and wrote it on a napkin. "I'll see you in twenty minutes." she said as she put the napkin in her pocket.

Bum went up to the room to straighten up a little before she came up. J. Brown was still asleep, snoring. It was 9:15 pm when he heard a knock at the door. He answered it knowing it was Jazmeen. "I'm going to take my shower now." She said as she walked in past Bum. She walked right to the main bathroom, knowing exactly where it was, being an employee there for two years now.

"Okay." Bum said as he watched her walk by with her bag in her hand. *Damn I love that walk.* He thought to himself.

Bum sat with the television on as he looked over the menu waiting for Jazmeen to get done with her shower. She came out of the bathroom wearing jeans, a polo shirt and sandals. Bum hadn't seen her outside of her work clothes before. She was sexy with her work clothes, but she looked even better in regular clothes. The jeans were tight enough to show every curve from her hips down. She had nice shaped legs and the sandals showed her pretty feet. The polo shirt hugged her perky titties as the top buttons were undone exposing a little cleavage. Bum admired her body as she walked over and joined him on the couch. "You look nice outside of your work clothes." Bum complimented Jazmeen.

"Thanks." she responded while blushing.

"So…" Bum exhaled as he focused back on the menu. "What do you want to eat?" He asked as he handed her a menu.

She placed it on the coffee table without looking at it. "I know the menu by heart, you forgot I work here?" She reminded Bum.

"You're right." He put the menu down, "Why don't you order for the both of us." He suggested.

She agreed as she called their orders in.

After eating, they continued to talk and watch TV as she tried to teach him a little Portuguese. They laughed and enjoyed each others company. "I know you're leaving tomorrow morning, and I would like for you to remember me." She spoke as she looked into his eyes.

"I will." Bum said.

Jazmeen then leaned in and gave him a kiss on his lips. Bum stood up and grabbed her hand as he guided her to the bedroom. He turned on the light as he began to slowly undress her while kissing her neck. She put her hands behind his neck as she began to caress it. She was now totally nude. He backed up to check her body out from head to toe. He took her hand as he slowly spun her around to see her back side also. Her body was perfect, a perfect 10. He then came out of his clothes. Jazmeen then walked closer and wrapped her arms around his neck. "Turn the lights off," she whispered in his ear.

He turned them off and walked her to the bed. He laid her on the bed as he grabbed a condom. He placed the condom on and then got on top of Jazmeen as he placed the tip of his dick on Jazmeen's pussy lips. With his hand he rubbed his hard dick over her pussy. She was wet. He heard the moisture as he rubbed his dick over her pussy lips. He then inserted it in her. Her pussy was tight and moist. She clasped her legs around Bum as he pumped in and out of her. As Bum continued to fuck her, he felt her shaking and her pussy began to squeeze his dick as she began to cum. Bum started fucking her faster then he came. Bum pulled out, rolled over and laid on the bed next to her. *Damn her pussy is good.* Bum thought to himself. She then rolled over and pecked him on his lips.

After Bum got cleaned up, Jazmeen took another shower. Bum liked Jazmeen, he kind of wished that she wasn't so far away. He then thought he was just glad to have met her. Jazmeen stayed for a few more hours as they fucked once more. She then said her last goodbyes to Bum.

Bum laid down after seeing Jazmeen off, and went to sleep prepared for the morning when he and J. Brown headed back to New York.

Chapter 20

It didn't take long before Billy D saw the kid who was watching him outside of Trixie's house. He noticed the kid along with someone else sitting in a car outside of his house. Billy D wanted to go out there and wet the whole car up, but he didn't want to do that outside of his house. He grabbed the Mac 10 machine pistol and hopped in his truck which was parked in the driveway. As he pulled out of the driveway, the kid immediately started his car. Billy D acted as if he didn't even notice them as they began to follow him.

"This nigga 'bout to die homey." The driver spoke to his man with an angry look on his face.

"You know I'm riding out wit you homey." His man agreed as he paused then looked over at him. "So who is dis nigga?" He asked wanting to know who and why they were about to kill a man.

"He's a fucking dead man, that's who he is," the driver spoke as he continued to drive while looking straight ahead with a spaced out look on his face.

His man just cocked his gun and placed it on his lap still unaware of the reason of his friend's anger.

Billy D continued to drive as he turned into a dark alley. He then pulled into a driveway just off the rode of the alley and cut the lights off.

"Where the fuck that nigga go?" The driver asked as he turned into the alley not seeing Billy D's truck anywhere in sight. He and his man looked from side to side as they continued down the alley. The headlights of their car were the only sufficient light in the alley. Billy D watched as they slowly passed his truck. He grabbed the Mac 10 and got out the truck.

"Yo just back up outta here, I don't see the nigga nowhere." His man demanded as he began to worry. As they began to back up slowly, Billy D stepped from out of the driveway as he waited for the car to get closer. The driver was looking over his right shoulder as he backed up, and his man was looking around still searching for Billy D. They had no idea that Billy D was waiting for them. When the car got close enough, Billy D tapped on the driver's side window with the barrel of the Mac 10. Both the driver and his man were startled as they looked over at Billy D with the Mac in his hand. When the driver's man saw Billy D he immediately knew who he was. "Oh shit that's Billy D... what the fuck you got me out here fucking wit dis nigga for?" His man asked in a panic as he looked straight ahead scared to death trying to avoid eye contact with Billy D.

"Man he fucking ma bitch." The driver screamed with a hint of anger and fear in his voice.

"We 'bout to die over Trixie ass… nigga everybody fucked dat bitch." His man angrily responded as his eyes began to water.

Billy D then swung the gun at the driver's window shattering it. He saw the gun on the passenger's lap, so he began to shoot him. The kid just started to scream. Billy D grabbed him up out of the broken window with one hand as he aimed the Mac at his head with the other hand. "What the fuck was you following me for?" Billy D screamed angrily with his teeth clenched.

"Man you fucking ma bitch," The driver cried as he now laid on the ground just outside his car.

"Who. WHO?" Billy D screamed, now even angrier as he realized all this was over a girl.

"Trixie." The kid responded as he realized he was about to die. Billy D was so disgusted with the kid at this point; he no longer wanted to look at him. He hated to see niggas get emotional over a whore. He raised the gun and shot him in his head several times.

***

When Billy D woke up the next morning he checked his phone. He had several missed calls from his grandmother. He knew something was wrong. So he immediately called her.

"Hello," she answered on the first ring.

"Grandma what's wrong, is everything alright?" Billy D asked worried.

She began to cry. "Your uncles in jail."

Chapter 21

When Bum got back in town, he had a lot of business to handle. He wanted to go see his kids first and Keisha's mother. Although he and Keisha didn't get along, he always respected her mother.

Bum made his way to Keisha's mothers' house. There were cars in the driveway, and cars in front of the house, so he parked a little up the street and walked to the house. He rang the door bell and an older man answered the door whom Bum had never seen before.

"Can I help you?" He asked Bum as he stared him up and down.

"Oh, that's Brandon the kid's father," Keisha's aunt told the man as she walked past him and pulled Bum in the house giving him a hug. "How are you doing Brandon?" she asked with tears in her eyes.

"I'm ok." He responded as he looked around at all the different faces in the house, some which he had never seen before. "How are you?" He asked now looking at her.

"Been better." She responded.

"Where are the kids?" Bum asked looking around the house again.

"They're upstairs with the rest of the kids?"

"Where's Ms. Kimberly?" He asked referring to Keisha's mom.

"Oh she's in the kitchen." She turned and pointed to the kitchen.

When Bum walked in the kitchen, Keisha's mom immediately walked over to him and gave him a hug. "Hi Brandon, it's good to see you." She whispered to him.

"You too." He whispered back. "So... how are you?" he asked as they broke their embrace, looking at her with compassion.

"I'm hanging in there." She said as her eyes started to tear up. She forced herself to smile; this caused the tears to fall from her eyes and down her cheek. Bum started to wipe them away. "I'm ok… did you see the babies?" she asked.

"No."

"Come on," she grabbed his hand and guided him upstairs.

When they made it upstairs, Bum heard kids laughing and playing. Their innocence didn't allow them to mourn the death of a loved one. When his son and daughter saw him they immediately stopped what they were doing and ran over to him. "Daddy!" They screamed.

He picked his daughter up and hugged her as he put his arm around his son who was hugging his waist. "Hey," he said to them both. Keisha's mom started smiling as she saw how happy her grandkids were to see Bum. "Y'all want to hang out for a little while." He asked. "How about Chuck E Cheese?" All the kids in the room jumped up and yelled. "Ok, Ok," He said attempting to calm them down. "Everybody can go, soon as I'm done talking to Grandma." He told them.

She walked him into a room and closed the door.

"I know your just getting back from out of town, but did you hear what happened?" She asked Bum. He shook his head no. She then put her head down and started to cry. He walked over and hugged her. "She burned to death Brandon. They believe she was alive as she burned to death." She continued to cry as she told him what the investigators told her. "They said she tried to burn the house down with two bodies in it and accidentally ignited herself…and burned alive." She continued to sob.

Bum just shook his head as he listened. "Here, this is to help with the funeral." Bum said as he handed her $6000 dollars.

She hugged him again. "Thank you Brandon," she said as she wiped the tears from her face.

***

After dropping the kids off back at Ms. Kimberly's, Bum was tired. All of the kids wore him out at Chuck E Cheese.

He then rode to the trap to check on Mojo and Bumpkin. When he walked in, he saw Uno and Pete.

"Bra…you back." Pete walked over and hugged him.

"What up?" Uno smiled as he hugged him.

"So how many of dem Brazilian bitches you fucked?" Pete asked eager to hear about it.

"Just two." Bum answered. "Y'all niggas burned her up huhn?" Bum changed the subject as he asked while looking at both of them. They nodded their heads yes. Bum then nodded his head in agreement. "Well, you know what they say..." Bum looked at each of them. They stood there waiting for him to continue. "…You play wit fire you get burned!"

Chapter 22

Bumpkin sat at the kitchen table bagging up the last two ounces when he heard a loud crash and the sound of glass breaking coming from the front of the house. *What the fuck.* He thought to himself as he jumped up. He grabbed his pistol and headed to the front. He then heard a sound rumbling as he reached the living room and saw fire growing. It fed off everything in its path. He immediately ran back in the kitchen, grabbed the two ounces and ran out of the kitchen door. The flames grew fast; the fire covered the entire front portion of the house. Bumpkin stood in a daze and watched as the fire continued to grow throughout the house. The sound of sirens snapped him out of his daze as he made his way to his car. He looked back at the house as he proceeded to pull off and ride down the street.

Bumpkin rode the streets with no destination. He was vexed. He couldn't believe someone threw a Molotov cocktail at the house and burned it down. The only thing that was on his mind was finding out who did it and seeking revenge.

He ended up in Niagara Falls at the water. He sat in his car staring out into the water; his mind was in another world at the moment as he thought about what had just happened. The house was pumping. They were moving well over 30 ounces a week easy. Now to watch all of that just burn up made him sick and he felt violated. He didn't know who did it, but he had an idea, he was going to find out and whoever was involved had to pay. The whole time Bumpkin sat in his car, his phone was blowing up. He paid it no mind as his thoughts continued to race.

***

"Yo Bum, the house burned the fuck up!" Mojo yelled as he was on the phone with Bum.

"What?" Bum asked with concern.

"Man I just rode past, all them damn police and fire investigators was out there so I kept riding... man I called Bumpkin 'bout 10 times, he ain't answer," Mojo continued to yell. "I hope he wasn't in the house." Mojo added as he simmered down thinking of the possibility of his friend being dead.

"Yo son, just calm down, I'ma call him right now." Bum said as he hung up. "Fuck!" Bum banged his fist on the dashboard of his car. Shit just wasn't going his way he thought. First Keisha and the nigga King try to set him up to get robbed and killed, now Mojo was telling him the trap house burned. He pulled over so he could call Bumpkin. Bum sat in his car as the phone continued to ring. Bumpkin wasn't answering. He began to worry that he may have actually been in the house. He sat there thinking of what to do next, and then his phone began ringing. It was Bumpkin. Bum saw his number pop up on his caller ID and immediately answered the phone "Hello." he answered anxiously.

"What up Bum?" Bumpkin sounded somber.

"You, man you alright?" he asked Bumpkin.

"I'm good just thinking about how many niggas gone have to die behind this shit."

"So you know 'bout the house?" Bum asked. "

Yeah, I was there when it happened." Bumpkin told Bum.

"Where you at now?"

"I'm in The Falls…at the water."

"I'ma be there in about 25 minutes, don't leave." Bum demanded as he started his car back up. He then called Mojo back. "Yo son. I talked to Bumpkin, he in The Falls at the water. I'm headed there now, so meet me there."

"Alright." Mojo agreed as he hung up.

When Bum made it to The Falls, he parked next to Bumpkins truck. He then got out and got into the passenger side of the truck. "So, what happened?" Bum asked Bumpkin, as he turned and saw Mojo pulling up. Mojo then hopped in the backseat.

"Yo son I been calling you like crazy, you alright?" Mojo asked Bumpkin as he leaned towards the front seat to see his friend.

Bumpkin nodded his head yes. He then turned to Bum "The niggas cocktailed the house." Bumpkin began to tell Bum and Mojo what happened. "I was in the kitchen. I heard the glass break so I went to see what the fuck it was, when I got to the living room I saw fire. So I grabbed the work and bounced."

"Who did it?" Bum asked.

Bumpkin shrugged his shoulders. "I don't know."

"Man its Roney and them punk ass niggas from up the block." Mojo yelled from the back. "I knew I should have killed that nigga that day at the store." he continued on angrily.

"What day, what happened at the store?" Bum asked looking from Bumpkin to Mojo not aware of what Mojo was talking about.

"The nigga Roney said we had to bounce because we was making too much money. I guess that was his way of saying leave or else." Mojo responded.

"So you think the cocktail shit was the or else?" Bum turned and asked Mojo.

"I know them niggas did it son," Mojo responded as he looked at Bum "I just know." Bum began to think back to how shady the niggas up the block have been acting lately. He knew it was going to be animosity, but now wasn't a good time. They threw the first blow, now it was on. War.

Chapter 23

Lex was up at 6 o'clock in the morning. He sat at the edge of his bed with just his boxers on. He was beginning to get a little nervous as he sat in anticipation of his 9 o'clock phone interview with ESPN. He then got up and headed to the small bathroom located in his dorm room. He looked into the mirror as he began brushing his teeth. He started smiling at his reflection as he thought about all the attention he'd been receiving lately. Almost every week he made a play that appeared on ESPN. He was becoming a household name, as he was being mentioned as a possible first round pick in many of the mock drafts he had seen on television and the internet. He was the star player, the face of the program as the Buffalo Bulls were ranked 19th in the nation with 7 wins and just 1 close loss in overtime to the number 8 ranked team in the country. He was considered the second best safety in the country. Although he played defense, he had more touchdowns than many offensive players in college football. In 8 games he had 62 tackles, 5 forced fumbles, 10 interceptions, 7 sacks and 8 total touchdowns. He was already being mentioned as a front runner for the Jim Thorpe award, which was given to the best defensive back in college each year.

***

It was now 8 am when Lex made his way to the coaches' office, where his phone interview was to take place. As Lex stood at the door of the office he saw the coaches watching film for the upcoming game. "Hey Lex." The head coach looked over at Lex. He then looked at his watch. "You're early. You might as well come on in and watch this film with us until they call." He waved Lex in as he turned his attention back to the film. "So Lex, You nervous about the interview?" The coach asked as he continued to watch the screen.

"Not really," Lex responded as he got more comfortable with the upcoming interview. He knew they were going to talk about him and football, and those were two things he was very comfortable with.

"Just remember to mention your teammates and how great your coaches are." The coaches in the room began to laugh. "And be yourself." He added as he looked Lex in the eyes.

***

After the interview, Lex couldn't wait until Sports Center came on so he could see the interview on television, along with the millions of other people who were going to see it. The interview went perfect. The man who interviewed him complemented Lex on his talent every chance he got. Lex was on cloud nine. He felt like a superstar. He then made a promise to himself that he would go even harder the rest of the season. He knew the expectations of him were high now and he wasn't going to disappoint.

***

"Oh shit that feels good, right there…don't stop." Lex ordered in pleasure as Michelle straddled his lower back while massaging his upper back and shoulders. He laid on the small twin sized bed as he enjoyed Michelle's golden touch. She continued to massage him with just her panties on. Her perky round 34c titties were on display. She didn't put her bra back on after they had sex. She just put her panties back on. Her long hair hung over her right shoulder covering the top half of her right breast. She was looking oh so sexual. If Lex was in his right mind, he would have stood at attention in anticipation of round two. However, his mind was elsewhere. He had sex with her to get his mind off of all the excitement and attention. It worked, but now all he was thinking about was Iyani. Only 20 miles separated them, but he hadn't seen her in over a week. They talked almost every night, yet he missed her and she would let him know the same every night before they hung up.

"Did you hear me?" Michelle asked as she reached back and smacked him on his ass. Lex then focused his attention back on Michelle while he shifted his head as it rested on his hands.

"My bad, what you say?"

"I said…" Michelle continued with a slight hint of an attitude. "If one of my friends tried to fuck you would you fuck them?"

Lex just shook his head no. He wasn't really answering the question; he wasn't trying to hear that shit. "Hey, hand me ma phone." Lex raised up almost throwing her off his back as he pointed to the phone on the night stand. He just realized that he forgot to turn his phone on that morning. With the excitement of the interview, it slipped his mind. Michelle reached over and grabbed the phone and handed it to him. When he turned it on he saw that his voice mailbox was full. "Watch out." He demanded for Michelle to get off of him as he rolled over and sat at the side of the bed.

He had several messages from Iyani, Billy D and his grandmother. His phone began to ring. It was Billy D. “Yo, what’s good?” Lex answered.

“Yo, what up doe, I been calling you all day.” Billy D responded with his voice raised. Lex could tell that something was wrong by Billy D’s voice.

“I forgot to turn ma phone on, what’s happening, everything alright?” Lex stood up from the bed asking with concern in his voice.

“Everything alright?” Michelle whispered while putting on her clothes as she observed Lex’s posture. Lex just waved her off as he waited for Billy D’s response.

“Naw son, Unc got knocked.” Lex wasn’t expecting to hear that his father got arrested. With the phone to his ear, he put his other hand over his face as he shook his head. Michelle began to worry as she watched Lex’s reaction. “Lex... Lex.” Billy D called his cousins name as he got silent.

“Yeah...I’m still here.” Lex answered as tears began to fill his eyes. “Yo son, he gon be alright.” Billy D tried to reassure, but deep down he was worried for his uncle. “Meet me at grandma’s house in a hour,” he demanded.

“Alright,” Lex responded as he hung up.

“Lex, you ok?” Michelle asked as she walked over to comfort him.

“Yeah I’m good.” Lex said as he walked around her and grabbed her bag. “Come on, I’m gon drop you off at your dorm, I have to go.” Michelle was worried for him, but the only thing she could do was follow him out of his dorm room and to his car.

***

When Lex got to his grandmothers house, he saw Billy D's truck already in the driveway. When he walked in the house, it was dark except for the kitchen. Lex walked in the kitchen and saw Billy D peeling an orange.

When Billy D saw Lex he got up and hugged him. "What up son, you alright?" He asked Lex as he backed up to observe his cousin.

"Yeah I'm good." Lex responded sitting down at the table. Billy D sat back down and continued to peel his orange. "So what happened?" Lex asked Billy D hoping he knew.

"I really don't know yet." Billy D answered as he put the peeled orange to the side. "But I think it's the Feds." He continued as he tried to wipe away the sticky mess the orange left on his fingertips. Lex placed his elbows on the table and leaned his face into his palms as he began to realize the seriousness of his father's situation. "I think somebody snitched on him, and if I find out…" Billy D said as he began to squeeze the orange out of anger. The juice squirted on the table. Billy D didn't finish his sentence, he didn't need to. They both knew what he was capable of. "I'ma go holla at Unc soon though…I can't go now, maybe next week." Billy D changed the subject.

"I feel you." Lex responded as he removed his hands from his face.

"I know he would want us not to worry." Billy D said trying to keep his cousins spirits up. "You just concentrate on you. You got a lot going for you, so stay focused and don't worry about it." Billy D's eyes began to water as he thought about how proud he was of his cousin. He didn't want him to worry about Bank. He wanted his cousin to succeed and accomplish his dreams. He loved Lex to death.

Lex looked up and saw this in Billy D's eyes. "I love you." Lex said as he got up to hug him. "I'm 'bout to go so I can get ready for class tomorrow." He added as he walked towards the door. Lex knew Billy D was right. Bank would be alright, and he needed to focus on himself, the only thing he had control of.

Chapter 24

"Roney, Roney, nigga get up." Fred said as he stood over Roney trying to wake him up. "Get up nigga," he said again, this time shaking him by his shoulders.

"Yo, nigga chill," Roney said groggily as he squinted while looking at Fred.

"Get up and take yo ass home, you ain't been home in three days." Fred said as he tried to pull Roney up from the couch. Roney was at the trap faithfully now that business was picking up ever since they burned down the trap house around the corner. It had been three weeks since they cocktailed the house, and they were seeing the benefits from it. They heard that Mojo and the rest of his crew set up shop at a crack head's house on the same block, but they weren't concerned for now with the boost they were seeing in sells thus far. They were surprised Mojo, Bumpkin and Bum hadn't retaliated yet. "Look at you…you can't even stand up straight." Fred joked as Roney almost fell back into the couch.

Roney grabbed his coat from the couch and put it on. "I'ma see you niggas in the morning." he said as he walked towards the door.

"Alright nigga." Fred and the rest of his crew said as he walked out the door.

It's cold as a bitch. Roney said to himself as he flipped his hoody over his head, walked off the porch and headed to his truck. It was

3:30 in the morning; the streets were empty except for a few crack heads that wandered. Roney saw Pammy walking up the street heading to the trap, so he stopped her. "Yo." He called out to her. She immediately walked over to him.

"Hey what's up Roney, I need a twenty," she said as she handed him the money. Pammy was 26 years old and strung out on crack. She used to be a weed head until she started experimenting with laced blunts. Now she's a full fledged crack head. The only thing that remained decent on her was her body, even though she was about 10 pounds lighter now. Her face showed the effects of a rough life. She had scars on her face from various razors and fingernail marks from the many fights that she had been in, and she was missing two teeth, from the top and bottom of her mouth.

"This only eight bucks." Roney responded as he looked at the money. "I ain't got nothing for dat." He added as he handed the money back.

She put her hand on her hip and smacked her lips. "That's fucked up Roney, after what you did to me last week."

"What I do to you last week?"

Pammy put both hands on her hips as she tilted her head looking at Roney as if he were stupid. Roney held his ground. She smacked her lips again as she turned around and began to walk away. He knew exactly what he did last week, and he definitely remembered what she did, and he wanted her to do it again. "Hold on." Roney said as his dick began to get hard thinking about her head game. Pammy began to walk back smiling at Roney exposing her gapped mouth. "I'ma give you the twenty for the eight bucks…only if you do what you did last time." Roney said while rubbing his dick, Pammy handed him the money. "Let's go to ma truck." Roney demanded as Pammy followed behind him, knowing it wouldn't take long. She figured she should be back home in about 10 minutes, since he always came in less than 5 minutes.

Roney looked around to make sure no one saw him getting into the truck with Pammy. He then unlocked the truck and let her in. Roney turned the truck on and turned the heat all the way up. He then unzipped his pants and pulled out his dick. Pammy immediately leaned over and began sucking his dick. "Oh shit…sss, slow down." Roney whispered as he laid his head back on the headrest with his eyes closed. Pammy continued on, trying to get it over with as quick as possible. Roney opened his eyes as he reached to turn the heat down. Out of the corner of his eye he saw a silhouette and the light from the end of a lit cigarette through the rearview mirror. Someone was in his back seat smoking a cigarette watching him get head from Pammy. He was shook. He pushed Pammys head away and reached for his pistol, which was under his seat. As he felt for it, he began to panic. *Where is it?* He thought to himself as he continued to frantically feel for it. Pammy looked at him like he was crazy since she had no idea what was going on.

"Roney." The man in the back seat called to him. Pammy was startled as she turned and looked to the back seat. "Roney, relax." He added as he took a pull from his cigarette. "Go head and get ya nut off. Its gon be ya last one anyway." He added. Roney then stopped searching for the pistol and rose up. He recognized the voice now. "Go head and suck the nigga dick," the voice ordered Pammy. He then put the gun to Roney's head and leaned up close to him. "She suck good dick?" He asked Roney with the pistol still to his head. "I said...do...she...suck...good...dick?" He asked again this time louder with the gun pressed harder to the back of his head. Roney began to nod his head yes. The man then leaned back, his arm extended with the gun still at Roney's head. He looked at his watch, then back at Roney. Then he shot him in the back of his head causing his head to slump over onto the steering wheel. Blood and flesh scattered onto the dashboard and windshield.

Pammy ducked down onto the floor of the passenger seat in shock, in fear that she was going to die next.

"Damn Pammy..." He said as he sat comfortably in the back seat. "That head of yours must be good...Shit, its fucking mind blowing." He began to laugh.

She became even more frightened, because he knew her name. She was still crouched down on the floor when she heard him get out the car and slam the door behind him. Slowly raising her head up to see if he was gone, she peered up at the window, and saw him looking right at her. She immediately ducked back down. He opened the passenger door and she now looked him in his face as she began to cry out, "Mojo please." She sobbed. "Mojo please don't kill me." He looked at her as he raised his gun at her head. *Pop pop pop pop* He shot her four times in the head. *Pop pop pop pop* He then shot Roney four more times.

Chapter 25

It was the first of the month, payday. Nobody could tell Darlene anything on payday. She thought that she was the shit this time of month, she had on her Sunday's best. Today was the one day that she didn't have to ask a nigga for shit, she could buy it herself. Tomorrow, now that's a different story. Today, *"Kiss ma ass,"* was her motto. She had $375 dollars, all to herself, well except for the $150 she owed out. She was going to get drunk and high all by herself without having to suck dick or kiss ass. *Not today,* she thought as she walked up the street in her high heels thinking she was the shit. When a car rode past and blew its horn, she waved without looking, as though she was blowing them off. Even if they weren't looking at her, she felt like they were.

When she made it to the store, she knew exactly what she wanted. She walked to the cooler and got two forty ounce bottles of Silver Thunder, then headed to the counter.

"Hey Darlene." The Arab behind the counter greeted her.

"Hey." She spoke with an attitude. "Give me a pack of Rogers and a rose." She demanded as she grabbed a lighter off the counter. The Arab put the pack of cigarettes along with the rose on the counter. The rose was actually a glass stem, used to smoke crack with. It was sold with a tiny plastic rose in it to conceal its actual purpose. Darlene now had her kit. She was good to go, off to the crack spot. As she was about to turn the corner she realized she forgot the chore boy which was used as a filter in the crack pipe. She was about to turn and head back in the store, when she overheard Fred and his homeys talking about burning down Mojo's and Bumpkin's house. She stood there eavesdropping.

"Yeah, shit nigga we should have just shot all them niggas, Mojo, Bumpkin, them young niggas and the nigga Bum instead of burning the fucking house down." Fred continued on, "Now ma nigga dead."

"How you know dem niggas did it doe?" One of his boys asked.

"Them niggas had to do it, shit who else?" Fred responded.

"We got to see them niggas now." Another one of his boys added.

Darlene stood there gathering in all she heard. She was going to tell Mojo and them everything she heard, shit she didn't like them niggas anyway, their crack was garbage.

***

Uno, Bull and Pete posted on the porch of the home in which they now designated as their new trap. This was only temporary until they found another house in the area where they could set up shop. They already had a good clientele in the area. They were making so much money in the hood they wanted to remain as close as possible to the original trap. While they posted outside, Mojo and Bumpkin held the work inside. The crack head whose house it was enjoyed this setup. He got to smoke for free everyday. They weren't making as much money as before, but this would have to do for now.

"Shit nigga it's getting cold out here." Pete said as he sat on the couch on the front porch while trying to bury his face into his coat as he raised his shoulders and tucked his chin into his chest.

"I'm just glad it ain't snowing yet." Bull responded as he stood while shifting his weight from side to side trying to generate heat by staying in motion. It was December 1st, the temperature was dropping and before long the snow would be falling. Buffalo was known for its harsh winters, but occasionally the winters provided days with decent temperatures. Uno sat next to Pete bundled in his heavy winter coat thinking today wasn't one of those days.

"Look at this bitch." Bull said as he saw Darlene walking up the street like she was cute.

"Who dat?" Pete asked as he raised his head up trying to see over the banister while still sitting on the couch.

Uno then stood up to see. "What the fuck..." Uno said as he saw her walking towards the house. "She look cold as hell, wit that old ass lime green dress on." He added. "Oh shit!" they all began to laugh as she almost fell trying to walk in her high heels.

"She a hot mess." Pete said while still laughing.

"Yo chill." Bull said as she approached trying to stop them from laughing as she got closer.

"Hey ya'll," she said as she walked up the porch stairs slowly holding onto the railing to maintain her balance.

"Hi Darlene, you look nice today." Pete said as Uno and Bull looked at him, all laughing on the inside.

"Thanks honey," she responded while adjusting her wig. "Where Mojo, I need to talk to him?" she said.

"He inside." Uno motioned towards the door.

She walked in the hallway and knocked on the door. The crack head who owned the house answered the door. "Hey Rusty, Mojo here?" She asked already knowing the answer.

"Mojo." He turned and called out Mojo's name. He then turned back towards Darlene. "Damn gurl, you looking good." He complimented while looking her up and down. Rusty was an old timer for real. He was a Vietnam vet. He did every drug in the book and fucked every crack head in the hood.

Darlene gave him a fake smile. She knew he wanted to smoke with her and fuck her, but she wasn't trying to hear that today. Not today, *kiss ma ass,* she thought to herself.

"Hey what up?" Mojo said to Darlene. Rusty moved out of the way and winked at Darlene as he walked towards the back, giving Mojo and Darlene their privacy.

She handed him the money she owed him. He began to count it. "And let me get something for this hundred." She added as she handed him the hundred dollar bill.

Mojo took the money and walked towards the back to get her two grams. "Here you go." Mojo handed her the drugs.

"Thanks Mojo. I probably will be back later on." She said as she turned to walk out. Mojo nodded his head. "Oh yeah." She turned back facing him. "I almost forgot to tell you…" She began whispering. "I was at the store, and I overheard Fred, Rev and the rest of them boys talking about they should have just shot ya'll."

"Hold on." Mojo stopped her. "They said what?"

"They said they should have shot ya'll he named all ya'll even Bum, but then he said something about they burned the house up." She looked at Mojo who was looking angry now. "I wanted to tell ya'll because I love ya'll, you know I don't fuck wit dem niggas. I don't want to see nothing happen to ya'll."

Mojo nodded his head yeah. "Alright...good lookin'." He responded as he opened the door for her and let her out. He closed the door behind her and stood in the hallway for a minute thinking about what he had just heard. He wasn't worried about them; he wished he would have killed all of them already.

Chapter 26

"I'm really feeling you…you hear me?" Bum said while holding the phone to his ear with his shoulder as he continued to count the first of the two large stacks of bills. He put a rubber band around the first stack as he started to count the other.

"Yes, I hear you; I just would like to spend more time with you," Misa responded. Bum continued to count the money. "You're not even listening to me." Misa said as she waited for Bum to reply.

"Yes I am." Bum responded while still trying to count the money and pay attention to the conversation. He had just hit his man with a half a key. He knew the money was right, but he always counted his money out of habit. "I understand, shit been a little hectic lately. When things calm down I'ma make it up to you." He wrapped a rubber band around the second stack of money not counting it all. He decided to count it later as he talked to Misa. "Ok?" He asked.

"Ok, and you know I'm going to hold you to that right?" She replied.

"I hope so." He responded. "But I have something to do right now, I'm a call you later ok?"

Misa sighed. "Ok, bye." she hung up.

Bum was feeling Misa, but he didn't really have time for her right now. He had a lot of bullshit to deal with, plus he still had to make money. He wasn't going to allow anything or anybody to interfere with that. *Money over bitches.* He thought to himself.

***

Bum was looking for another house to setup for Mojo and Bumpkin. He wanted to get one in the same neighborhood, but had no luck. Half the houses were either abandoned or occupied. He didn't want them to pump out of the crack head's house, but they didn't have many options. He was now headed over to the new trap to drop off some more work. When he pulled up he saw Bull and Uno on the porch looking as though they were freezing. "What up?" Bum asked as he slammed his car door shut. The impact caused pieces of rusted metal to fall off the door of his 92 Bonneville.

"What up bra?" They both greeted Bum.

"Y'all niggas look cold as hell." He said as he walked over to slap them up as they sat on the couch.

"Hell yeah, its fuck'n brick out here." Bull replied.

"Yeah," Bum agreed as he leaned against the banister across from the two. "Money been coming through?" He asked.

"It's picking up... but it ain't like it used to be." Bull answered shaking his head. Bum than stood up and walked toward the door.

"Shit, its gon be alright." He assured them as he walked in the hallway. He knocked on the door.

"What up bra?" Pete answered the door.

"Shit. What up wit you? I see you ain't fucking wit that cold." Bum joked.

"Shit, I came in here to warm up."

"I hear you." Bum then walked toward the back.

"Bum, what up fam?" Mojo greeted as he got up from the kitchen table.

"What up Bum?" Bumpkin said as he stood over the stove cooking the coke up.

"Shit...How much coke you got in there?" Bum asked him as he sat at the kitchen table.

"This the last 3 ounces…you brought some more right?" Bumpkin turned and looked at Bum. Bum pulled a plastic bag out of his coat pocket containing 6 ounces and threw it on the table.

"Cool, how much is this?" Mojo asked.

"Six O's." Bum said.

"But yo…" Mojo now looking right at Bum. "The crack head Darlene put me on to the niggas who burned the house up." Mojo eagerly told Bum.

"Thought you said the nigga Roney did dat shit?" Bum asked.

"It was, but all them niggas had something to do wit it, Fred, Rev, the lil nigga Belly, all dem faggits." Mojo spat as he said their names. "She said she even heard dem niggas talking 'bout they should have shot all of us." He added.

"Well…them niggas got to get it." Bum said as he looked into Mojos eyes.

***

"See y'all tomorrow." Bum said to Uno and Bull as he walked down the steps. "Try to stay warm." He added.

"One bra." They said as he walked towards his car. A cherry red Range Rover crept up the street as Bum reached his car. Uno immediately noticed this as he grabbed the tech 9 from under the couch. Bull pulled his 357 magnum from his waistband just in case. They had no idea who was in the Range. As it pulled up to Bum the driver lowered the window.

"What up fam?" J. Brown yelled out to Bum. Uno and Bull stood down when they saw it was J. Brown.

"What up nigga?" Bum said as he walked toward the truck.

"Get in homey." J. Brown demanded.

"This shit hot." Bum complimented as he looked around the interior of the Range Rover. The seats were a dark blood red. He had TV's in the dash and headrest, and custom made red carpet on the floors to match the exterior.

"You like?" J. Brown asked while smiling. "What you been up to doe homey?" J. Brown changed the subject.

"Tryin' to make money ma nigga that's it." Bum answered.

"I feel you...But yo you heard 'bout OG Bank?" J. Brown asked Bum.

"Yeah I heard he got knocked, that's fucked up. He been at it for a while."

"Yeah, but shit that was ma plug."

"Word?"

"Word. He the only nigga in the town that can get me what I need except for OG Regal... but I don't trust dat nigga, he seem grimy." J. Brown said.

Many of the younger hustlers called Bank and Regal OG because all the work they put in throughout the years and all the money they made. They were two of the few that had longevity in the game. Regal used to get money with Bank and Big Bill back in the day until he started doing his own thing. He was a bad luck nigga, everybody around him either got killed or got arrested. Bank still fucked with him through the years but from a distance.

"What you gon do?" Bum asked as he looked at J. Brown.

J. Brown turned and looked at Bum. "I'ma switch it up." He said. "But I need to holla at Gutt." He added.

"I'll call him and give him yo number later tonight." Bum told him.

"Man good look'n." J. Brown slapped him up and embraced him. "I need to get this money homey, heroin or Cain it's all the same, I'ma hustler baby."

"I feel you, I'ma call him tonight and do that for you." Bum said as he slapped J. Brown up.

"Ma man, I'ma holla at you."

"No doubt, be easy." Bum said as he got out of the Range Rover and hopped in his Bonneville.

Chapter 27

Bank laid on the hard surface, they called a bed. It was basically a three and a half by six foot slab of concrete with a half inch of mattress laid on top of it. After laying on it for the past two weeks, it caused havoc on his back. He laid on his back inside the cell gazing at the ceiling, his mind racing. He had avoided this predicament for the last 45 years. Now he was in a situation in which the rest of his life could be in the hands of people who didn't or couldn't understand his life or his circumstances.

As kids Bank and Big Bill knew first hand what it was like to go days without eating. Their father worked in the steel mill until they started laying people off, and he was one of the first. This put his family in a situation of despair. There was no money saved up, all his money paid the bills and put food on the table. They moved from families' houses to homeless shelters and even slept in cars. With no high school education his father couldn't find another job. Desperate for money his father turned to the streets. Before long they were living comfortably. Seeing this as kids made Bank and Big Bill believe that the only way to eat was to hustle. That's all they knew. It cost his father and brother their lives and now him, his freedom.

The sound of his cell door opening paused his thoughts. Every cell on his block began to open as they let the inmates out to go to recreation. This allowed the inmates to socialize with each other. Some watched TV, others played spades, poker or chess.

Everyone knew who Bank was. He was like a living legend in the streets. Every time he stepped out his cell eyes were always on him. *"That's OG Bank."* He would hear other inmates whispering. People respected Bank in the street as well as in jail. He never had to wait to use the phones. Every time he walked towards a phone, whoever was on it would hurry and get off the phone.

"Yo I'ma get back at you. OG Bank got to use the phone," the young man said into the phone as he turned and saw Bank walking towards him.

"Naw, Shorty go ahead and finish ya conversation." Bank demanded. He appreciated the respect everyone showed him but he wasn't on it like that, he was cool as hell. Many people didn't know him personally they just heard about him. The many stories people told of him caused a lot of people to fear him, but he was one of the coolest, most down to earth niggas you would ever meet. That's why he was not only feared but loved as well. He took care of a lot of people through the years. A lot of people got rich with his help. Now a lot of people were going to be fucked up with him incarcerated.

"You sure." The young man held the phone in his hand as he extended it towards Bank.

"Yeah go ahead." Bank smiled at him letting him know it was okay.

"Thanks." he nodded at Bank.

"Ma muthafuckin' man Bank." Bank turned as he heard someone say his name.

"Oh shit. Ace?" Bank embraced his man whom he hadn't seen in fifteen years. Ace was Bank's right hand back in the day. Ace and Regal were brothers. He's been in jail for fifteen years now on a murder charge in which he was setup. "What you doing in the holding center?" Bank asked now looking at his friend noticing how much he has aged over the years. Even though they were about the same age, Bank looked about 15 years younger than Ace.

"My mom finally got enough money for ma lawyer, so know I'm trying to fight this shit all over again." He responded looking stressed.

"Ya mom?" Bank looked puzzled. "Regal ain't take care of that, all that money he sitting on?" Bank asked.

Ace looked down as he shook his head no. "Man I ain't heard from him since they moved me up state." He responded with disappointment in his voice.

"Hold up..." Bank adjusted his stance as he tried to comprehend what he was hearing, "You mean to tell me all that money I was giving him and the letters I had him send to you, he wasn't sending them?" Bank asked.

"Nothin'." Ace shook his head no. "That's ma brother and all, but he's a fuckin' snake." Ace angrily said. Bank looked shocked. "He the reason I'm in this muthafucka." Ace continued on angrily. Bank stood there taking it all in in disbelief. Ace looked at Bank shaking his head. "The nigga set me up…and the nigga did some otha foul shit." Ace added as tears filled his eyes.

"What?" Bank asked as he stepped in closer on Ace as if he was trying to hear him better. Ace looked up now with tears falling down his face.

"Inmate Michael Ferguson report to the officer's desk." the officer called over the intercom. Bank looked over towards the officer's bubble as he heard his name. "Yo Bank I think you got a visit." One of the inmates yelled while walking towards him. Bank nodded his head as he looked at the fellow inmate." I'ma talk to you next rec." Bank said to Ace now looking at him. He then walked towards the officer. “Excuse me.” Bank spoke to the officer trying to get his attention as he sat at the desk reading the newspaper. “You just called my name over the intercom?”

“Michael Ferguson?” the officer asked without looking up from his paper.

“Yes.” Bank answered.

“You have a visit.” He informed Bank as he continued to read the paper.

***

As Bank headed to the visitors room he began to think about what Ace had just told him. He couldn’t believe Regal would shit on his own brother like that. He always knew Regal had shit with him, but he didn’t think he was capable of setting his own brother up causing him to do a twenty to life bid. Damn. He now wondered what else it was that Ace had to tell him about Regal.

When Bank reached the visiting room, after getting searched he saw his nephew Billy D. He walked over to him and gave him a hug over the partition, then sat down across from him. “So…how you doing?” He asked Billy D.

Billy D shrugged as he sat in the chair looking at his uncle. “I’m alright, how you doing?” he then asked his uncle.

“I’m alright. I just worry about ya grandma, you and Lex.” He answered. “How is she doing, have you been over there at all lately?”

“Almost everyday, she doing okay though.” Billy D informed him.

“What about Lex?”

Billy D began to smile. “He doing real good, the conference championship game is this weekend. You know he amped up.”

Bank smiled as he shook his head. "Tell him I love him and good luck, and make sure he ball out."

Billy D nodded his head yes. "So what's going on with this shit?" Billy D asked referring to his charges.

"My lawyer trying to find out everything, so next time I see him he should hip me to exactly what's going on…all the charges and if any niggas snitched or anything like that." Bank told Billy D as he leaned up closer toward him lowering his voice.

"What you think…" Billy D looked him in his eyes as he began to talk "Do you think somebody talking or something?"

Bank shrugged his shoulders. "We'll see." He said as he leaned back in his seat now. "We'll see."

Chapter 28

"Why you always trying to smoke when we got business to handle?" Bull asked as he drove the car while looking in the rear view mirror at Pete in the back seat rolling a Dutch.

"Nigga I ain't trying to smoke." He responded as he licked the Dutch while twisting it in his hands. "I'm just rolling it so I can blaze it when we done." He added as he sat the marijuana filled Dutch Master in the astray of the back seat.

"You need to worry about blazing that steel." Bull said referring to the tech 9 Pete had next to him on the back seat.

"Oh don't worry about dat nigga." Pete responded as he picked the tech 9 up from off the seat and held it in his hand shifting it from side to side admiring his weapon of choice for the night.

"Ayo...keep going straight." Uno told Bull as they neared the unsuspecting group of men. Uno looked as he counted how many men were now standing on the side of the store. "It's about six of dem niggas out there." Uno informed Bull and Pete as they passed the side street. "The nigga Fred not even out there." Uno said, now gripping his own tech 9. He then grabbed his 38 revolver from the glove compartment and tucked it in his waist. They always did this, because the techs were known to jam. The revolvers were always reliable. "Circle back around." Uno ordered as he flipped his hood over his head. He then turned towards the back seat. "Soon as he turn the corner we hopping out." He told Pete.

Pete shook his head as he inserted the long clip back into the tech after double checking it. "Let's go." Pete said now looking up at Uno.

***

Mojo laid in the cut, just behind the store. He was dressed in all black and armed with an AK 47. He held the rifle to his side, it looked almost as big as him. He laid in the cut for the past 20 minutes, listening to the young men talking, laughing and telling jokes, not knowing that death was literally just around the corner. They usually didn't keep their guns on them because of the harassment by the police. They would stash their guns in the cut. The same cut Mojo now occupied.

***

"I'm telling you son…" The young man spoke extremely loud to the rest of the men on the side of the store. "All these bad bitches out here fucking the same niggas." He continued on animated making sure everyone listened. "And all these niggas out here get'n money fucking the same bitches... so if any of these bitches got something then all them niggas got it too, and if any of them niggas got something then all the bitches got it... you know these niggas ain't wearing no condoms." He continued on as his friends began to debate with him.

"Nigga I don't fuck none of these hoes raw." One replied.

"Nigga I ain't talking 'bout you, I said niggas dats getting money." The rest of the young men began to laugh. "You ain't getting no money nigga." He added now getting personal.

"Nigga fuck you." The other one responded angrily as he was embarrassed.

"Yo, chill." Another one stepped in looking at the car slowly turning the corner. "Them niggas just rode past." He said to the rest of the men as he began to slowly back pedal, instincts leading him to the cut. Uno and Pete hopped out the car as soon as Bull braked. With no words said they began shooting at the group of men as they ran towards them. The group of men were caught off guard as Uno and Pete ambushed them. Four of the men barely made it 10 feet as the tech 9's bullets penetrated their bodies. Uno and Pete stood over them and continued to shoot.

The two men that got away ran right towards the cut. They both knew they were less than one hundred feet from their weapons. They didn't know they were less than fifty feet away from Mojo and less than five minutes away from death. Mojo heard the whole scene play out as he waited for the men to appear in his sight. The two men came around the building frightened as they avoided the hail of gun fire in which their four friends couldn't. They both stopped in their tracks as they saw Mojo standing in the middle of them and their weapons. They were scared shit-less as they seen the barrel of the riffle aimed in their direction. Mojo stood there for about 10 seconds looking at the two men. He wanted them to realize their fate before he ended their lives. The 10 seconds seemed like 10 minutes to the two men as they stood still. Mojo then pulled the trigger as the bullets ripped through their flesh. Mojo walked up on their lifeless bodies as neither one was recognizable any longer.

Chapter 29

The University at Buffalo was up 28 to 21 with three minutes and four seconds remaining in the fourth quarter. They were three minutes and four seconds away from becoming Mid American Conference champions. Their opponents had just scored a touchdown to pull within seven points of tying the game. Now they were preparing to kick the ball off to the Bulls. Lex stood outside his own end zone waiting for the kickoff. The coaches of the other team were putting the pressure on their special teams to stop Lex inside of his own thirty yard line, and then rely on their defense to stop UB's offense with enough time remaining for their offense to tie the game. Lex had other plans.

He stood on the field in his own world as he began to get amped up. He began to bang his fist against his chest, nodding his head aggressively as though he were listening to some hardcore hip hop music. He knew his team needed a big play, and he was determined to provide it. The kicker kicked the ball and Lex watched as the ball began to soar in the air in his direction. The kicker had kicked the ball hard as he could, trying to kick it out of the end zone. Lex back peddled quickly as he caught the ball in the back of the end zone. He watched the opposing team players approaching, everything and everybody suddenly appeared to be moving in slow motion except for him. He quickly cut up field as a couple of his teammates made good blocks allowing him to glide through the middle of the pack of would be tacklers untouched. He then pivoted on his left foot as he quickly cut to his right without loosing speed. This movement caused two players from the opposing team to collide into each other. He was running as fast as he could toward the sideline to avoid a couple of linebackers who had an angle on him. They couldn't match his speed as he avoided their attempts at tackling him. All he saw now was the kicker in between him and the end zone. The kicker tried to angle him towards the sideline, but Lex immediately cut back in towards the middle of the field as he raced toward the end zone. Lex raced toward the end zone with no one in his path. He looked up at the huge screen watching himself running towards the end zone. The screen was a couple of seconds slower, as he crossed the end zone the screen showed him still running as he watched himself cross the end zone again.

Everyone began to go crazy as he turned to face his teammates running towards him in excitement. They began to jump on him as he collapsed under the weight of all his teammates celebrating with him.

"Yeah nigga, you did it!"

"Way to go Lex!"

"It's a wrap!" The players yelled as they piled on top of him. They finally got off of him and helped him up as they walked off the field to their sideline. Everyone on the sideline was excited as they began celebrating. Everyone except the coaches as it was still two minutes and fifty seconds left.

"Everybody get off the field now." The coach screamed as he began pulling the players toward the sideline. "Kickoff team get out there now…this games not over guys, we still have almost three minutes to play, so let's go special teams, get out there and make a play." He screamed while clapping his hands. "Hey Lex…" The coach said now walking towards Lex who was sitting on the bench celebrating with the rest of his teammates while trying to catch his breath. "Way to make a play, hell of a run, now catch your breath because we need you back on defense in a minute to make another play and end this game." He winked at Lex as he patted him on the shoulder pads.

The special teams did their job, now it was up to the defense to do theirs. "Let's go fellas, we can end it here!" Trevor screamed to the defense as all the players huddled around him. On first down the Quarterback threw an incompletion as he felt the pressure coming from the defense. "Don't get scared now mutha fucka!" Trevor yelled to the Quarterback as they lined up for second down. The Quarterback completed a short pass to the Runningback from out of the backfield. Lex ran up and tackled him after he gained five yards. The offense rushed to the line as the clock continued to run. They hiked the ball as Trevor came on a blitz right up the middle, untouched as he sacked the Quartback. "Fumble." The sideline yelled. Everyone ran to the football which was rolling on the field as both teams began to dive after it. Lex dove on it, and the defense began to celebrate as well as the coaches now with only one minute and twenty four seconds to go in the game. It was pretty much a wrap, the game was over.

As the final seconds ticked off the clock "5,4,3,2,1." The team began to celebrate as they drenched the coaches with a Gatorade bath. Lex was named MVP of the game. He ended with a punt return and a kickoff for a touchdown, 9 tackles and a fumble recovery.

Chapter 30

"*Come here Billy D.*" Big Bill said to Billy D as he stood in the middle of the living room. A young Billy D stood in front of the old floor model television, which stood higher than his 3 year old frame. He looked over at his father once he heard his name. *"Come look at the baby."* Big Bill said. Billy D stood still as he watched his father rocking the baby slowly as he cradled the tiny baby. Billy D began to slowly walk over to the two of them as his father kneeled down to allow Billy D to see the baby. *"You want to hold him?"* Big Bill asked as he extended the baby towards Billy D. Billy D looked at the babies face and realized he had seen the baby before. In the picture at his grandmother's house. The picture he asked his grandma about, the one that she seemed as though she didn't want to talk about. Billy D then looked up at his father as he noticed the blood seeping out of the many bullet holes that lined Big Bills torso.

Billy D woke up sweating profusely, the dream startled him. Out of all the dreams he had about his father, this one really had him confused. He sat up on the bed wondering who the baby was in the picture, now in his dreams.

"What's wrong?" Trixie asked groggily, Billy D's sudden movements awakened her.

"Nothing," Billy D responded as he laid back down on the hotel bed. He noticed the sun was up; its brightness penetrated through the small cracks in the hotel rooms blinds.

He turned the television on and tuned to the weather channel. *"Damn."* He said out loud to himself as he saw the forecast for the upcoming days. It was December 30th and the weather was going to be unusually pleasant for that time of year. The temperature was going to be in the 50's going into the New Year. He saw the time at the bottom of the TV screen. 9:57am. "Yo, get up." Billy D nudged at Trixie as she fell back to sleep. She rolled over looking at Billy D with her eyes half open. "Time to go." He told her. Billy D wasn't going to fuck with Trixie at all after what he went through with her crazy ass dead ex-boyfriend, but he decided he would fuck her one more time before he cut her back. Trixie got out of the bed with just her thong panties on while covering her titties with her arm. Billy D watched as her round ass jiggled while she walked to the bathroom. He shook his head as he admired her fat round ass. *I might have to fuck her one more time.* He said to himself as he thought about how her ass jiggled when he hit it from the back. When Trixie came out of the bathroom, she saw Billy D lying on the bed with his boxers off. She went right over and began giving him head. He then put a condom on and fucked her for the last time.

***

"I'm so tired." Trixie said as she leaned her head on the passenger side window of Billy D's truck.

"You can sleep all you want when you get home," he told her as he sped up trying to make it through the light before it turned red. The black Cadillac truck that was behind him also sped up as it ran the light. Billy D thought the truck might be following him, so he switched lanes and the truck did the same. He thought to himself. *Here we go again...every time I fuck with this bitch I got niggas following me. I'ma fuck around and kill these niggas and her this time.* He then looked over at her with an angry look on his face as she laid up against the window with her eyes closed. He wanted to smack the shit out of her. When he pulled up in front of her house he noticed the Cadillac truck turning the corner. "Get out." He demanded as he hit Trixie on her arm to wake her.

"Ouch, what was that for?" She responded as she rubbed her arm.

"Just get out." He said again while looking in his rear view mirror as the truck began to approach.

"Bye." She said as she got out. Billy D leaned over and pulled the door closed. "Call me." She said to herself as she stood there watching him drive off.

Billy D rode up the street as he continued to look in his rear view while reaching in his glove compartment to get his gun. He then pulled over and jumped out of his truck as the Cadillac truck was now on the side of him. He raised his gun as the truck stopped and the passenger window rolled down slowly.

"Be easy little Billy." The man spoke know with his identity exposed.

Billy D tucked the gun in his waist as he saw who it was. It was Regal, his Uncle Bank's friend. When Billy D was younger, Regal used to be like an uncle to him. He was always around when Billy D was a kid. Regal and Bank were tight. As Billy D got older he didn't see Regal as much. He just knew his uncle didn't deal with him like he used to. "What up?" Billy D said as he walked toward the truck and gave Regal a pound.

"Naw nephew...show me some love." Regal said as he got out the truck and hugged Billy D. "Get in the back I need to holla at you." Regal demanded as he opened the back door of the Cadillac.

"Hold on." Billy D said as he hopped back in his truck and turned it off, then and got in the truck with Regal.

"Billy D this ma man Paul... Paul this ma nephew Billy D." Regal introduced his driver to Billy D. "I like to call him lil Bill." Regal added as he turned around to Billy D while smiling. "His dad was the realest, one of the realest niggas I ever met." He continued to talk to the driver making sure Billy D also heard him. "And he had all the bitches." He laughed. "He even stole ma girl from me." He added not laughing anymore. "Billy D..." He yelled as he changed the subject now smiling as he turned to Billy D in the back seat. "Ma mutha fuck'n nephew." He added while still smiling. "How you been?"

"I been good." Billy D answered.

"How ya Uncle?" He asked referring to Bank.

"He good."

"Yeah... I got to go see ma nigga." Regal added as he turned back around facing the front of the truck. "But, nephew..." He then spoke out. "I need a favor from you." He added now looking back at Billy D again.

"What up?" Billy D asked.

"I need you to take care of a problem for me...this nigga bad for business, he hit a couple of ma spots, and he robbed a couple of ma little mans, he almost killed ma nephew Pretty Mone, you remember PM don't you?" He asked Billy D. Billy D nodded his head yes. "Anyways...I want this nigga dead...and you the only one I know thorough enough to do it, all these otha niggas scared of this nigga." Regal continued on. He then turned back towards the front. "I'll give you seventy five G's, twenty five now and fifty after you do it.

The twenty five in that bag on the floor back there, that's yours," Regal said referring to the bag on the floor next to Billy D.

Billy D leaned to pick up the bag; he saw the stacked bills inside the bag. He then looked up at Regal as he put the bag of money on the seat next to him. "Ok... who is it?"

Chapter 31

"3, 2, 1 HAPPY NEW YEAR!" Everyone in the night club yelled as confetti and balloons fell from the ceiling. The music began to thump as the bass pulsated through every angle in the club.

"A toast to all ma niggas, and to getting this money." Bum raised a bottle of champagne in the air as Mojo, Bumpkin, Uno, Pete, Bull, Lex, Billy D and J. Brown and his four man crew all joined in as they raised their bottles up also, tapping them in the air. They were in the VIP section of the club sipping bubbly along with the other patrons who dished out the extra money to have access to VIP. There were a few Buffalo Bills players and other dudes from the town who were getting money also in VIP. All the women that had access were gorgeous. They strolled around in their tight outfits, ass and titties damn near exposed. They knew this was where the ballers were.

***

Uno, Bull and Pete walked the club checking out all the ladies as they sipped on champagne. At 17 they weren't supposed to be in the club, and definitely not drinking, but Bum gave the man at the door a few bills, so he let them all in without IDing them.

"Ma nigga… good look'n on dat." J. Brown screamed over the music as he put his arm around Bum's shoulder. "I just got back from Florida the otha day...he looked out lovely." J. Brown added as he smiled at Bum. Gutt hit J. Brown with 30 birds for $15,000 a piece. He also fronted him 15 extra. J. Brown was happy now that he had work. He had to switch it up to cocaine after Bank got arrested, but he knew it would still move fast.

"You good now?" Bum asked. J. Brown nodded his head yes as he tilted his bottle up and began drinking.

***

"What's been good witchu?" Mojo screamed in Billy D's ear as he slapped him up and hugged him.

"Same shit, just cooling out…what you been up to?"

"Nigga you already know how we used to do." Mojo smiled at Billy D.

"Nuff said homey." Billy D smiled back, knowing Mojo put some work in.

***

"Yo, you see that nigga King lately?" Bum asked J. Brown. "Cus I ain't seen him since we got back from Brazil."

J. Brown stood there looking as if he was thinking. "Oh yeah, I almost forgot." He shouted. "This little bitch I be fucking wit got a friend dat fuck wit one of his mans, and she said the nigga bounced, he took all his shit and left town without saying shit to anybody."

Bum looked at J. Brown puzzled. "She didn't say where the nigga went?"

J. Brown shook his head no. "They don't know where the nigga at…I guess the nigga got shook after Keisha and his mans got burned up…the nigga pussy." Bum looked upset. "Don't worry, he'll probably be back… niggas always come back." J. Brown added as he looked at Bum.

"I hope he enjoy his self wherever he at, 'cause when I catch up to him it's a wrap." Bum responded.

***

"What up?" Billy D yelled in Lex's ear as he sat on the couch in VIP. "You alright?"

"I'm good, just thinking 'bout the game coming up." Lex told Billy D

"Don't drink too much." Billy D said as he pointed to the bottle of champagne in Lex's hand.

"I only took like two sips. Only reason I got it is because Bum gave it to me." He responded while looking at the almost full bottle.

"What up Fam?" Bum walked over to Lex and leaned down to give Lex a hug.

"Shit...cooling." Lex yelled back.

"I seen yo last game…you looking like a young Deion Sanders out there." He joked.

"Good looking man." Lex smiled.

"I'm 'bout to go fuck wit a couple of these bitches." Bum said as he slapped Lex up. "I'll be back."

"Alright." Lex said.

"Give me that bottle if you ain't gon drink it." Billy D reached for Lex's bottle. Lex laughed as he pulled it away from Billy D. "Yo, what up wit cha man?" Billy D asked Lex.

"Who?"

"Gravy…you still fuck wit him?" Billy D asked.

"That's gon always be ma man." Lex answered as he took a sip from the bottle. "But I know he did a lot of dirt, I know his time is short."

Billy D watched as Lex was raising the bottle to take another sip. "Thought you ain't want it." He tapped Lex on the side.

Lex continued to sip from the bottle as he looked over at Billy D and smiled.

***

As the club began to let out, Bum was looking around the club for Uno, Pete and Bull. "Yo where them little niggas?" Bum asked Bumpkin.

"Oh, them niggas left wit some bitches about a hour ago." Bumpkin informed Bum.

"Alright, ya'll niggas gon meet me at the hotel right?" Bum asked Bumpkin and Mojo as they began walking towards their vehicles.

"Yeah." Mojo responded.

"Alright, the bitches on they way there now." Bum added. He then turned towards Lex and Billy D "Ya'll coming to the hotel. We got three rooms at the Sheraton, its gon be some hoes there." he asked Billy D and Lex.

"Shit I can't I have to get ma shit packed up cause we headed to our bowl game tomorrow and I need to rest." Lex informed Bum.

"What about you Billy D?" Bum looked at Billy D.

"Yeah I'ma be there after I drop Lex off." He answered.

"Cool, see you there." Bum said.

***

"Man I'm fucked up." Mojo told Bumpkin as they walked to the truck.

"Nigga you should be, all them bottles you had." Bumpkin responded. "Just don't throw up in ma truck." Just as he said that Mojo put his hands on the side of the truck and bent over as he started throwing up on the sidewalk. Bumpkin walked over to see if he was alright. "Damn nigga, that shit look nasty as hell." Bumpkin said as he began to back away from Mojo who was still throwing up. N.either one of them saw the two men walking up the street with hoodies on headed right towards them. "Nigga if you done then get in the truck." Bumpkin demanded as he walked over to the driver side door.

Mojo lifted his head up and reached for the passenger door and saw the two men pull out guns. Before he could react the gun men began shooting *blat blat blat blat blat blat blat blat blat blat*. The bullets pinned Mojo up against the truck as some went straight through Mojo's body and hit the truck. Bumpkin opened the door and grabbed his gun from up under the seat. When he rose up he began to shoot at the two men who were now running through the dark parking lot. Car alarms started going off as Bumpkin shot through a couple of car windows trying to shoot the two gunmen as they fled. Bumpkin continued to shoot as the police rode up on him with lights flashing and sirens blaring. "Freeze, put the gun down!" The officers yelled as they kneeled behind their open doors with guns aimed at Bumpkin.

"Look like they got a nigga." Lex said as he and Billy D headed up the street.

Billy D stopped his truck as the police had the street blocked off. "That look like Bumpkin truck." Billy D said as he began to worry that Bumpkin and Mojo might have been involved in whatever was going on up ahead. "I hope ma niggas alright." He added with concern in his voice.

"Oh shit is that Bum running over there?" Lex asked pointing at Bum running towards Bumpkin. "Oh shit that's Bum and Bumpkin." Billy D said as they watched the event unfolding in front of them.

"Stop right there." The police yelled at Bum as he ran over towards Bumpkin. Bum stopped and put his hands in the air as the police pointed their guns at him and Bumpkin.

"Bumpkin." Bum screamed. "Put ya gun down." he demanded.

Bumpkin held his gun as he looked over at Bum. "They killed Mojo...them niggas killed Mojo!" Bumpkin screamed.

"Put ya gun down Bumpkin!" Bum said again with his hands still in the air while looking at the police then back at Bumpkin. "Put it down bra, please." Bum begged Bumpkin as Bumpkin began to cry. He then dropped the gun. The police rushed in and handcuffed him. Bum slid off back into the crowd as the police concentrated on Bumpkin. Bum hopped in his truck and rode off.

Chapter 32

"*And the University at Buffalo wins the bowl game behind the outstanding play of Lex Ferguson whom was named the MVP."* Lex watched ESPN as he and Iyani laid cuddled up on the couch. Iyani turned her head and looked up at Lex as she smiled at him.

"If Lex Ferguson comes out and enters the draft what round do you see him going in?" The commentator asked his colleague.

"Well he's actually a third year sophomore so if he wanted to stay at Buffalo he could for another 2 years, but I was informed that he will enter the draft. I believe he will be a mid to late 1st round pick, only because he took a year off, some teams would have liked to see him perform at this level another year, but there's no doubt in my mind he is one of the top 5 players in the upcoming draft." The man continued to praise Lex.

"Oh my god!" Iyani screamed as she sat up on the couch and turned facing Lex, still laying there with a huge smile on his face. "So you're going to play football in the NFL?" She asked excitedly. Lex nodded his head yes as he continued to smile. "Oh babe I'm so happy for you!" She screamed as she hugged Lex. "Why didn't you tell me." She playfully hit him.

"It slipped my mind." Lex said as he sat up. "I was focused on you." He joked as he stood up and grabbed her and put her in a bear hug.

"Ouch, put me down." She giggled. Lex put her down and she gave him another hug. "I can't believe your going to be playing football in the NFL." She gushed as they continued to embrace. "You know what?" Iyani began to speak as she walked towards the back. "We have to celebrate." She walked into her bedroom and grabbed some money and her car keys. "I'm going to get some things." She walked towards Lex and kissed him on the lips. "I'll be back in about thirty minutes." She added as she walked out of the door. Lex sat back down and continued to watch TV.

***

Lex began to doze off, he was tired, he and the rest of the football team just got back in town the previous night from the bowl game. The sound of the phone startled him since he was half asleep. "Hello." He answered the phone groggily.

"What up Mr. NFL?" Billy D playfully responded. "What you up to?"

"Shit..." Lex answered as he stood up and walked to the bathroom. "I'm tired as hell."

"You need to take a vacation, shit you earned it." Billy D suggested.

"I wish…" Lex said. "Wednesday I gotta go to Chicago and train so I can be ready for the NFL combine in Indy." Lex added as he walked to the refrigerator to get a bottle of water.

"Damn son, you don't get no time off?" Billy D asked.

Lex twisted the cap of the bottle and consumed the whole contents in three gulps. *Ahh* he said as the water quenched his thirst. "Shit… this is ma time off." Lex answered matter of factly.

"How long you gon be gone for?" Billy D asked.

"I probably won't be back in town 'til after the draft."

"Damn son…I'ma miss you man." Billy D sounded sad.

"If I be in New York City on draft day, I'ma bring you and grandma wit me." Lex told Billy D as he noticed the sadness in his cousin's voice.

"Surprise!" Iyani shouted as she walked in the door holding a football shaped cake, a bottle of champagne and four balloons. One of the balloons was shaped like a football, another said *Congratulations*, another said *It's a boy* and the other said *It's a girl.*

"Yo cuzin, I'ma holla at you when I get in Chicago." Lex told Billy D.

"Alright cuzin." Billy D said as he hung up.

"Thanks." Lex said as he walked over and gave her a hug. "But….what's this about?" Lex asked with a lost look on his face as he pointed at the two baby balloons. "Oh…they were buy one get one free." She answered as she looked up at the balloons as they hovered in the air. "These were the only two they had left." She added now looking at Lex while smiling. "You like the cake?" She handed it to Lex as she walked and put the bottle of champagne down on the table and headed towards the back while taking her coat off. "I was going to get lobster and shrimp from the grocery store, but I don't really know how to cook seafood that well." She screamed from the bathroom as she washed her hands. *You don't know how to cook anything well,* Lex chuckled as he thought to himself. "You want me to order a pizza and wings?" She asked as she walked out of the bathroom drying her hands off on the hand towel.

"Go ahead." Lex answered as he put the cake on the table, then sat back down on the couch and watched TV.

"You want a glass of this now?" She asked Lex as she held the champagne bottle in the air.

"Yeah, pour me a glass." He responded as he held the remote in his hand flicking through the channels. Iyani came back in the living room and handed Lex the glass of champagne. "Where yo glass at?" Lex asked her as she sat down next to him.

"I don't want any." She answered as she took the remote from him.

"You said WE have to celebrate." Lex emphasized. "So you have to drink with me." He smirked as he got up and walked to the kitchen. He came back to the living room with another glass of champagne. "Here you go." He smiled as he handed her the glass. Iyani took it and sat the glass on the coffee table. "Drink it." Lex demanded as he sipped from his glass.

Iyani sat with her arms folded and legs crossed as she aimlessly flicked through the channels with the remote. She then looked over at Lex. "I'm pregnant." Lex almost choked on the champagne shocked by what Iyani just told him.

Chapter 33

Shit was beginning to get real hectic. Mojo was dead, yet no one had a clue as to who killed him. On top of that Bumpkin was in jail without bail for reckless endangerment and a slew of other charges. Bum was stressing. He lost two friends on New Years day. A night of celebration turned into a night of misery. There was no amount of money that could bring Mojo back from death, and the judge ruled the same as he ordered Bumpkin be held without bail. Bum felt helpless. He couldn't do anything to help his friend regain his freedom at this point besides pay for the best lawyer money could provide.

***

The Y.G's also lost two of their big brothers. Even though they had no idea as to who killed Mojo, they did know who burned down the house, and they intended to make them pay. Their anger became intensified after Mojo's death, and they suspected the same people of Mojo's murder. "So yo..." Uno began to speak as he loaded the AK's banana clip to capacity then inserted it into the assault rifle. "Dem niggas should be in front of the house...so soon as Bull pull up on dem we got to hop out quick and dump on dem niggas." Uno stressed as he looked at Pete who was loading the clip to the tech 9.

Bull began shaking his head no as he heard Uno layout their plan. "Somebody else gon have to drive or we just park and come through the yard." Bull said as he grabbed the shotgun and threw the barrel over his shoulder as it pointed at the ceiling.

Uno looked Bull in his eyes, knowing Bull wanted to let off some stress. He nodded his head in agreement, not wanting to get in the way of a raging Bull. "Alright we gon park the car around the corner and come through the yard...Pete you ready?" Uno looked over at Pete who just inserted the 32 shot clip into the tech 9.

"Born ready." He said as he stood up and walked past Uno and Bull and headed out of the door.

***

"Yeah, park right here." Uno pointed as he looked at the house. "We cut through this yard and we should be right in they back yard, so we can creep up on dem upfront." He added. "Pete hand me da chopper." He demanded as he turned facing the back. Pete handed him the AK 47 from the back as he grabbed his tech 9 and handed Bull the shotgun.

"Let's go." Bull said as they all got out of the car and walked casually through the drive way leading to the backyard toward their marks.

They made it to the wood gate separating the two yards. They squeezed through a hole in the fence which allowed them access to the other yard without having to hop the 10 foot high fence. "Hold on." Bull whispered when his coat got caught on the wood that outlined the opening in the fence. Uno and Pete turned and helped him to get untangled.

"Come on." Pete said as they unhooked Bull from the fence. They crept on the side of the house and could overhear the group of men talking from the front porch. As Pete reached the edge of the house leading to the front, he motioned for Bull to come in front so he could set it off. The shotgun was loaded with buck shots, followed by slugs. Bull walked past Uno then Pete as he prepared to set it off.

"Let's go." Uno whispered.

Bull ran to the front where the group of 5 men were on the porch and let off the first buck shot. Quickly he cocked back the huge slide on the bottom of the twelve gauge shotgun engaging the next shot as he pulled the trigger. This all happened so fast that the men in front of the house didn't have time to react. Uno and Pete now stood on the side of Bull as they ran towards the group of men and began letting off several shots from their weapons. They stood less then five feet from the men as they continued to shoot. One of the men managed to get away as he ran through the driveway towards the back. "Let's be out." Pete yelled at Bull as he stood over the men unzipping his pants.

"What da fuck you doing?" Uno looked back in shock as he saw Bull pull out his dick and began pissing on the dead bodies.

Pete looked at Uno as they watched him piss on the bodies. "Dis nigga wildin' out." Pete said.

"Let's go nigga!" Uno screamed.

Bull zipped his pants up and followed Uno and Pete through the backyard. Uno and Pete slid through the hole in the fence and grabbed Bull to help his big ass through. His coat got caught again. "Damn ma shit stuck again." He said as he tried to wiggle through the hole. He then backed up still on the other side of the fence, when he saw the kid from the group who got away. "Oh shit!" He said as the man started shooting at him catching him a few times in the body.

Uno and Pete immediately began shooting through the fence not knowing where the shots were coming from as wood began to splinter off of the fence from the shots. They then noticed Bull laid out at the hole in the gate with blood seeping from his body as he began to gasp and choke on his own blood. "Bull, nigga hold on!" Pete screamed as he kneeled down next to his friend.

Uno stepped over Bull as he went back through the hole to see if they hit the gun man. No one was in sight. "Fuck!" He screamed in anger. "Bull don't die ma nigga!" he looked into his friend's eyes, seeing life escape through them as his eyelids closed slowly. Pete reached in the pockets of his blood soaked coat, and took the car keys from his lifeless friend. He and Uno then ran towards the car as they heard sirens approaching.

Chapter 34

Lex sat inside the booth, which was more like a small cubicle, surrounded by partitions on both sides. It was just high enough to give one a feeling of privacy, yet allowed for the officers throughout the visiting room to observe your every move. In front of Lex was another partition which separated him from the empty chair in which his father would soon occupy.

As he waited for Bank to join him, he looked around at the prisoners interacting with their loved ones. The atmosphere was a mix of emotions. Some sad, mad, anger but mostly despair showed on the prisoner's faces. The atmosphere had Lex feeling a little upset. Then he thought about how perfect his life was at the moment. In three months his dream would come true, he would officially be an NFL player; he was expected to be a first round pick. He then thought about what Iyani had told him. He was going to be a father. He smiled to himself. The smile disappeared as soon as he saw his father walking towards him with his prison issued orange outfit on.

Bank approached him with a huge smile on his face. Lex stood as Bank reached over the partition to give him a hug. "So how you doing? I didn't get to see yo game but I seen the highlights. Mr. MVP." Bank said as he smiled proudly at Lex.

"Yeah, I'm good." Lex smiled back as he looked into his father's eyes. "How you doing?" Lex asked with a serious face.

"I'm good." Bank answered. "Just a little in the dark until I hear back from my lawyer…So what you been up to?" Bank smiled as he changed the subject. "Tell me what's going on in ya life... I haven't seen you since that day me and Billy D went to ya game."

Lex took a deep breath. "I've been busy since then…now that the season's over I have to go to Chicago and train so I'll be ready for the combine in Indy." The NFL Combine was a week-long showcase in Indianapolis where college football players perform physical and mental tests in front of NFL coaches, general managers and scouts for evaluation of prospects for the NFL draft.

"Yeah Billy D was telling me about that, he said you leaving Wednesday." Bank said as he looked at the clock.

"Yeah I was supposed to leave Wednesday, but I changed it till next Sunday." Lex informed Bank as he prepared to tell his father the other news. "I'ma stay in town a few more days so I can spend some time with Iyani." He said as he looked down at his hands.

"I feel you." Bank nodded his head in agreement.

Lex then looked up at Bank. "She's pregnant." Bank looked in shock. "Yeah?" He asked as he began to smile. "Congratulations, So I'ma be a grandfather huhn man?" Lex nodded his head. "Man I'm too young to be a grandfather." Bank joked. "But for real." He leaned in closer towards Lex. "I'm proud of you…you setting ya own path...you always did yo own thing…you're a natural born leader. I respect you for that, and I love you." He said as he looked into Lex's eyes. "I'ma try my hardest to be up outta here so I can come to yo first game, and be there when my grandbaby born." Bank added.

"Come on Mr. Ferguson, times up." The officer informed Bank.

Bank looked at the officer then back to Lex. "While I'm in here make sure you take care of ya grandmother and Billy D." Bank demanded as he stood up and reached over to hug Lex. "I love you." He added.

"Love you too." Lex said as they separated. Lex stood there as he watched his father walk through the door in which he came out of thirty minutes ago. He then walked out the visiting room as his eyes began to tear.

***

Bank made it back up to his cell block, as the other cells began to open for rec. "On the rec." The officer screamed as the prisoners began filing out of their cells.

Bank was hoping to see Ace as he made his way through the yard. He hadn't seen him since the first day Billy D came to visit. He figured they may have sent him back upstate. "Yo Bank." Someone called.

He turned to see Ace. "Where you been, I thought they sent you back upstate." Bank said as he looked at Ace.

"Naw…I had to go in front of the judge and they moved me across the street for a few days." Ace informed Bank.

"So how it go?" Bank asked.

"Man, I can't tell…I don't want to get ma hopes up either, I been through this shit before." Ace responded.

"I feel you…Now what was you saying about Regal?" Bank asked as they began to walk.

"I don't know how you gon take dis, but when I found out I wanted to kill da nigga." Ace said as he looked into Bank's eyes. "Now Regal came to visit me once since I been down, and that was about 10 years ago, and at that visit was when he told me he set me up." Bank looked at Ace in disbelief. "But what he told me next is what made me want to jump through the glass and kill his ass." Ace said with anger.

"What he say?" Bank stopped and faced Ace.

Ace put his head down as he prepared to tell his best friend what his brother Regal had done many years ago. "Remember we was beefing wit dem niggas in 92, and we thought dem niggas killed Big Bill?" Ace asked Bank. Bank nodded his head yes. "Well after Regal told me he the one who set me up... he told me to be glad he ain't kill me like he did Big Bill."

Bank backed up in shock as he looked at Ace who was now crying. He couldn't believe what Ace had just told him. All these years he was eating with the snake that killed his brother. Every emotion went through his body as he relived his brother's murder. He stood there trying to comprehend what he had just heard.

Chapter 35

Bum's thoughts wandered as he drove his car while on the phone with Misa. He thought about his friends. Bumpkin was in jail without bail, and Mojo and Bull whom were casualties of the streets.

"Hellooo." Misa said with an attitude feeling as though Bum was ignoring her.

"Yeah I'm still here." Bum replied. "I'm just stressing a little right now." He added with stress obvious in his voice.

"Why don't you come over here...I'll give you a massage to relax you, and we can watch a movie or something. I'm pretty sure I can make you feel better." She suggested in a sexy, sensual tone.

"Oh yeah?" Bum replied as he noticed the tone of her voice.

"Um huhm." She agreed.

"I'll be over in about a hour."

"Ok." Misa responded as they hung up.

***

Bum was headed to his stash house to drop some money off. He decided that he would shower and change before heading to Misa's house. He was riding up the street when he saw Rev hop out of his truck approaching a young lady headed into the neighborhood pizza spot. *"All them niggas had something to do wit it Fred, Rev, the lil nigga Belly, all them faggits."* Mojos words replayed in his head as he thought back to the conversation they had. *Rev,* he said to himself. His conscience wouldn't allow him to keep riding. It wouldn't allow him to spare this mans life. Not after his friends had been murdered.

Bum turned the corner as he circled around the block and parked on the side of the building that Rev and the young lady had entered. He pulled out his .50 caliber Desert Eagle from up under the seat and he put his hoody over his head. After tucking the large hand gun into the waist band of his pants to conceal it, he stepped out of the vehicle, walking alongside the building slowly. Peeking around towards the entrance of the pizza spot, he saw that the street was empty, no one was in sight. He then leaned up against the side of the building and waited for Rev to exit.

"Call me up, I'ma take you to the Bahamas, take you shopping, you know all dat good shit." Rev told the young lady as they exited the pizza spot. Bum peeked around the building as he heard Revs voice. "Shit...ma money long, you heard?" Rev added as he pulled a stack of bills from his coat pocket.

"Fuck'n clown!" Bum mumbled to himself as he watched. The young lady just laughed at him as she began to walk back to her car.

"Fuck you den bitch." He screamed at her as he watched her walk away. *"She got a fat ass."* Rev mumbled to himself.

Bum stepped from the side of the building; he reached in his waistband and grabbed the handle of his desert eagle. He walked towards Rev as Rev continued to admire the young ladies physique. Rev didn't realize Bum was behind him until he was right up on him. As he was turning around he saw the huge triangular shaped barrel pointed at his head from out of the corner of his eye. He didn't even get a chance to turn all the way around before Bum pulled the trigger, shooting him in the temple. The huge bullet took off the entire left side of his forehead as he fell to the ground. Bum shot him four more times as his motionless body laid awkwardly on the sidewalk. The young lady looked back when she heard the first shot and hurried to her car and sped off. Bum walked casually to his car and rode off as if nothing had happened.

When Bum made it to the stash house, he put his money up and took off his clothes and put them in a bag next to the garbage. After his shower, he got changed and put the desert eagle up as he grabbed his 357 magnum and headed to Misa's house.

***

"Hey." Misa hugged Bum as she greeted him at the door.

Bum was pleasantly surprised as he slowly put his arms around Misa. She had on some boy shorts and a tight wife beater. Nothing else. Bum continued to hug her as he looked down at her ass. He wanted to palm it so bad that his hands began to slowly gravitate towards it involuntarily.

"Bad boy," Misa joked while hitting Bum on his back as she felt his hands cupping her ass. "Come in." Misa demanded walking towards the living room.

Bum watched as she walked. Her boy shorts hugged her ass as her smooth reddish brown, slightly bowed legs were shaped perfectly.

"Sit down, make yourself at home." Misa said sitting down on the cream colored couch. Bum took off his coat as he looked around the house. There was matching cream colored couch and loveseat. The coffee table was glass with a cream leather boundary, and two matching end tables on each side of the couch. The floors were light oak hardwood throughout, and she had a 52 inch flat screen television with a surround sound system across from the couch in the living room.

"Nice house." Bum said as he put his coat on the loveseat and walked over toward the couch to sit next to Misa.

"Thanks, there's nothing on." Misa said with the remote in her hand while flipping through channels as she sat on the couch with her legs crossed.

"Turn on the radio." Bum said as he looked over at the stereo system. Misa leaned over the arm of the couch and grabbed the remote control for the stereo from the end table. They looked over at each other simultaneously as Mary J. Blige played. "Here you go with that Mary." Bum smiled.

Misa began to laugh. "I told you that's my girl." She began to lip sync as she closed her eyes and moved slowly to the melody. She then slowly opened her eyes as she felt Bum looking at her. "What?" She laughed as Bum stared at her.

"You crazy." Bum responded as he smiled at her. *Sexy Mutha fucka.* He thought to himself as he continued to stare at Misa. "What up wit that massage?"

"Scoot up." She motioned as she slid behind him on the couch as he sat in between her legs with his back to her. She began to rub his shoulders. "So, why are you so stressed?" She asked as she caressed his shoulders.

Bum relaxed with his eyes closed as he enjoyed the rub down. "Just a little bit of everything." He responded, not wanting to talk about it.

"Well I hope you feel better by time you leave here."

Bum turned to look back at her, "Thank you." He said as he smiled. He then began to rub her thighs as she continued to rub his shoulders and back.

"You want something to drink? I got a bottle of Cristal in the Fridge that's been in there since, forever." Misa asked Bum.

"Sure."

"Ok…get up." She said as Bum stood up and pulled her up from the couch. "Come in the kitchen with me." She grabbed his hand and led him into the kitchen. "Have a seat." She pointed to the bar stool along the counter.

"This is a nice kitchen." Bum said as he looked around. There were granite counter tops, stainless steel appliances and oak cabinets.

"Thanks…is this enough?" Misa asked as she handed Bum the glass of Cristal.

"Yeah, this good." Bum lied as he took the small wine glass. Bum wasn't an alcoholic, in fact he rarely drank, but when he did he usually drank a bottle of champagne by himself.

"Let's go back into the living room." Misa said grabbing the bottle of Cristal and another wine glass and walking back into the living room. "Oh this is my song." she said excitedly as she grabbed the remote and turned up the volume. She sat on the couch and poured the champagne into her glass, then took a sip before she placed the wine glass on the coffee table next to the bottle of Cristal. She stood up and began to move sensually to the music.

"Anybody ever tell you that you look like her?" Bum asked as they listened to Amerie sing. Misa turned to Bum and gave him a sexy look as she nodded her head yes, and continued to dance. Bum tilted his head back as he finished the glass of Cristal off and poured some more.

As the stereo continued to change from CD to CD and from song to song, they downed the whole bottle of Cristal. As they talked, the alcohol began to affect Misa, she began to joke more and giggle at everything said. Bum was surprised that he was also a little tipsy. "See I told you that you were going to feel better before the night was over." Misa smiled at Bum as she moved closer to him on the couch and then rested her head on his shoulder.

"Yeah, thanks for inviting me over." He said as he put his arm around her.

"Thanks for coming," she responded as she looked up into his eyes. He lowered his lips to hers and started to kiss her. She grabbed the back of his head and pulled him on top of her as she laid under him on the couch. "I want you," she moaned in his ear as he began to kiss her neck. He then stood up and grabbed her hands to pull her up. They continued to kiss as she held his hands and back peddled towards her bedroom. As they made it to the room, they paused just long enough to take their clothes off. Bum then laid her on the bed kissing her neck and her breast as her nipples began to harden. She moaned in anticipation as Bum's stiff dick rubbed her thighs. "Do you have a condom?" Misa moaned as Bum sucked her nipples. He held the condom up to show her. He took it out of the wrapper with one hand and placed it on his dick. He found pleasure in Misa's pussy as he held her smooth legs in the air while he stroked in and out of her. She moaned with each stroke. Bum kissed her legs as her ankles rested on his shoulders. Misa reached up and grabbed him by the back of his neck as she pulled his lips to hers and began kissing him aggressively as she grinded her pussy on his dick. *Oohh,* she let go of his neck and grabbed the sheets on the bed as she began to cum. Bum rose up as he grabbed her legs and spread them wider as he penetrated even deeper into her. Her moans became loader. He let her legs down as she began to backup towards the head board, Bum followed as he came. She grabbed his neck again and started to kiss him. "Thank you." She whispered.

"No…thank you." He whispered back as he laid on top of her.

***

"You should stay the night." Misa suggested as she hugged Bum at the door.

"Naw…I have to go…next time." He said as he walked out the door.

"Bye, drive carefully." She added as she waved.

"I'ma call you in the morning." He said walking toward his truck.

Bum wanted to spend the night, but he had to much shit on his mind. He preferred to be at home in his own bed where he would feel more comfortable. He was glad he had chilled with Misa. She took his mind off the streets the whole time he was with her. Now it was back to reality as his mind began to wander. His mind was elsewhere as he ran the stop sign. A police car immediately pulled behind him as it threw its lights on. *"Fuck!"* Bum mumbled to himself as he put his blinker on to pull over. The officers approached Bum; one was on each side of the truck. Bum rolled the window down as they got closer.

"How are you doing sir?" The officer asked.

"I'm good, yourself?" He replied.

"Can I see your license and registration please?" The officer asked as he and his partner held their flashlights towards the inside of the truck. "You know you ran a stop sign back there?" He added as Bum reached for the glove compartment to grab his registration.

"Oh, I wasn't aware of that officer." He responded as he opened the glove compartment. *Oh shit* He said to himself as he forgot about the 357 he had put in there because he didn't want to take it inside of Misa's' house. The officer's flashlight beamed on the chrome revolver.

"Sir put you hands on the steering wheel now!" They screamed as the one on the drivers side opened the door and pulled Bum out of the truck. He began to pat Bum down as his partner held his gun at Bum's head. He then read Bum his rights as he cuffed him and walked him to the police car.

Chapter 36

Bum sat in the Bullpen with the other prisoners, after the judge ruled that he be held on a $100,000 dollar bail. The bail was set higher than usual, because of the increase in gun violence throughout the city, and this was supposed to be a way of controlling it. However this wasn't much money to Bum. Through a bail bondsman, he needed just $10,000, and he would be released until sentencing. He knew he would be walking out of the jail in a matter of hours. He just hoped it would be sooner than later. He was tired of hearing everyone's war stories and all the lies he'd heard thus far.

"Them muthafuckas ran up in the crib guns out, nigga I was shook." Bum looked at the man as he continued to tell his story to the rest of the prisoners. "I had four birds of coke on the table when they ran in…" He continued to lie. Bum knew he was exaggerating because he bought his work from Bum. He never bought more than 4 ½ ounces. Bum just looked at him as he continued. "So I grabbed the four bricks and ran to the bathroom bust them shits open and began to flush the shit, the police run in behind me, threw me on the floor and these muthafuckas grabbin' shit up out the toilet and shit." He paused as the officer opened the door.

"Brandon Williams." The officer yelled. Bum immediately walked towards the officer at the door.

"That's me." He said as he stood in front of the officer.

"Let me see your wrist band." He demanded as Bum raised his arm displaying the wristband with his name and prison number on it. The officer checked Bum's wristband then looked at the paper he held in his hand to make sure the information matched. "Come on." The officer began to pull the door as Bum walked out from the bullpen.

"Be easy Bum, I'll see you in a minute!" The man yelled from inside the bullpen as the officer closed the door. Bum just nodded his head at the liar. "So anyway…" he continued on with his lie as he turned back facing his audience.

"Raise your hands." The officer ordered Bum as he uncuffed him, then he cut his wristband. "You're free to go." He said pointing to the door. Bum looked at the door then the officer, and then he headed towards the door quickly as he opened it. *Freedom.* He thought to himself as he saw people walking about the court building freely. Then he turned and saw Jasmine and his Cousin Tamika standing there smiling at him.

"What's good?" He said as he walked towards them. "What you doing in Buffalo?" Bum asked Tamika as he hugged her.

"I came up here to talk to you, then I found out you got arrested, so here I am." She responded as Bum now hugged Jasmine. "Gutt out front in the truck." She added.

"Word!" Bum asked, he was surprised. "Let's get the fuck up outta here." He said to Tamika and Jasmine as they began to walk.

"Where did you park?" He asked Jasmine.

"In the parking garage." She answered.

"Thanks." he said to Jasmine as he stopped walking.

Jasmine then pulled out $10,000 from her purse as she handed it towards Bum. "She told me to keep it, because she was going to bail you out." Jasmine told him referring to Tamika.

Bum looked at Tamika then at the money then back at Jasmine. "Keep it." He said as he smiled at her.

Jasmine's eyebrows rose as she was surprised. "Are you sure?" She asked as she held the money and looked at Bum.

"I'm positive." He added as he hugged her again. "Thanks for being there." Bum then walked with Tamika towards the Range Rover with the Florida license plates. "Hurry up and get home wit all that money on you." He turned and yelled at Jasmine as he continued to walk.

As they made it to the truck, Bum went to open the back door. "Naw Bum, you sit in the front." Tamika demanded, as she walked around Bum and hopped in the backseat.

"Cuzo..." Gutt screamed as Bum opened the door. "What's happening wit you?"

"Man I'm just happy to see you." Bum said as they embraced. "So what up doe, why you come up to Buffalo?" He now asked curious to their visit. Tamika would come up often to handle business, but Gutt rarely ever came, especially unannounced.

"Man..." Gutt started to speak as he made his way through the busy downtown traffic. "I came to see what's up witcha boy J. Brown." He continued.

"What you mean?" Bum asked unaware of what Gutt was talking about.

"The nigga was suppose to get back at me two weeks ago wit dat bread he owe me." Gutt told Bum as he looked over at him.

"Last time I seen him was on New Years, he told me he went to see you, I don't think he would be on shit wit ya money or nothing like that."

"Well that's why I came up here, to see why he lost communication wit me."

"Just chill cuzin, I'ma see what's up wit him…the nigga caked up so I know he got ya money." Bum said as he tried to relax Gutt.

"Alright… but if I got to leave wit out ma money I'm taking him wit me." Gutt said with all seriousness.

"No," Bum shook his head. "If he don't pay you, I'ma make sure he pay…one way or another." Bum said as he looked at Gutt. "Now that that's out the way…Cuzin we got to hit the town tonight, you know how we do!" He yelled in excitement.

Chapter 37

Bum was awakened by his cell phone when it vibrated in his pants pocket. It was eleven in the morning. He didn't get in til six am, after him and Gutt hit the town. They partied all night as they went from club to club enjoying the nightlife. They rarely got a chance to hangout together, so when they did they made the most of it. Bum was now paying for it as the alcohol he consumed throughout the night caused his head to throb as it matched the phones vibration.

Fuck! He put his hand on his forehead as he began to massage his temples. He sat on the edge of his bed as he reached in his pocket to get his phone. He had several missed calls, and voice messages. His doorbell began to ring as he looked through all the missed calls. As he walked towards the door he dialed Uno's number to return his call. Bum looked out the window and saw Uno standing at the door. Bum hung the phone up as he opened the door. "What up? I was just calling you." He greeted Uno as he slapped him up and hugged him.

"What up bra, I've been calling you all morning." He walked in behind Bum.

"Lock the door." Bum demanded as he pointed back at the door.

"I know you be up with the sun, so I got a little worried when you didn't answer ma calls." Uno said to explain his presence at Bum's door at this time of day.

Bum didn't mind the unannounced visit, because he wanted to holler at him anyway. "Just tired as hell." Bum yawned as he walked to the kitchen. "Want something to drink?" He yelled to Uno who was sitting on the couch in the living room.

"Naw bra, I'm good." Uno yelled back.

"Come in the kitchen." Uno walked in the kitchen as Bum sat at the table and threw two Tylenols in his mouth and chased it with a bottle of water. "Ma fucking head is pounding son." Bum said as he laid his elbows on the table and rubbed his temples with the palm of his hands.

"You must have been drinking." Uno responded as he sat in the chair across from Bum at the table, knowing the affects of too much alcohol.

"Fucking wit Gutt." Bum nodded his head in agreement.

"Cuzin Gutt in town?" Uno asked excitedly.

Bum shook his head "Yeah...he came up to check J. Brown."

"What's that about?" Uno asked confused.

"He owes Gutt damn near a quarter mil." Bum informed Uno.

"Word?" Uno looked surprised.

"I guess J. Brown lost contact wit him." Bum talked as he walked to the refrigerator. "So now Gutt think he trying to walk him..." Bum pulled two bottles of Tropicana orange juice from the fridge and walked back to the table. Bum sat down and slid Uno a bottle and opened his as he took a sip. Bum shook his head. "I told him to chill, and let me holler at him and see what's up," Bum looked at Uno. Making sure he had his undivided attention. "But this is what I want to do." Bum began to explain. "I want you and Pete to go check him...don't let him know Gutt in town, don't even let him know I'm out of jail, just holla at him and see where his heads at…" Bum paused as he leaned back in his chair "Now that's ma man, but if he get to frontin', then get at him…shit he know the consequences of this shit, the streets is ill." Bum said in a menacing tone.

"I gotcha bra." Uno responded in his likeness.

"Oh yeah…" Bum began to speak as he leaned in towards Uno, "And that faggot ass nigga Fred gotta get it too."

Uno smirked. "That's already in motion…he's a fucking dead man walking."

***

"Come on Rusty, wait til we get back to do that shit." Uno said as he stood at the doorway to the kitchen watching Rusty put flame to the end of the crack pipe. Uno shook his head as he walked to the living room and sat on the couch next to Pete.

"What you expect…" *uh uh* Pete choked on the weed smoke as he puffed the Dutch. "The niggas a crack head." he said as he blew the smoke into the air.

Uno just shook his head as he watched Pete continue to smoke the weed. "Both you niggas should have waited." He said as he stood up from the couch and walked towards the kitchen. Rusty met him at the door way with a muddled look on his face. "Man you ready?" Uno asked impatiently as he looked into Rusty's eyes. Rusty nodded his head yes, avoiding eye contact as he squeezed past Uno. "You look paranoid nigga." Uno said as he walked behind Rusty toward the living room.

"Na naw young b blood…thathaat shiit got me on point, I'm on point." He stuttered as he looked toward the floor while checking his pockets.

"What you looking for?" Pete asked Rusty as he stood up and grabbed his tech 9 from off of the coffee table.

"Ah, noonothing…I'm ready he responded as he now looked Pete in the eyes looking more focused.

"Nigga I hope so." He said as they walked to the door.

***

"Rusty, you good man?" Uno looked to the back seat at Rusty making sure he wasn't too high to fuck up what they had planned. "All you have to do is knock on the door, make them niggas think you there to buy something so they open the door that's it."

"I told you I'm on point." He assured him. "Let's go." They all got out the car and walked towards the house. As they made it to the house they crept toward the side door where the men handled their transactions. Uno stood with his back to the house holding his AK 47, while Pete stood on the other side holding his tech. Rusty stood in front of the door ready to knock on it. Uno shook his head letting Rusty know to knock now.

"Who dat?" A voice on the other side of the door yelled.

"Rusty." He yelled back. The man on the other side of the door looked through the small hole to confirm it was Rusty, and then he began to unlock the locks on the door.

"Who dat?" Fred asked the man opening the door as he and his man sat at the table counting money.

"Crack head nigga Rusty." He responded still unlocking the locks.

Fred sat there thinking to himself. "*That's the crack head that was fuckin' wit Mojo, Bumpkin and them…what the fuck he doing here?*" It didn't sound right to him. It sounded kind of fishy. "Ayo hold on, don't open the …." He tried to tell his man not to open the door but it was too late. Uno and Pete rushed in as they shot the man at the door. Fred and the other man at the table tried to grab their guns from off the table, but Uno and Pete shot as they reached for them. They then ran towards the back as Uno and Pete followed. Fred pushed his man down as he jumped over him and ran into a room. Uno and Pete shot his man as they followed Fred into the room. Fred jumped out the window but was hit with several bullets before he could hit the ground. Uno and Pete walked to the window and saw Fred trying to crawl away. They both raised their guns and began shooting as he collapsed to the ground with over twenty holes in him from the gunshots. *Pop pop,* Uno and Pete turned, startled by the gun shots. They walked out the room, guns drawn as they saw Rusty standing over a dead man next to a shot gun. Rusty put two shots in the back of the man's head with the old luger pistol which he held in his hand. Uno and Pete looked to each other in shock and then back at Rusty "I guess you was on point." They began to laugh.

Chapter 38

Lex was scheduled to leave for Chicago the next afternoon. He wasn't going to be back in town for a few months, so he wanted to go over his grandmother's house and spend time with her. He tapped on the back window of his car to get Iyani's attention as he pumped the gas. She rolled the window down as she looked back at him on the side of the car. "Hand me my phone." He said as the window rolled down. She grabbed his phone from the console and handed it to him through the window. Lex began to dial Billy Ds number so he could meet him over their grandmother's house and spend time together before he left. As he was dialing he saw Gravy pull into the gas station in his Jaguar.

"Ma mutha fuck'n homey." Gravy hopped out the car with his arms extended as he walked toward Lex.

"What up fam?" Lex stopped dialing as he put the phone in his pocket and embraced Gravy.

"Shit. You nigga." Gravy answered as he jabbed him playfully. "What you doing out here pumping gas for, Superstar?" he added as Lex proceeded to pump the gas.

"Ahh, gone head nigga." Lex laughed as he put the pump up and turned to face Gravy. "But what's good wit you doe homey. You know I leave tomorrow?" Gravy tilted his head as he looked confused. "Yeah, I got to go to Chicago and train, so I can be ready for all this running, jumping and all this other shit they gon have ya boy do." He informed Gravy.

"Damn homey, how long you gon be gone for?"

"Probably till April, then I'ma have to go to whatever city I'm drafted to."

"The Bills might draft you." Gravy laughed.

"I doubt it, but you never know...wherever I go I'll be happy." Lex smiled.

"Damn," Gravy shook his head as he smiled. "Ma man 'bout to bounce, why don't you ride wit me, hang out witcha boy for a minute… who knows when I'ma see you again." Gravy said with sadness in his voice.

Lex looked at him and thought about what he had just said. He knew the next time he might see Gravy may be standing over him as he laid in his casket at his funeral. Gravy's days were numbered in the streets. He robbed, shot and stole from a lot of people. Lex was amazed he managed to survive this long, but then again he knew Gravy was a strong nigga, and niggas respected him or feared him. Despite all the dirt he did, he still played the streets with no fear. "Come on." Lex said as he walked to Iyani in the passenger seat of his car. "I'ma have ma girl take ma car to the crib." He said to Gravy as he opened the door for Iyani. "Hey drive ma car home, I'ma ride wit ma man for a minute." Lex said as he held the door open so Iyani could get out and walk to the driver's side.

"When you coming back?" She asked as she got out the car.

"'Bout a hour, I'ma have him drop me off at yo house." He said as they walked to the driver side. He opened the door for her and gave her a kiss.

"Ok, hurry up."

Lex closed the door and winked at her. She blew him a kiss as he walked towards Gravy's car.

***

Billy D was getting ready to go to work, or put in work. This was nothing like a job to him since it came natural to him. Ending lives actually made him feel alive, it was therapeutic to him, a way to relieve stress, and getting paid for it made it that much more enjoyable. He looked at the Mac 10 pistol as it laid on his bed next to the 32 shot clip. Billy D began loading up a second 32 shot clip which he was going to take with him for this hit. He had every intention of emptying both clips into his victim. He laid the full clip next to its twin as he walked into the bathroom. Billy D looked in the mirror; his eyes reflected the hate and coldness stirring from deep inside his soul. He then leaned toward the sink splashing water on his face. He looked back into the mirror as the water dripped from his face. Now he was ready. Ready to feed that animal inside of him, the beast that fed off bloodshed.

***

Gravy had an ice blue XJ Jaguar sitting on 23 inch rims, with mirror tinted windows. His car definitely stood out. "This shit hot, I ain't never seen the inside of this joint." Lex complimented as he sat in the custom made ice blue and cream Louis Vuitton seats looking around the interior. The blue parts of the seat were leather and the cream parts were suede. The dash was oak and leather, with the steering wheel matching it.

"Yeah, compliments of these pussy niggas in the town." Gravy replied with a look of disdain on his face. "I don't even have to rob these niggas no more." Gravy said as he looked over at Lex. "I rarely pull the toast out, niggas see me and just start handing shit over…money, jewels, work everything…these niggas is feeble." He added as he turned to watch the rode as he drove.

"Niggas ain't gon keep going for that shit homey, somebody gon try to get at you if you keep that shit up." Lex said as he looked over at Gravy.

"I'm not worried about it…" He looked over at Lex "To be honest witchu...that's what I want, I only do this shit 'cause I can, niggas let me… it's too easy. Don't get me wrong niggas have shot at me, but when they see a nigga walking towards them dumping back and not even worried about they shots they get spooked and get da fuck up outta there… I'm not scared of dying; sometimes I think I want to die." Lex looked at Gravy and noticed his eyes watering. "I think about dis shit sometimes… You know… like what the fuck am I here for… I don't have shit to live for… I wake up every morning with nothing to look forward to. Just these rotten ass streets… that's it."

Lex never knew his friend felt this way. They were two different sides of the same coin. They both were products of the street and the bullshit that came with it, but they shared different outlooks on life. Lex looked forward to each morning with excitement and anticipation, as he had the entire world at his hands. His future was as bright as the sun, while Gravy's was dark and gloomy. Lex felt sorry for his friend. "Ayo…when I make it to the league, why don't you come wit me, get the fuck outta this city." Lex proposed as he looked over at Gravy. He wanted to help his friend. He knew if he stayed in Buffalo he would be killed.

Gravy shook his head no, "Man as much as I hate it here, I love it." Lex understood exactly what he meant. "This all I know." Gravy added. Lex nodded his head in agreement as he promised himself that when he made it, he would come back and get Gravy. "Yo man you hungry?" Gravy screamed animated as he changed the subject in order to change the mood.

"Naw I'm good."

"Shit I'm starving, I'ma go to Destini's and get a steak sub or something alright?" He looked over at Lex.

"Let's go."

***

"Yo, you sure you don't want nothing?" Gravy asked as they sat in the car parked in front of the sub spot.

"Hold on." Lex pulled out his phone. "Let me see if Iyani want something." He dialed her number.

"Where you at?" She answered the phone with an attitude.

"I'm still wit ma man. I was calling to see if you wanted a sub or something from Destini's."

"Yeah get me a chicken hoagie with everything on it and some French fries..." She blurted out. "Oh and two tacos and a single order of mild wings,"

"Damn...is that it?" Lex asked sarcastically.

"And some pickles." She added.

"I'm not getting you no damn pickles." He said while laughing. "I'ma see you in a minute." He said before hanging up.

"Pickles, she wanted a order of pickles..." Gravy looked confused. "What the fuck, that's some new shit or something, fried pickles?" He asked while laughing.

"Naw...she pregnant." Lex told Gravy.

"Word, Damn nigga dats what's up, congratulations." He smiled as he slapped Lex up.

"Thanks man, but just get her a chicken hoagie wit everything on it, some fries, two tacos and a order of wings."

"Oh yeah, she pregnant or just greedy as hell." Gravy joked as he got out the car.

***

Billy D watched as his mark got out of the car. He had been following him ever since he saw the flashy car pull out from the gas station. He knew exactly where to find him. He was headed there, when he spotted the car leaving the parking lot of the gas station. *Perfect timing.* He thought to himself. He was like a predator stalking his prey as he sat in his car observing his Mark. He sat his Mac 10 on his lap as he waited for the Mark to come back out from the building. Now was the time. When he walked out the building, Billy D would attack. He felt his heart racing as the blood rushed through his veins. His senses became heightened as his eyes locked on its target like an eagle on a rodent. He started the car back up as he prepared to attack.

***

"Ahh man…" Gravy said as he got in the car and closed the door. "I can't wait to bust this sub down, huhn hold this for me too." He said as he handed Lex the three bags of food. He looked in the rear view as he pushed a button from under his seat and he hit the ignition. A small compartment opened up from the dash as a chrome 45 Smith and Wesson was in it.

"What's dat for?" Lex looked at Gravy confused.

"Dat fuck'n car back there been following us ever since we pulled out from the gas station." He said as he grabbed the gun while looking in the rear view.

Lex looked back over his shoulder to see what Gravy was talking about. The car was now on the side of the Jag as it angled in front of Gravy's car pinning him in not allowing him to open his door. The driver hopped out with the gun aimed at the Jag and began shooting. Lex ducked down as Gravy began firing shots back at the shooter. This seemed to make him angry as he rushed toward the

Jag. Gravy was surprised by his actions, it reminded him of himself. He knew this man meant business. He wasn't scared of dying either. He then noticed he couldn't shoot anymore as the shots stopped. He looked over at Lex whose body was riddled with bullets. Then the shots started back up as the gun man inserted a full clip. Everything seemed to move in slow motion as Gravy looked down at his body and saw all the blood coming from his chest. He was dying and his best friend was dead, sitting next to him. He knew it was his fault. The bullets were meant for him and him only. His friend was in the wrong place at the wrong time.

***

Billy D rode off as he sat the Mac 10 on the passenger seat with its now empty clip. He grabbed the other clip from his coat and tossed it on the seat as it was empty also. He snatched the mask off his face and looked in the rear view mirror at his reflection. As he looked into his own eye's he saw nothing. It was as if his soul had escaped. He began to get nauseas as he drove. He had no idea what was going on. He never felt this way after killing someone. Somehow things felt different, he was sad. He didn't feel right.

He fought through the tears as he made it home. He threw the gun and the clip on the bed as he ran into the bathroom. He immediately kneeled down next to the toilet as he began to vomit. Standing in front of the mirror, he looked at himself. His eyes were bloodshot red and his pupil's looked soulless. He leaned over the sink as he splashed the cold water on his face. He looked in the mirror and began to cry. He was confused. He had no idea why he was reacting this way. He walked back into the room and sat on the edge of the bed as he rocked with his hands on his head thinking.

"LEX!" he shouted as he jumped from the bed. "No…can't be…he's out of town." He told himself. "He's in Chicago getting ready for the combine." He continued to try and convince himself. He paced the bedroom. "He left Wednesday; he told me he would call me when he got there." He said to himself. "But he didn't call me…maybe he been busy, yeah that's why he didn't call me." He continued to pace the room like a mad man. "I'ma call him." He walked to get his phone from off the dresser. He dialed Lex's number. "Pick up cousin, come on pick up." He said out loud. "Fuck!" The voice mail came on. He dialed again. "Pick up cousin." He cried out. He got the voice mail again. He then dialed Iyani's number. "She got to know where he at." He said as he waited for her to answer.

"Hello," she answered.

"Iyani!" he screamed nervously. "Did Lex leave for Chicago?" he asked impatiently.

"Uhn un." She responded. "He changed it for tomorrow, why?" She asked.

Billy D began to cry. "Where is he?" he asked.

"He's with his friend…Gravy, why Billy D what's wrong?" She began to worry. Billy D just hung up the phone as he cried uncontrollably.

Chapter 39

Uno and Pete rode on the west side to see what was up with J. Brown. They knew he was either fucking with some women, or at the gambling spot because all he did was chase money and women.

They pulled in front of the gambling spot hoping he was there. It looked like a luxury car dealership with all the expensive imported cars out front. "I don't see the niggas truck out here." Uno said as they looked around at all the cars.

"You want to keep driving?" Pete asked as he started the car back up.

"Naw, one of these probably his, he switch cars like drawers." Uno answered as he sat back in the seat.

"Let's go see if he in there, if not somebody gon know where he at." Pete turned the car back off and followed Uno as they walked towards the old building which was once a beauty salon, but now used as a gambling spot.

Uno walked to the door and pressed the button on the intercom. "Who?" A mans voice asked from the intercom.

"Uno."

"Who?" The voice asked again confused, not recognizing the name or the voice.

"Uno, Bum's man, I'm looking for J. Brown." *Buzzzz* the intercom sounded as he let Uno and Pete in. When they walked in the large room, it still resembled a salon, as sinks and chairs with blow dryers attached lined the far walls. Couches lined the other side. One man sat in one of the salon chairs, while another sat on the couch as his pistol laid on the coffee table in front of him. The room was filled with weed smoke. "Y'all can go in back." The man that was sitting in the chair said as he walked over to the man on the couch to hand him the weed. He pointed to the door leading to the backroom. Uno nodded his head as he and Pete walked through the thick cloud of weed smoke toward the door.

When they opened the door they saw everyone surrounding the pool table as the dice game was being played. "Come on in." J. Brown waved them over.

The other men looked over at Uno and Pete. "What up Uno, what up Pete." A few of the men greeted them as they slapped them up while walking over towards J. Brown.

"What's good?" J. Brown asked as he embraced the both of them. "What up wit ma man Bum, he get a bail yet?" Uno shook his head no as he backed up slightly.

"You boys came to gamble or what?" J. Brown asked as he turned back towards the dice game. The pool table was littered with piles of hundreds, fifties and twenties all the way around.

"Naw." Uno said. He then leaned in towards J. Brown and whispered. "I need to holla at you."

"What up?" He turned to face Uno.

"Can we talk somewhere in private?" Uno asked as he pointed towards the door.

J. Brown paused for a minute as he stared at Uno trying to figure his intentions. "Come on." He walked towards the door leading back upfront. Uno followed him. "So, what's up?" J. Brown asked as they walked through the door.

"I'm here to see what's up wit dat money you owe Gutt." Uno said as he looked at J. Brown eye to eye.

J. Brown looked aggravated as he shifted his weight and folded his arms. "He sent you to ask me dat shit?"

"He didn't send me to ask you nothing…" Uno replied calmly. "...he asked me to ask you what's up wit his money."

"Come here." J. Brown said as he walked to the door leading outside. "Where he at?" J. Brown asked with his arms spread out and looking around as they both stood outside in front of the building. "Where the fuck he at?" He asked sarcastically.

"He ain't around." Uno responded as he watched J. Brown's anger set in.

"You see dat Benz right there?" J. Brown pointed at a white Mercedes Benz S63 AMG with chrome and white rims. Uno looked at the car, then back at J. Brown and nodded his head yes. "You see this shit?" J. Brown then pulled up his sleeve exposing a platinum and diamond watch. Uno looked at it then back at J. Brown. "Yeah!" J. Brown said as he nodded his head cockily. "That's where his fucking money at." He puffed out his chest as he spoke. "And tell da nigga good look'n." He added as he spit on the ground and looked at Uno. He then walked back into the building.

Uno walked in after him as they walked to the back. Uno stood at the door. "Yo Pete, let's be out." He called to Pete.

As Pete reached the door, J. Brown added. "And tell da nigga to suck ma dick!" He screamed in anger.

Uno looked at him and calmly asked. "Is it anything else you want me to tell him?"

"Just get da fuck up outta ma shit." He waved them off.

***

"What the fuck dat nigga talking 'bout, suck his dick, don't he know niggas get killed fa say'n shit like dat?" Pete asked as they walked to their car.

"I'm not gon even tell Bum and Gutt that he said dat shit. I'm just gon let them know he ain't trying to give Gutt his money." Uno said as they got in the car. "I'm 'bout to call dem boys now and see what they want to do." Uno said as he pulled out his cell phone and called Bum.

***

Uno and Pete walked into the restaurant as the hostess greeted them.

"Hello, a party of two?" she asked as she grabbed two menus from the podium.

"No, we're joining a party." Pete told the waitress as they looked around the restaurant for Bum and Gutt.

"There they go." Uno tapped Pete in the side as he spotted Bum with his hand raised waving them over.

"Thank you." Pete took the menus from the hostess and walked with Uno towards Bum and Gutt.

"What up?" Gutt spoke to the both of them as they stood at the table.

"What up Gutt?" They both slapped him up.

"Y'all want something to eat?" Bum asked them as they grabbed two chairs from the table next to them.

Uno shook his head no, and then looked at Pete who held the menus in his hands. "They got take out?" Pete asked as he looked at Bum.

"Yeah." Bum answered as he turned to locate the waiter. He got the waiters attention, and then waved him over.

"Can I get you something sir?" He politely asked. Bum pointed at Pete as he proceeded to eat.

"Yeah, umm..." Pete hesitated while looking at the menu, not really knowing what to order. He put the menu down and free styled. "Just bring me some chicken and shrimp." The waiter looked confused.

"Get him the same thing I had. But to go." Bum simplified the order for him.

"Will that be all?" He asked.

Bum nodded his head yes. The waiter nodded, and then walked off. "So..." Bum wiped his mouth. "Did y'all see him?" He looked from Uno to Pete.

"Yeah... We seen him." Uno responded.

"What he say?" Gutt then asked.

Uno shook his head. "Basically, he ain't trying to give you yo money." Uno told Gutt as he watched his reaction.

"I knew I should have just went to go kill dat nigga." He huffed.

Bum put his hand out to relax Gutt. "Chill cuzin." He looked at Gutt.

"How was he actin'?" Bum looked at Uno now.

"Real fucking cocky...the nigga got the new Benz and all dat." Uno turned to Gutt. "He even told me to tell you thanks for that."

Gutt sat back in his chair looking upset as he looked at Bum. "That's ya man huhn cuz'n?" He asked sarcastically.

Bum looked at Gutt as he fumed. He then looked back to Uno and Pete. "Get him." With those two words Bum knew it was a wrap for his friend.

Chapter 40

Billy D sat in the booth with a blank expression on his face. The last three days were hard on him, as he dealt with the fact that Lex was dead. He was at the holding center to visit his Uncle Bank. He wanted to tell his uncle face to face that it was him who had murdered his only son, his own cousin. He was sure that his uncle had already knew this being as he knew of everything that happened in the streets, but he felt he had to tell him personally. Lex's funeral was in a couple of days, and Billy D didn't want the first time he and his uncle to see each other since the incident, to be at the funeral with his uncle shackled and escorted by armed officers. So, he was there to do the hardest thing he ever had to do in his young life thus far. Billy D felt as though he had lost a part of himself after Lex's death. He felt empty inside, as though his heart and soul were missing. His eyes were bloodshot red, his face was dry and rough from the dried up tears that stained his face.

He looked up to see his uncle approaching. "How you doing Billy D?" Bank asked as he sat across from his nephew. Billy D's eyes watered as he looked down at his hands.

"I know it's hard, but you have to keep living." Bank said as his voice cracked. He lowered his head to try and make contact with his nephew.

Billy D still had his head down looking at his hands. He then raised his head and looked his uncle in the eyes as tears fell from his. He then shook his head from side to side. "Unc…Unc, I killed Lex." Bank nodded his head knowingly as his eyes watered. "It was an accident. I didn't mean to Unc, I loved him more than I love myself..." He continued to cry. "It should have been me, not him…not him." He shook his head as he sobbed.

"Billy D." Bank said quietly as he tried to make eye contact with Billy D. "Billy D…look at me," He looked up slowly into his uncles eyes. "I know what happened…I know you wouldn't hurt your cousin, and I know how you feeling right now." Billy D looked down avoiding eye contact with his uncle as he started to cry again. "Look at me Billy D." He demanded as Billy D raised his head. "I still love you. I'ma love you no matter what…and I forgive you, now I need you to be strong…strong for your grandmother and for me…you are all that we have Billy D." He spoke with sincerity. "It wasn't your fault." Bank added as he shook his head. "The person responsible for what happened is the snake dat paid you to get at Gravy." Billy D looked at his uncle confused. "That nigga need to die a thousand deaths from all the grimy shit he did." Bank whispered.

Billy D leaned in toward his uncle with a puzzled look on his face as he whispered. "I thought dat was ya man Unc, I mean y'all use to be real tight back in the day." Bank shook his head.

"Anybody that set they own brother up is a fucking snake…and anybody dat fuck wit ma brother need to die." Bank's voice cracked.

"What you mean by dat Unc." Billy D asked as his uncle's words made no sense to him.

"Regal has to die." He whispered. "He killed your father."

Billy D shook his head in disbelief from what his uncle had just said. "Naw…"

"Yes." Bank nodded his head as he leaned in as close as he possibly could. "I would never have you kill anyone, but this shit is real personal, this is a family matter, I would do it myself if I could…but..." He paused as he wiped the tears from his eyes with his hand.

Billy D sat there looking at his uncle as he felt his insides bubbling from the anger escalating inside. He wanted to get at Regal in the worst way. He wanted to kill him twice, once for his father and again for Lex. He knew when the time came he would make him suffer. Just as he did after his father's death and now Lex's death.

Chapter 41

"Hold on." Uno put his hand over Rusty's to stop him from starting up the car. They watched J. Brown as he exited the strip club. "Wait until he pull off." He added as they watched J. Brown get into his Benz. Uno sat in the back. They had Rusty drive the car so he could drive it back to the house, as they planned on riding with J. Brown.

"Dats a cold ride there." Rusty said as he watched J. Brown pull out from the parking lot.

"Come on man, follow dat nigga." Pete tapped Rusty on the shoulder as they watched the Benz ride past them. Rusty turned the car on and made a U turn in the middle of the street as he attempted to follow J. Brown without being noticed.

"You can get closer, don't want to fuck around and lose the nigga." Uno told Rusty as the distance between them and J. Brown widened.

"I don't want to get too close, he gon know we following him."

"By time he realize we following him, this eagle gon be in his grill." Uno responded as he held the Desert Eagle in his right hand.

As Rusty sped up, J. Brown turned down a side street as if he were headed towards the expressway. Rusty did the same as he tried to keep up with the Benz. "Yo speed up, soon as he stop at the stop sign do it." Uno told Rusty as he looked to the back at Pete.

"Hopefully the nigga jump right out, soon as he do, we hop out on him." Pete nodded his head while looking over Rusty's shoulder through the front window as the car got closer to the Benz. J. Brown slowed up to stop at the stop sign. *Boom* Rusty hit the back of the Benz just enough to cause it to jerk a little. Uno and Pete waited a second hoping J. Brown would jump out of the vehicle in anger after his brand new Benz just got rear ended. They saw the door began to open.

"WHAT DA FUCK!" He hopped out the car screaming angrily, as his arms flailed in the air. "YOU BANGED MA SHIT!" He continued to scream as he approached the car.

Uno and Pete hopped out the car simultaneously with their twin Desert Eagles aimed at a stunned J. Brown. He stood in the middle of the street, frozen with his mouth wide open and hands in the air obviously concerned about his current predicament. "What up?" Uno said as he walked closer to J. Brown with the gun pointed at his abdomen.

"Get in the backseat nigga." Pete demanded as he walked past J. Brown and hopped in the driver seat of the Benz.

J. Brown stood there with his hands still in the air as Uno held the pistol close to his ribcage. "You heard the man, get in the fucking car." Uno said while pushing him towards the back door of the Benz. J. Brown opened the back door and got in. "Slide over." Uno motioned with the gun as he sat in the back next to J. Brown.

"What up, y'all little niggas tryna rob me…what's dis shit about?" He asked nervously as he looked at the gun in Uno's hand, then back up at Uno.

"Naw, just want my mans money…get dat to us and you can ride off in ya Benz..." Uno said as he looked around the interior of the Mercedes Benz. "...this shit is nice, what it cost you?"

"Man, I got da nigga money. We can go get dat shit right now, its noth'n." J. Brown relaxed a little bit, wanting to believe that they just wanted Gutt's money and then they would let him go. He didn't really respect them. He looked at them as little niggas. He figured with Bum and Bumpkin in jail, and Mojo and Bull dead they really were out of their league fucking with him. He thought to himself he would give them the money, then they would let him go and he would kill them ASAP.

"Where it's at?" Uno asked J. Brown. "Ma little spot on the west. 7th near Porter." He said with an attitude. "Matter of fact I got a few bricks of coke there, y'all niggas can have dat shit too." He added feeling himself, as he thought about what he was going to do to them when this shit was all over.

"Let's ride Pete. 7th and Porter" Uno said as Pete turned the music up and put the Benz in drive.

These little bitches must don't know who they fucking wit, I know they heard… shit I'm a fuck'n Don…shit I piss out what these little niggas worth… they fucking dead! J. Brown smiled as he thought to himself.

***

"Yo bra, we pulling in front of ya house right now." Uno told Bum as he held the cell phone to his ear.

"Ok, the door open, just come on in." Bum responded as they hung up.

Uno and Pete grabbed the two bags from the back seat and walked to the front door of Bum's house. As they opened the door they saw Bum and Gutt sitting on the couch in the living room smoking weed.

"What's good?" Bum said as Uno and Pete stood at the door. They walked over to the couch and placed the two bags on the coffee table in front of Gutt as he sat on the couch puffing on the weed.

"Ok, Ok," Gutt said as he leaned up and blew the smoke out. He opened one bag and saw stacks of bills with rubber bands wrapped around them. He then opened the other bag and saw four keys of cocaine. "What's this for?" Gutt looked at Uno and Pete as he pointed to the cocaine. They both shrugged their shoulders.

"The nigga gave us dat too…shit why not, let me hit dat weed." Pete said as he reached for the weed.

Gutt handed it to him. "Bum where dat money counter at?" Gutt asked Bum as he stood up and grabbed the bag of money.

"In the kitchen, in that cabinet under the sink." He pointed towards the kitchen.

"Pete help him count dat shit." Bum told Pete. Pete smoked the weed as he followed Gutt into the kitchen.

Uno sat on the couch across from Bum now. "I talked to my lawyer today." Bum told Uno.

"What he say?"

"He said it's looking like I might have to do a little bid, they want me to do 3 years, but he told me he can get it down to one and a half."

"Why don't you just take it to trial?" Uno asked, not wanting Bum to do any time.

"I would, but I got them two other gun charges and you know they on shit now with them gun charges." Uno shook his head in disappointment. "I'ma probably take the one and a half and try to get my lawyer to speed this shit up so I can start the shit soon, that way I can be out by next summer." Bum said as he walked over and locked the front door. "So what happened when y'all seen J. Brown?" he asked as he sat back down.

Uno sat up on the edge of the couch as he began to tell him what happened. "Ok, so we sat outside the strip club fa about a hour and waited fa the nigga to come out, soon as he come out I tell Rusty to follow da nigga."

Bum looked confused. "Rusty. The crack head Rusty?" He asked.

"Yeah, don't sleep, Rusty get's it in…so anyway the nigga hop in his Benz and we following him."

Hold on, this the same Benz he said he bought wit Gutt's money?" Bum asked.

"Yeah, Same joint, so we behind him and he turn down the little side street and I tell Rusty to get up on him and bang da Benz in the back when he stopped at the stop sign. So we hit da nigga shit and he hop out mad as hell screaming and shit. He walking towards the car, that's when me and Pete hop out on him wit da Desi's pointed at him."

"Oh shit!" Bum began to laugh. "I wish I could have seen the nigga face."

"Yeah he was shook…So we hop in the Benz; I'm in the back seat wit J. Brown and Pete in the driver seat. So I tell the nigga give us Gutt money and he good. That's when he started getting all cocky and shit again. So the nigga like *"I got da nigga money, lets ride to ma spot on 7th and Porter."* Then he say he got a few bricks there also and we can have them too. The nigga was talking real greasy though like he was better than us or something." Bum shook his head. "So we ride on the west side to his spot. Pete pull in the driveway and park the Benz. We get out, I got da pistol pointed at da nigga stomach while he opening the side door to the house. Soon as we get in the door I hear dogs barking and shit from the basement. I'm thinking the whole time "*I hope dis nigga don't got the money down there, cus I ain't tryin' to fuck wit no dogs.*" Bum laughed. "So I ask the nigga if anybody in the house, he like *"Naw"* I grab him and we walk through the house anyway to make sure ain't nobody in there. Wasn't nobody in there, so we walk toward the basement and I tell him if one of them damn dogs come at me I'm gon shoot him and da dogs. He try to get us to let him go down there by his self to tie them up. Me and Pete look at each other then back at him. Pete then hit the nigga in the head wit the barrel of the Desi. He was like *"What the fuck, you think we stupid, we all gon go down there together and you gon control dem dogs then tie them up."* So we go in the basement, the dogs run up sniffing us and shit, he grab them and tie them up. Then I ask the nigga where da money at? He walk to the back, it's like a little room back there wit a door on it wit big ass locks and shit. So he open the locks and we go in the room. In the corner it's a big ass safe. You know one of them old joints wit the circle spin handle and shit. I got the pistol to his back while Pete on the side of him with the pistol to his head while this nigga trying to open the safe. It's taking the nigga forever, so I poke the pistol in his back hard as hell, he like *"Ouch!"* I tell da nigga to hurry the fuck up. He scream *"What the fuck... you niggas got pistols to ma head and shit, how the fuck am I suppose to concentrate."* Pete hit him in the head again wit the pistol, sweat dripping from the nigga head. So he finally open the shit up, and he got mad pistols and old ass rifles in the safe. Then at the bottom he had the two bags stuffed on the shelf. Pete grabbed the bags and opened them, and there it was…the coke and the cash." Uno said with excitement.

"How much money is it?" Bum asked.

Uno shrugged his shoulders. "I don't know."

"So what happened wit J. Brown?" Bum asked curiously.

Chapter 42

"You like how I work that dick?" The young lady asked Regal as she proceeded to suck his dick. She was a pretty light skinned girl with a nice body, and long straight black hair. Young, fresh and straight out of high school, just the way Regal liked them. Even though he was well into his 40's, he had a thing for the young girls. He would take them shopping, get them whatever they wanted, and in the bedroom he would have his way with them. He would have them perform all his sexual fantasies. Regal had a thing for kinky sex. He enjoyed all types of sexual fetishes, from whips and chains, role play, blindfolds and handcuffs.

"Give me dat pussy now." Regal demanded as he laid in the huge bed blindfolded with his hands handcuffed to the bed post.

The young lady obliged as she mounted his dick. "You like this pussy daddy?" She asked as she rode his dick.

"Yeah." He raised his pelvis to penetrate her even deeper. "Give me dat tight pussy baby." His lower body squirmed in pleasure as his vision and hands were restricted.

Billy D stood in the large walk in closet as he watched the two through the slightly opened door. He noticed that Regal was really beginning to enjoy himself and didn't like that one bit. He wanted to make him suffer in the worst way. He opened the door wider, making his presence known. The young lady became startled as she saw Billy D appear from the closet. Billy D was dressed in all black, and held the Glock pistol to his lips motioning for her to be quiet as he approached the bed. She began to shake and whine as fear consumed her body.

"Yeah baby cum on ma dick." Regal moaned thinking she was about to cum. Billy D grabbed the back of her hair and turned her to face him. He looked her in her eyes sympathetically as she began to cry. "Yeah...I got you crying huhn baby. You like dat dick don't you?" Regal asked braggingly, unaware of imminent death. Billy D didn't want to kill her, but he knew he had to. She would become a casualty of Regals treachery. Billy D positioned her head next to Regal's, as he pulled her hair causing her head to arch up. He then shot her in the back of the head causing skull bone, brain and blood to splatter all over the head board, pillows and Regal's face.

Regal inhaled in shock as her thoughts leaked on his face. "What da fuck is going on?!" He screamed in fear as he began to spit out the flesh from the young lady as it spilled into his mouth when he spoke. He yanked at the handcuffs desperately trying to free himself. "Look…" He began to calm down. "I have a million dollars cash; if you let me go you can have it. I don't have to know who you are or what this is about, just let me walk." He pleaded desperately.

"That's not enough." Billy D spoke. Regal turned his head, trying to catch the voice and shake the remains of the young lady off of him. Her lifeless body still straddled him.

"What do you want? I'll give you whatever you want."

"Can you give me my father back?" Billy D asked angrily. "How about my cousin, huhn nigga? I want both them back since you gon give me whatever I want."

"Look young bra, I don't know what you talking 'bout, but whatever happened wit yo people I'm sorry, but I can't do nothing about dat." Regal acted as if he had no idea who or what he was talking about, but he knew exactly who it was. He couldn't figure out how Billy D found out that he had killed his father.

"Why you do it?" Billy D asked sternly.

"Look here little Billy I told you I don't know what you talking about." Regal screamed out angrily.

"Then how the fuck do you know who I am?" Billy D asked suspiciously.

Regal was unaware he had said Billy D's name. "What you talking about? I don't know who…"

"Shut the fuck up, you said my name, you know who I am because you killed ma father!" Billy D cut him off as he screamed in anger.

"Nephew," Regal began to speak as he felt Billy D removing the girl from off of him. He lifted her body from Regal's, and sat her on the ottoman, placed his fingers over her open eyelids and closed them. He then walked back towards the bed. "I didn't kill yo father, that was ma best friend." Regal tried to make himself cry. "I would've died for him…I loved him." He continued on.

Billy D snatched the blindfold off his face. Regal had no tears in his eyes. "Don't worry…I'ma take care of that." Billy D smiled at him vengefully.

"Get these fucking cuffs off of me." Regal began to jerk about frantically as he tried to free himself of the restraints used for his fetish. "If I was out of these cuffs I would tear yo punk ass up." he yelled out angrily as he looked at Billy D hatefully. Billy D pulled a carpenters hammer from his waist and swung it at Regal's knee smashing his kneecap. "Ouuua shit you punk bitch!" Regal screamed in pain.

"Shut da fuck up…why you kill him?!" Billy D screamed as he swung at his knee again.

"Ouuua!" Regal screamed through clenched teeth as spit flew out his mouth. "Fuck you and your father!" He screamed with his teeth clenched. Billy D hit him in his other kneecap. "Ouuua…fuck, he fucked ma bitch!" Regal screamed. "The nigga stole ma girl…he knew she was ma bitch, he didn't care he fucked her anyway." Regal screamed out angrily with hate in his voice. Billy D shook his head as he couldn't believe Regal killed his father over a bitch. "He got the bitch pregnant…ma bitch, he got ma bitch pregnant…" He cried out. Billy D looked at Regal as he said that. "I went to see the baby and the little nigga looked just like Big Bill, just like the nigga, and yo ass." He looked at Billy D in disgust. "Soon as I seen dat shit, I killed dat Puerto Rican bitch." He added as he stared at Billy D.

"What about the baby, did you kill him too?" Billy D asked.

"I should have." He said coldly. "And yo ass too." He added meaning every word.

Billy D smashed the hammer into Regal's head with all the force he could garner. His skull cracked like an egg. He continued to bang the hammer into his skull as he thought about his father and Lex. With each blow he felt a sense of relief.

***

The next morning Billy D woke up with mixed emotions. He was excited yet confused. Regal told him that his father had another baby, a son, his brother. Growing up he never saw or heard of this. He was his father's only child, so he thought. He made it his business to find out one way or another. He was going to ask his grandmother if it were true.

Billy D pulled into his grandmother's driveway, hesitant. He didn't know how he would ask, but he knew he had to. He needed to know if he did indeed have a brother. That word *Brother* made him feel good, as if he wasn't alone in this world. After Lex's death that's exactly what he felt, alone. He put his key in the door and walked in. Walking to the living room, he saw his grandmother sitting on the couch watching television.

"Hey baby." She extended her arms as Billy D walked over to give her a hug; she kissed him on the cheek. "So how are you?" she asked.

Billy D sat down on the loveseat. "I'm good, how are you?"

"I'm fine…what's up?" she asked sensing he had something on his mind.

"Grandma," he eased up in the loveseat. "Remember that picture I asked you about not to long ago?" He asked while looking his grandmother in the eyes. He had seen how she became uneasy as he asked.

She put her hands over her face as she began to tear. The phone began to ring. "Oh, let me get that." She felt relieved. She didn't want to talk about it, and Billy D wondered why. He wasn't going to let it go, he had to know. She rushed in the kitchen to get the phone. There was a phone in the living room right on the end table next to the couch, but she went in the kitchen to answer the phone. Billy D sat on the loveseat for about 10 minutes waiting for his grandmother to return so he could get the answer he so desperately needed. "Billy D." She came into the living room. "Pick up the phone, it's your uncle." She pointed to the phone on the end table.

"Hello." he said.

"What up? I heard what happened to ol boy." Bank said referring to Regal. "That's what's up… he deserved it, but ya grandma told me you've been inquiring about that baby picture she has…" Bank paused. "Shit, he should be about what, 16,17,18? Somewhere around that, but yeah I want you to look after him…make sure he alright out there…after all he's family." Billy D just listened as he took in his uncles words. "He's your brother." Bank sounded relieved after revealing what was a secret for so long.

Billy D's eyes began to water. "Who is he?"

Chapter 43

"So what now?" Pete asked from the passenger seat as Uno drove.

Uno shrugged his shoulders. "I don't know, probably go holla at Bum and have him hit us wit some work to get the block jumping again."

Pete nodded his head in agreement. "I'm feeling dat, shit big bra Mojo dead, ma nigga Bull dead, Bumpkin in jail, Bum 'bout to go to jail…" Pete said as he paused and looked over at Uno. "It's just me and you oh baby." He began to sing jokingly the old Tony Tone Toni song. "Naw just fuck'n wit you." He got serious as he thought about his fallen comrades. "But yeah doe…it's so much money around the way, ain't nobody over there to get it, all the doe that came through the trap, and dem niggas up da block was getting cake too. Roney, Fred, shit damn near all dem niggas dead."

"Yeah…the nigga Belly still living, he really the only nigga still around there getting money. He the only one I really respected out of all dem niggas." Uno responded.

"Dat nigga must got a horse shoe up his ass, as many times as we came through clapping at dem niggas. He was the only one really trying to shoot back, we should pull him in, get him down wit da team." Pete suggested as he looked at Uno.

"Pump some life back into the block before we do anything. It's our time to get this money." Uno looked over to Pete with a determined look on his face. Pete nodded his head in agreement.

"Ayo I got an idea." Pete said as he looked over at Uno.

"Let's ride on the west side." Uno looked at Pete skeptically. "Let's go." He agreed as he drove to the west side.

***

"Ain't nobody seen him?" Rico asked the three men who stood on the corner as he sat in his blue Range Rover. "Man dis ain't like da nigga not to answer ma calls. I've been calling him since yesterday, he still ain't answering." He said as he got out his truck and joined the three men on the corner. He pulled out his phone and dialed J. Brown's number again.

Rico was J. Brown's right hand man. He had a feeling something was wrong with his friend after not seeing or hearing from him in almost two days now. J. Brown would sometimes disappear with a lady friend for awhile, but he would always answer Rico's calls and let him know what was up.

"What the fuck." He hung the phone up after getting J. Brown's voice mail once again. "I hope ma man alright." Rico paced the sidewalk nervously.

"Yo, Rico, there he go right there." One of the men said as he spotted J. Brown's white Mercedes approaching from up the block.

Rico turned to see the Mercedes pulling up towards the group of men. He began to smile with relief at the sight of J. Brown. "What da fuck ma nigga." He smiled as he walked toward the Mercedes. The window began to roll down. "Where you been at?" He shouted as he walked toward the driver side of the vehicle. The window rolled down enough for him to see that it wasn't J. Brown behind the wheel or in the passenger seat. He was shocked as Uno and Pete stared out at him from the Benz. J. Brown's Benz, but where was his man. He backed away slowly and took another look at the vehicle. He thought maybe it wasn't J. Browns, maybe it just looked like his, but after looking again he realized it was J. Browns.

"What up homey?" Uno asked Rico with a smile on his face.

Rico shook his head. "Aaaint nothing…wha what up Uno, what up Pete?" He stuttered in disbelief. He knew now that his friend was dead.

"Be good homey." Pete yelled as the window rolled back up. Uno then rolled off.

Rico still stood there stuck. He couldn't believe these two little niggas killed his man and were now riding around in his Benz.

"Rico, what the fuck them niggas doin' wit J. Brown's Benz?" One of the men asked.

Rico walked over to his truck angrily. "Them little niggas killed ma man." He screamed as he opened the door of his truck and leaned in and grabbed his gun. He then got back out and slammed the door. "I'ma kill dem niggas…dats ma word, dem niggas dead." He screamed as he brandished the gun in the air.

***

"You see that nigga face?" Pete laughed. "Yo the nigga looked like he saw a ghost." He continued to laugh.

"Yeah." Uno laughed. "It's time to get rid of this mutha fucka doe," He said seriously.

"Yeah, it's about time." Pete agreed.

"Ayo answer this, its Bum." Uno threw his phone over to Pete.

"What up bra?' Pete answered.

"Uno?" Bum asked thrown off by Pete's voice.

"Naw its Pete."

"Oh what up. Where Uno at?" Bum asked.

"He right here, he driving."

"Oh, well y'all boys come to ma building when y'all get a chance I got to holla at y'all."

"Alright bra."

"Alright." he said hanging up.

"What he say?" Uno asked.

"He want us to stop through and holla at him."

"You want to get rid of this joint first or you want to go holla at him now?" Uno asked Pete.

"Let's go get the hooptie, get rid of this bitch now and ride back in the hooptie." Pete responded.

"Bet." Uno said as he rode Pete to get the hooptie.

They drove an hour south of Buffalo to get rid of the Benz. Uno got out of the Mercedes and Pete got out of the hooptie stretching and yawning, "Aahhh shit."

"You tired nigga?" Uno asked as he opened the back door of the hooptie and got the gas can.

"I feel stiff as hell in this little mutha fucka...I'ma miss riding in that shit," he responded while pointing at the Mercedes.

"Yeah this shit is comfortable." Uno said as he walked towards the Benz with the gas can in hand. He began to douse the interior of the Benz with the gasoline, then the exterior.

"Hold on nigga, pop the trunk." Pete demanded. Uno walked to the back of the Benz where Pete was standing. He popped the trunk. They began to cough. "Damn, this nigga stink." Pete said as they looked at J. Brown with his severed dick in his mouth and body decomposing. They held their arms up to cover their nose from the stench.

"This shit smell better than this nigga." Uno said as he began to throw the gasoline onto the dead body.

"Hold on." Pete stopped Uno. He then reached for J. Browns watch.

"Naw, leave dat shit alone...after all he did die for that shit and this car, let him burn wit dat shit." Uno said as he began to pour the gasoline on J. Brown again. Pete then pulled out the matches, lit a couple and threw them in the car and in the trunk to ignite J. Browns dead body. "Shit...that's that." Uno looked over to Pete.

"Yup...that's that." Pete responded as they got in the hooptie and drove off.

***

It took them a little under an hour to make it back to the city. Uno pulled out his phone to call Bum as they pulled in front of his house. "Ayo bra, we out front, we getting out the car now." Uno told Bum through the phone.

"Alright." Bum said then hung up.

"Yo man I really liked that watch." Pete said as he and Uno walked to the front door of the house. "I should have took that shit, he ain't need it." Pete continued on talking about J. Browns watch. Uno just shook his head as he laughed.

"What's good wit' you boys?" Bum opened the door and slapped them both up.

"Tired." Pete responded.

"Yeah, well me and you both." Bum replied as he walked toward the steps leading upstairs. He turned towards Pete. "Lock that door." He told him.

"Yo bra we need to holla at you." Uno told Bum as he watched him walk up the steps.

"Go ahead, I can hear you." Bum shouted as he walked upstairs.

"We need you to front us a half a joint, so we can get the block back to jumping." He shouted making sure Bum heard him.

Bum walked down the steps with two large Louis Vuitton bag's on one shoulder and a Fendi bag in his hand. "A half a joint." He laughed as he walked toward the couch. He threw the Fendi bag on the love seat, and then took the Louis Vuitton bags off his shoulder and dropped them on the coffee table. "Get the block to jump'n huhn…" He smirked as he looked at Uno then at Pete. "How 'bout y'all flood the block." He said as he pointed at the two Louis Vuitton bags. They both walked over to the coffee table.

"What's this?" Pete asked looking confused.

"Shit, open them." He ordered. Pete began to open one bag. "Open the other one." He ordered Uno. They unzipped the bags and saw several keys of cocaine. "I want you boys to get the whole hood jumping. Its six bricks in each bag. When y'all done with that then holla at Gutt, he gon work wit y'all. I already spoke to him about it. He fuck'n wit y'all, he appreciate what y'all did for him." Uno and Pete were not expecting that. They never moved that much work before. "I'm not hustling anymore. I'm chilling until I get sentenced. Dat shit is all y'alls, just make sure you boys keep ma commissary right and send me some packages when I get upstate." Uno and Pete looked at each other in disbelief. "The hood is y'alls…I know you boys are more than capable of holding it down, I'm only gon be gone 'bout a year." Bum said as he went to sit down on the loveseat. "Oh yeah." He picked the Fendi bag up from the loveseat. "I almost forgot." He threw the bag to Uno.

Uno caught it. He then looked at Bum confused. "Open it." He said as he sat down.

Uno opened it and was shocked by its contents. It was stacks of bills inside. "That's $200,000 right there y'all split that." Bum said. Uno and Pete stood there in shock. "That was $400,000 y'all bought over here. J. Brown only owed Gutt $225,000. I threw in a extra $25,000 so y'all can get a $100,000 apiece."

"That's what's up!" Pete screamed out as he walked over to Bum. "Good look'n bra." Pete said as him and Bum embraced.

"No doubt, it's y'all time to shine." he told them.

Uno walked over to Bum. "Good look'n bra." He said as they hugged.

"Alright." Bum said as he slapped his hands together. "Go get that money." he said as he smiled at the two of them. They zipped the bag's back up and headed out the door.

"Make sure y'all be careful driving wit all that shit in the car." Bum warned them as he let them out the door.

"Definitely." Pete said.

Uno turned to Bum as he proceeded out the door. "We appreciate this bra, we ain't gon let you down." He told Bum, meaning every word of it.

"I know, y'all ready for this." He smiled at Uno. Uno then turned away and walked behind Pete headed for the car. "Ayo, Uno you still ain't tell me what happened wit J. Brown." He said as he stood in the doorway.

Uno looked at Pete, they smiled at each other. Uno then looked back to Bum. "Remember what you said about playin' wit fire?" He smiled at Bum.

Yeah." Bum nodded his head at first confused. "Oooh." He smiled. "Say no more."

The Finale

Billy D couldn't believe it when Bank told him who his brother was. He had literally been in arms reach of him on several occasions. He saw him often in the city. He was good friends with one of his friends. Billy D had the opportunity to spend time with his father as a kid. Even though their time together was short, he did enjoy the little time they did spend together. His brother never got this opportunity. Big Bill was murdered when he was just a baby. His mother was killed also a few months before Big Bill got killed. He was considered a ward of the court after his mother's murder. His maternal grandmother didn't want anything to do with him, because he was the son of a black man. She was an old fashioned Puerto Rican woman. After his mother's murder, Big Bill tried to get custody of him, but all he was left with was a baby picture of his son. He grew up in the system, being moved from one group home to another. The only family he ever really had was his street family, his brother's.

***

Billy D followed his brother from a distance, yet close enough to keep an eye on him. He watched as his brother drove the streets. He followed him as he got on the expressway heading downtown. They got off the expressway and made a left on Niagara Street heading to the lower west side. He followed as his brother turned down Pennsylvania Street. His brother stopped at the corner in front of a group of men. A man smiled as he walked towards the car his brother was driving. When the man got to the driver side, his facial expression turned from excitement to disappointment. Billy D watched as the man backed away from the car. His brother then pulled off. He sat at the end of the block watching the man closely. The man's face now showed anger as he rushed to his truck. He opened the door and leaned in to get something. He reappeared with a gun in his hand as he slammed the door closed. He walked back towards the other men on the corner and waved the gun in the air furiously. Billy D couldn't hear what the man was screaming, but he knew his anger was directed toward his brother. He reached over to the glove compartment and grabbed his gun. He then put the car in drive and rode up toward the men on the corner. They didn't see Billy D as he pulled up; their attention was on their friend who was enraged. Billy D got out the car and walked past the men headed right at the man with the gun. The other men looked on in shock as the gun hung from Billy D's hand.

"I'ma kill dem niggas...dat's ma word, dem niggas dead." The man with the gun screamed as he looked in the opposite direction at the people responsible for his anger riding off. Billy D raised the gun to the back of the man's head and pulled the trigger. One shot was all it took as the single bullet penetrated the back of his head and opened the front of his head causing his brain to spill to the concrete just before his limp body joined. Billy D turned towards the group of men with the gun to his side. "Y'all see the nigga that just pulled off?" He asked the men as he looked to each of them. They all nodded their heads yes as they looked at the gun in Billy D's hand then to their friend who laid dead on the sidewalk. "If anybody fuck with him they good as dead." Billy D said malevolently. The men stood there careful not to move suddenly. They didn't want to incite Billy D. He turned around and walked back to his car. He sat in the car and looked in the mirror, and said "I am my brother's keeper!"

www.ingramcontent.com/pod-product-compliance
Lightning Source LLC
LaVergne TN
LVHW091125080826
845145LV00008B/2044

* 9 7 8 0 6 1 5 3 3 8 7 7 4 *